K. A. STEVENS

When Innocence Dies

ISBN: 0-6156-1653-4
ISBN-13: 9780615616537

DEDICATION

Like most authors, I need to thank many people for their support, love, and expertise. A great source of knowledge came from spending a weekend at the Borderlands Press Boot Camp for writers. They told me what was good, what was not, and to cut, cut, cut.

On a personal note I have to thank those who know me and who live with me. They were the ones who had to put up with me while I wrote this book.

First and foremost, I thank my children, for they taught me the important things in life, (and it isn't a clean house); my family, who supported me in all my crazy desires; and my friends Judy, Tommie, Sandra, Clarice, Martha, and Fran, who all took their turns giving me their time and support to make this book a reality.

And there's a special person I never expected. He crossed the dimensions of my soul, digging deep inside of me, and turned dying embers into a raging fire. He ignited my passion.

CONTENTS

ACKNOWLEDGMENT

The artwork on the cover is by The Art of Sandra Dee.

Chapter 1
Thursday

The defects and faults in the mind
are like wounds in the body.
After all imaginable care has been
taken to heal them up,
still there will be a scar left behind.

Francois de La Rochefoucauld (1613–1680)

"...If this is an emergency, please dial 911."

"Damn it, Liz, where are you when I need you?" Maggie slammed her phone on the desk. Whatever it took, she decided, and picked the phone back up. Selecting another number out of her contacts, she placed the phone to her ear. "C'mon, Benny, answer your phone." Maggie rubbed her forehead. The vise grip pressure was coming on strong, and she needed relief. She knew she shouldn't lean on Benny, but he understood the pain. He could help.

"Benny."

"Hey, Maggie. What's up?"

"I have another bad headache. I need to get away from work for a while."

"Sure. We can go now if you want. Want me to come get you?"

Maggie sighed. "Let me meet you. I've finished seeing my office patients, but I need to go to the inpatient unit. Zach's got a new patient, and he's out of town. I'd better get that done first if I can."

"Okay. Give me a call when you're ready. I should be able to get away; we're not too busy. You promise you'll call me back?"

"Cross my heart. Nothing I would like more than to get away. I'll call you."

"Okay, great. Hey, Maggie?"

"Yeah, Benny?"

"You know I love you more than life itself?"

"Yeah, Benny, I know."

"And you love me back?"

"Yeah, Benny, of course. Of course I love you. Bye."

Maggie put her phone in her pocket. *Liz is going to think I'm an idiot. Damn it, why didn't she answer her phone?* Shaking her head, Maggie set off on foot to the inpatient psychiatric unit. She usually enjoyed the walk, especially when the weather was good. But today the heat was unbearable. The glaring sun tightened the vise grip on her head as she attempted to shield her eyes. She never would get use to this crazy weather. One day it would be fifty degrees and the next day it would be eighty. Worse yet, it didn't seem to matter if it was December or June. It was only the end of May but already felt like August—hazy and humid. The azaleas had long lost their bloom and the pansies were wilting. Maggie wished to be anywhere else other than walking toward a psychiatric hospital to hear problems only God could solve. She let out a huge sigh and tried not to contemplate the kind of God that allowed for the suffering of people, especially children. She never could let go of that one argument whenever somebody wanted her to believe. She had been one of those suffering children, living through hell at the hands of her stepfather.

At the door of the psychiatric unit, she searched for something in her pants pocket, but came up empty-handed.

"Damn it." Maggie punched the intercom button on the wall.

"May I help you?" A tired-sounding voice responded on the intercom.

"Hello. This is Dr. Taylor. I forgot my key."

"Sure, Dr. Taylor. I'll be right there."

Maggie didn't have to wait too long before the charge nurse was unlocking the reinforced glass door.

"Hi, Dr. Taylor, am I glad you're here. I was just getting ready to call you about this patient Dr. Newton admitted last night." Judy locked the door behind them as she ushered Maggie inside. "His name is Davis Melvin. You know him? He's one of our frequent flyers." Not waiting for Maggie to respond, Judy kept talking. "He mainly got in because he said he was suicidal, but he was also drunk as a skunk. Blood alcohol, one point two. He's on the detox protocol. But his blood pressure is still too high, 160 over 100, and his pulse is 110. He's shaking and sweating up a storm. We've loaded him up on Valium but it's not holding him too good." Satisfied with having given a full report, Judy stood in front of Maggie, waiting for orders.

"Well, hello to you, too, Judy." Maggie attempted a smile, rubbing the temples of her head.

"Oh, gosh. I'm sorry, Dr. Taylor." Judy took a good look at Maggie. "You don't look so good yourself."

Without thinking, Maggie let out a big sigh.

"That's an awfully deep sigh. Are you okay, Dr. Taylor?"

Maggie shook her head, knowing better than to dump on a staff nurse. "I'm okay, nothing that a stiff drink—or a Valium—won't cure. Better living through chemistry, right?" She smiled at Judy, hoping the overused cliché would lighten Judy's concern. "Enough about me, Judy, let's get Davis's chart. I'll take a look at him."

Walking toward the nurses' station, they heard escalating chatter coming from the dayroom. Maggie and Judy peered into the noisy room. Jerry Springer's voice blared from the TV, as he refereed two women fighting over the same man. A small group of patients argued over which woman would stand victorious.

"Should they be watching that garbage?" Maggie asked Judy. Judy shook her head, detouring into the dayroom.

"Okay, you guys, I told you no Jerry Springer. I won't even ask who turned it on." Without thinking twice, Judy turned the television off.

"Miss Judy, c'mon, it's almost over." Through a toothless grin, an overweight, short woman with multiple tattoos on her arms and legs got up from her chair, trying to reason with Judy.

"Gladys, you know you are not supposed to be watching this."

"But Miss Judy, them women gettin' ready to go at it. We'll miss it."

"That's right, Gladys, you are going to miss it. TV is off." Judy looked to the whole group. "Every one of you should be in Dorie's exercise group. Now get on down there. You're late as it is."

Judy herded the five patients out of the dayroom and closed the door. Maggie stood at the doorway, watching Judy direct traffic down the hall. As Judy walked past Maggie, she rolled her eyes. Maggie couldn't help but smile back at Judy, giving her a small pat on the back. Once the patients were on their way to the exercise class, Judy and Maggie headed to the nurses' station. Maggie sat down next to a case manager with a phone to her ear and a stack of charts at her elbow.

"Hello, Dr. Taylor. On hold, as usual."

Maggie nodded to her. "Hello, Michelle. Seems as if every time I see you, you have a phone at your ear. You sure you weren't born that way?"

"Sure does feel like it some days. Looking for a place for some of our patients. No beds, nowhere. If you have any discharges today, it's going to have to be the Salvation Army. Sorry. We got a new patient in, too. Melvin is his last name. He might need a place. He's been here a few times, burned a lot of bridges."

"Don't worry. I know you're trying. I'll have to give extra this Christmas when I see those bell ringers."

Judy handed Davis Melvin's chart to Maggie.

"Thanks, Judy."

"Hey...Hey."

Maggie looked up from her reading.

"Hey. You seeing me instead of Dr. Zach? I need something to help me sleep."

Maggie saw two patients staring at her. She didn't know who asked the question.

"Hi. Are both of you Dr. Zach's patients?" Maggie looked past the two in front of her to see another patient coming her way.

"She's Dr. Zach's patient," the younger girl standing in front of Maggie said as she pointed to the one who spoke. "I'm not, but I wish I was. Dr. Zach is really cute."

Maggie smiled at both of them. "I can only see Dr. Zach's patients. But it will be later on this afternoon."

"You can't see me now? I want to go home. Can't I go home now?" The third patient who had walked up from behind attempted to get Maggie's attention.

"You can't keep me. Only Dr. Zach can. I'll stay only for Dr. Zach. I know my rights."

The craziness of a madhouse. Maggie looked to Judy for help. She had absolutely no desire to be here.

"Okay, everybody. It's getting so loud we can barely hear ourselves think. Go on to your group. Dr. Taylor will see you if she's supposed to. We'll find you when it's time. Promise." Judy once again herded patients to their appropriate places.

Once back at the nurses' station, Judy dropped into a chair. "I sure wish we would hire another day nurse. This place is exhausting."

"Can't talk Kristin into coming back?" asked the case manager, Michelle, who was still on hold.

"Wish I could, Michelle. But I think she's pretty happy in the operating room. We've got plans for dinner this weekend. Catch up on things. Maybe I'll get on my knees and beg."

Michelle started to respond but had to direct her attention to the other end of the phone. "Oh, yes. I'm still here.

I just about forgot I was on hold. What did you find out? Do you have a bed for a male?"

"How is she?"

"Pretty good. Wish she hadn't left, though. Guess she felt she had to, Dr. Newton and all."

Maggie nodded in acknowledgement without commenting. She worked hard not to discuss her partner's personal life.

"She did tell me her brother is coming back to town. His wife died, you know. Cancer. Kris's family is here, so I guess it makes sense."

Judy noticed the time. "Dr. Taylor, group therapy is going to be starting soon. You know how the social workers have a tizzy fit when we pull the patients out of their group."

"You're right about that. I really just want to see the new patient now, anyway; he probably isn't up to going to group."

Grabbing Davis Melvin's chart, Judy escorted Maggie down the hall. Opening Davis's door let just enough light in so they could see him curled up in a fetal position, blankets pulled up over his head. The curtains had been drawn, and all of the lights were off. Judy flipped the light switch.

"Ugh. Turn that damn light back off. I think I'm gonna puke." Davis grabbed his pillow, putting it over his head.

"Sorry, Davis. Dr. Taylor needs to see you."

Maggie impulsively took a step backwards. She was hit with a foul smell coming from the blankets.

"Hi, Davis. Dr. Taylor." Ignoring the smell the best she could, Maggie sat down in a chair next to the bed.

"You don't look so good. Just need to ask you a few questions." She could tell this guy was hurting. "What else have you been doing besides alcohol?" Drugs?"

Davis tried to focus his glassy, bloodshot eyes on Maggie. "Shooting u...ugh." He couldn't get the whole sentence out of his mouth before green spew projected itself toward the open door.

"Group time!" A pony-tailed blonde social worker announced at the doorway. "Group ti...oh shit, oh gross!" Vomit decorated her hair, face, and clothes. "Oh my God, oh shit!" Her face became a contortion of disgust as she ran out of Davis's room retching.

Maggie stood up, grateful not to have been hit with Davis's vomit.

"Judy, why don't we give Davis a shot of Phenergan fifty with two of Ativan. Once his stomach has settled, clean him up. Make sure he gets in a bathtub. I'll finish looking at his chart at the nurses' station."

Maggie settled back at the nurses' station to review Davis's record. She saw that he had a long history of abusing drugs and alcohol. She also saw what she thought was the beginning of the end. She saw it too often in the lives of people who landed in a psych hospital, especially the repeaters with no place to go.

"Maggie, I think Davis should stay at least three or four days. Through the weekend, at least, then a referral to a rehab facility."

Maggie glanced up from her reading. The lead social worker, Andrew, stood at her side, peering over his glasses. He stood there with his hands deep in the pockets of his Tommy Hilfiger pants. His dress was always the same: button-down shirt and khakis. He always wore his shirttail out to give an impression of ease, but it also helped to cover his lack of masculinity. Along with his slight, effeminate build, he was also graced with a slight swish in his walk. These two genetic characteristics made him the focus of ridicule when he was a young boy. To make up for his lack of muscle mass and manly strut, Andrew learned to become a master of mind games. While his dress was intentionally non-threatening, he worked at putting others on the defensive daily.

Maggie pointed to the history in Davis's chart.

"Andrew, this man is a child abuser, not just a drunk. He probably belongs in jail."

"Maggie, that sounds like a personal opinion, not a professional assessment. You know rehab is the only place he'll get any kind of treatment."

Without realizing it, Maggie was rubbing her head again. She stood up and looked eye to eye with Andrew. "Andrew, if you want to talk in professional terms, why don't you start with calling me Dr. Taylor?" She closed Davis's record and handed it to him. "We'll discuss treatment options after he detoxes."

Maggie walked out of the nurses' station. Between Andrew, Davis, and her exploding head, she couldn't handle much more.

Judy was coming out of Davis's room. "Gave Davis his meds, Dr. Taylor. Hopefully he'll be better in an hour or so. Who do you want to see next?"

"Judy, I've got to go. I forgot I had an appointment. If it's okay with you, we'll do rounds after lunch." Maggie walked as quickly as she could to the door and pulled on the handle.

"Crap." She turned back toward the nurses' station. "Judy!"

***

"Benny, I don't think I can take it anymore. My head is pounding. I feel like it's going to explode. What makes me think I can take care of child-abuse survivors? It's too much. I'm not sure if I can handle it anymore. When I saw that patient's chart and read that he had sexually abused his granddaughter, I was sick. More than that, I wanted to see him choke on his own vomit. I just don't get it. Why do the courts let these guys go to do it again?"

While Maggie talked, Benny rearranged his silverware on the table, careful to make sure the measurements were the same between the utensils. He preferred to have his ruler with him to make sure it was perfect, but he had been doing it for so long the ruler was not much more than an assurance. He had also learned many years ago that there were some things you just didn't do in public.

Benny loved Maggie, as much as anyone could love another person. She seemed to understand his soul; accept his quirks. He knew it was because they had experiences in common. A childhood path of secrets and abuse, tormented and tortured by the very people who were supposed to love and care for them. For Benny, it was his mother who had robbed him of his childhood and later his manhood. She was an expert at belittling him at every stage of life, constantly reminding him that "he was a no-good son-of-a-bitch just like his father."

Benny found it hard to believe in himself or anyone else. But when Maggie came along, things changed. He was on his way to becoming a nurse anesthetist, and she was finishing her residency. He'll never forget that it was the same year he saw Rod Stewart in concert. He and Rod had become friends by chance. They had parted promising to stay in touch, and Rod had signed his album cover, 'Everybody deserves one Maggie May in their life, Rod.'

When Benny met Maggie during the month of May, he knew she was the one. He even wondered if Rod had actually sent Maggie to him, as a gift. Rod was thoughtful that way, often sending signs of their friendship to Benny. Benny and Maggie had met at the library, both involved in pharmacology research. Benny had known he wanted to go into medicine ever since he and some buddies experimented with drugs in high school. The most fun was slipping girls date-rape drugs. Having that kind of power over people, especially women, excited Benny. He didn't always take advantage of them; he just liked having that kind of control. He gave his mother the date rape drug once and watched as his friends tore the buttons off her blouse, ripped her panties off.

Benny had started off as low man on the totem pole at the local hospital. Straight out of high school, he managed to get a job working nights in the transport office. He would push patients around on gurneys or hospital beds from the emergency room to the operating room to a nursing floor. He felt comfortable working at night, sleeping during the day. He liked seeing life illuminated by the moon instead of by the glaring sun. He quickly realized his medical career goal was the right one. He noticed that it was the folks in the surgical scrubs that got the respect, or at least the hand job. Benny enrolled in a two-month nursing-assistant course. Once he was working on a nursing floor, he learned all he could from the nurses and doctors around him. When surgical services needed an extra nursing assistant for a few months, he volunteered to work the extra duty. It was a decision that was pivotal in his choice of careers. He got to see the operating room in action. He also saw who ran the show, the real people with the power. He was fascinated by how much control the anesthetist had over the life and death of a person.

After Benny had been a certified nurse anesthetist for a few years, the thrill of anesthetizing people had worn off. In the beginning Benny could not contain his excitement. He felt all-powerful when he was pushing drugs. He would get wide-eyed, taking in how the patients succumbed to the drugs of sleep and helplessness. He could feel the sweat on his brow and his heart start to race as he slipped the breathing tube into their throat and taped their eyes shut, knowing he was in full control. He could even feel hardness in his pants that he could only dream about. During surgery, he would often fantasize about what he might do to patient if he were alone with them. Sometimes, if he was feeling bold, he would take a patient to the brink of death with drugs; all under a surgeon's watchful eye. Couldn't get better than that!

Benny loved Maggie. At first their relationship was slow to take off. Maggie spent a lot of her time at work and didn't seem to be in a hurry to get involved. She wasn't as demanding as so many women could be. The first time they tried to make love, he couldn't perform. But that was really no surprise to him. His mother had made sure he would not be like his "no-good son-of-a-bitch father using his manliness to screw anything with a skirt on." No, that would not be Benny.

After years of therapy he understood that the sickness in his soul was intertwined in his mother's discipline. But therapy could not erase the damage done by her demented philosophies.

He could still recall as if it were yesterday.

Benny, look what I have for you. This is a lesson you must learn in order to become the man your father never was. You must see the evils of the world and be punished for them. It will keep you strong when you are tempted by the corruption of women. His mother would show him pictures of nude women and men in various poses together, encouraging Benny to masturbate. As Benny reached the ecstasy of his orgasm and ejaculated into his hands, his mother would hold his hands over a hot stove until he cried out in pain. When Benny finally understood this torment would never end, he started to refuse his mother.

"No matter," his mother retorted. As long as his member was engorged, she would masturbate him and continue to hold his hands to the fire. Only until he lay flaccid at any stimulation—vision or touch—did she feel her duty was complete. After that, she acted like she barely knew him, not caring that she stole the innocence from his childhood, the sanity from his psyche.

Yes, Maggie was perfect. She almost appeared more relaxed when he couldn't enter her. That was when they shared their painful and abusive histories. After that night, he never had to try to please her, and she never had to pretend she wanted him. And they had other things in common. They both used alcohol to bury the pain. He liked it when Maggie drank with him; it was a wonderful way to keep the world out. Benny loved the world where only he and Maggie existed, along with their favorite bottle of booze.

Benny used a toothpick to swirl his olive around in his glass, so engrossed in thought of how his past and present had merged to this point. He had often thought about going out and killing the scum of the world. Just for fun. He was only a little startled that the idea aroused him as Maggie was talking. Doing it for Maggie, for both of them. Maybe even with Maggie. He could feel the arousal in his crotch. This would be honorable. He would be able to stop Maggie's suffering. As his love for Maggie grew, he felt he could sense every fiber of her soul—what she wanted, what she needed.

"You know, Maggie, we might be able to help him choke on his own vomit." Benny slowly looked up from his glass and into Maggie's eyes. It was important to read her thoughts correctly.

"What about hanging him by his balls in the mall?" Maggie started to giggle, her drink going to her head on an empty stomach.

"Yeah, that's a good one, too. But let's think about this. We wouldn't want to get caught, but we could pay this loser back with what he deserves."

"I wish, Benny, I wish." Maggie looked into Benny's eyes. "You do know that I'm just fantasizing, right? This is just fun and games to relieve some stress."

Maggie was disturbed by the intense look on his face. She felt her heart pound. A feeling of uneasiness overshadowed her silliness. The same feelings she had told Liz about. The reason she knew she shouldn't have called him. The red flag she had decided to ignore. "Benny, you almost sound like you mean it. And what's that look in your eyes?"

Benny tried to relax his face. He didn't want to scare her, but he wasn't sure how he looked.

"Look, Benny, I just wish my pain would go away and I've got to learn to deal with it. Some days are harder than others." Maggie glanced at her watch. "Let's get out of here. I've gotta get back to work."

Benny motioned to the waitress for the bill. As she laid the bill and the pen on the table, her hand accidently moved Benny's spoon so that it was not evenly spaced with the other utensils. Benny snatched them up, scowling at the waitress as she walked away.

"Damn it. What's wrong with her?" Benny had to re-align the silverware before he could pick up the bill. "I don't know that she's the best waitress I've seen. Seven percent is plenty for her," adding the amount to the bill.

Maggie studied Benny's reaction to the waitress. Immediately she saw Benny in a way she had never seen him before. If he always acted like this, she wondered, why was she seeing it for the first time?

When the waitress walked by Benny to wait on another table, he thrust the piece of paper in front of her.

The waitress glanced at the bill, then at Benny as she tucked it in her pocket. "Have a good day," she said out loud. To herself she added, "Cheap ass."

Benny and Maggie walked out to the parking lot, neither saying a word. At Maggie's car, Benny held Maggie at her shoulders so he could look into her eyes. "Maggie May, I love you so much, I would do anything for you. You know that, right? Anything. Whatever it takes to relieve your pain, you know I'll do it."

"Benny, you're great. I know you care about me. But you can't take me seriously. We were just joking around. Right?" Maggie tried to read Benny's eyes. "Look at me."

Benny looked deep into Maggie's eyes, searching for her love, for what she really wanted. Benny gave Maggie a quick kiss on the lips before she slipped into her car. As the car door closed Benny called out, "I'll give you a call this evening. Maybe I'll come over with a bottle of carmenere!"

Maggie barely turned toward him, giving him a quick wave as she drove out of the parking lot. Driving back to work, Maggie reflected on her relationship with Benny. She enjoyed his company when they met, but as their relationship developed, she was not so sure. She recalled the first time they'd shared the horror stories of their childhoods. He was so gentle, so loving, as she recounted the secrets of her past. And it had broken her heart to hear how his mother had tormented him. She wanted to save him. She wanted them to save each other. But instead of them becoming stronger together, she found he was sucking the energy right out of her. She was trying to get healthier, deal with her abuse issues; he seemed to cater to his past and allowed it to engulf him. She was starting to see that the only reason she was staying with him was because she didn't know if she had the energy to leave him.

Back at the hospital, she pushed her thoughts about Benny out of her mind and finished her rounds. She was happy to see that Davis had gotten a bath and was sleeping peacefully. At her office there were no patients in crisis, only phone calls requesting refills. She was grateful for the calm.

Her headache had become a dull annoyance and a reminder that Benny was not the right answer after all.

***

At her own therapist's appointment that evening, Maggie laid her day out, focusing quickly on her feelings about Benny. "Liz, I know I shouldn't have called him. I'm a damn psychiatrist and treat people just like me. But I can't even get it right." Maggie sat across from Liz, wanting answers for her own weaknesses. "He's bad for me, I know that. Why can't I let go?"

"What makes you think you can't?"

"Damn it, Liz. Just give me the answers to my craziness. I'm tired of thinking. And I'm tired of analyzing my feelings."

Liz was insistent. "Okay, let's break it down. What are the pros of staying with Benny?"

Maggie shook her head, trying to get serious. "Okay, I'll play the game...Why did I call him? He can be a tower of strength. And he's always there for me."

"What else?"

Maggie shrugged her shoulders.

"So what's the negative?"

"Sometimes when I'm with him I feel like I'm standing in quicksand. We start talking about our past and getting revenge. I'm just joking. I'm starting to think he might be serious."

"Interesting."

"He spooked the hell out of me today. When you didn't answer your phone, I called him. I had just seen a new patient of mine. It was like looking straight into my past. Even to the point of her dad stripping her naked to weigh her...putting her in front of a mirror...crawling into bed with her." Maggie eyes moistened. She tried to blink the tears away. "My head was ready to explode. And then on top of that, I had to go see a child molester on the unit for Zach. It was just too much."

"You did have a day. Sorry I didn't answer, but I was with a patient."

"It's not your fault. I know I have to figure this out." Maggie reached for a tissue from Liz's desk to wipe her eyes.

"The other night, I told him I was going to start therapy again. He didn't like that. He told me our spirits are so enmeshed that he could sense what I'm thinking, what I need. And that I don't need a therapist, I just need him. I didn't think too much about it at the time; we had been drinking. But today, I don't know, we were going back down the rabbit hole, chasing ghosts, but this time...I saw a look in his eyes. It ran a shiver though my spine."

Maggie's gaze drifted toward the window, thinking about her lunchtime conversation with Benny. Tears slowly rolled down her cheeks. Dabbing at her face, she wondered how she had let him get so close.

"Shoulda, woulda, coulda. Don't beat yourself up. You're ready when you're ready. You know that." Liz hated to see her patient in pain. She waited for Maggie to respond. Maggie looked at Liz as if she were hearing those words for the first time. When she didn't say anything, Liz continued, "Do you want me to use all my favorite therapy clichés in one session? I'll have to charge you double!"

Maggie smiled. "Just don't say, 'I see!' or I may not pay you...you therapist, you." She was glad that Liz was joking with her, making attempts to lighten the load. Liz was one of the best and as genuine as they came. "So, okay, know-it-all therapist, do I get to come see you twice a week, instead of once?" She knew she was going to need help filling the void.

"You can come see me every day if you want, but I don't provide any alcohol."

Maggie knew it was time to let Benny go for good. She was ready.

***

As Maggie opened the door to her home she heard the answering machine pick up a call.

"Hey, Maggie May, if you're home, pick up. I've been trying to reach you all night. You must have your cell phone off by accident or something. I can't get through. I'm worried about you. Call me as soon as you get this. Okay. I love you. Call me."

Maggie made no attempt to pick up the phone. In the beginning she thought these phone calls from him were endearing, thoughtful. She ignored the obvious, wanting Benny to be a good thing in her life. But the red flags were there, and she couldn't ignore them anymore. It was like a light switch had flipped in her head. Liz had helped her to see that she herself encouraged Benny's crazy behavior. The phone rang again. Benny was loud and angry, ranting into the machine. "Why won't you pick up the phone? Why is your cell phone off? You know you need me. Pick up the phone, damn it!"

She knew he wouldn't stop until he heard her voice. She changed her clothes while his tirade continued over the message machine, wishing phones had never been invented. It was impossible to hide from life anymore; no caves on planet Earth. She also knew she couldn't hide from telling Benny the truth: it was time for her to move on. She still didn't understand the emotional connection she had to him, or why it was so hard for her to break up with him, or even why she thought she needed him. And she knew she would miss him terribly, but he was bad news, and she couldn't ignore it any longer. She picked up the phone in the middle of Benny's fifth call.

"Here I am…I just got in, Benny. Sorry."

"Maggie, baby…Where've you been?"

"I'm sorry, Benny, I had to run a few errands. Traffic was worse than usual, I guess."

"You know you're supposed to let me know. We've discussed this before, have we not?" Without waiting for Maggie to answer, Benny kept on. "What errands did you have to run, Maggie May? You didn't tell me about them at lunch today. You told me you had a headache. It must have gotten better since you ran some errands. I told you I was coming over with a bottle of wine. Did you go drinking without me? Or meet someone for a drink?"

Maggie didn't tell him about her therapy appointment on purpose. When they first met he seemed to support Maggie's therapy work. But when she voiced her desire to start therapy again, he became visibly offended. It was best she keep Liz out of the conversation. "Benny, we need to talk." Maggie was not sure how to start. "I think maybe we need to spend less time together. You're a great guy and all. I think I just need some space for a while."

Silence.

"Benny, are you there?"

Still no answer. Maggie thought maybe he had hung up.

"What is it, Maggie May? You didn't want space earlier today. What happened after you went back to work? It's those creeps getting to you again. You had to see that patient. Did he bother you?" Benny didn't give her time to answer. "This did start at lunch, but you didn't want to say anything. Why don't you want me? I thought I saw something in your eyes. What did that pervert do? That's it, isn't it? Don't worry; I'll protect you, take care of you."

"No, Benny. It's not the patients, and it's not you. It's me. It's all me." Maggie wanted this conversation over as soon as possible.

"I can, you know. You don't need space. You just need me. We're made for each other. You know that. Our spirits belong together, Maggie. I'll come over now, make it all right."

Maggie rubbed her temples, her head screaming with pain. Let's see. On a scale of one to ten, with ten being the worst, what would it be? That was the question she asked her patients if they wanted pain medicine. What about emotional pain, how is that measured? By the number of razor slashes on the wrist, a thigh? Maggie had put on a pair of shorts and a T-shirt. She pulled up her shorts, exposing the inside of her thigh. One, two, three, four, five, six, seven, eight, nine, she counted. Nine old scars, her emotional pain always hurt to nine razor slashes. But she didn't slash any more. Now she had headaches, and one was coming on strong.

"No, Benny, I don't think it's a good idea for you to come over. I'm sorry."

"Maggie, Maggie!"

The phone went dead.

***

Benny went to his wine rack and pulled out his favorite carmenere and a wine glass. Maggie wanted space. Space for what? He kept thinking about their last few dates together, searching for any clues to this dramatic change in her behavior. The more he thought, the more anxious he became. He needed relief fast. Sipping his glass of wine, he reached into a kitchen drawer and pulled out a plastic ruler and a level. Did she meet somebody new? Could it be another guy, a guy with a hard cock? She always said she didn't need it—or even like it—but maybe she wasn't telling the truth. Maybe she was even ridiculing him behind his back. Maybe, just maybe, she was making everything up just to make fun of him.

Benny started on the kitchen walls. With the ruler he measured the distance between each wall hanging and with the level made sure each picture was hanging perfectly straight. He continued in the living room as his thoughts ran wild.

That's what Mother used to do. Build me up to tear me down. NO! Maggie wouldn't do that. What's wrong with me? Maggie's too sweet, too wonderful, too much like me. Think, think, THINK! What's happened lately? Was she seeing that stupid therapist again? She said she wanted to. Maybe it was the slob she was talking about at lunch. That patient she saw today. That's got to be it. She probably thinks I can't protect her. She can't stand the pain of seeing those jerks, much less taking care of them. She's testing me... All women do it. Maybe she needs to see that I'm strong enough for the both of us. She told me she wanted him dead. That's what she means by needing space. I bet she's seeing that therapist, too. Maggie must be talking to her, telling her things. Last time she wanted to shut down it was because she was talking to that fucking therapist. Maggie's talking to her instead of me about that pervert.

After he poured another glass of wine he continued to use the ruler to make sure all of the books on the bookcase and the coffee table were arranged symmetrically, spaced the exact same number of inches apart. Benny felt Maggie's soul slip from his existence. He moved to his bedroom with his level, ruler, and glass of wine. *She's upset at me because I haven't protected her, and now she has to go to that damn therapist for help. Those perverts keep hurting her. If I could just kill the pain, her pain.*

Instantly Benny got it.

That scumbag is her pain and she wants me to kill it; kill him. It's him. That's it, I know that's it. She wants him dead; she wants him to choke on his own vomit. Maggie wants me to make it happen.

This new insight into Maggie energized him. He downed what was left of his wine, got on his hands and knees, and brought out a lockbox that was under his bed. Going back to the kitchen, he retrieved his keys from the key rack. Eying the open bottle, he grabbed that as well before heading back to his bedroom. After he poured himself another glass of wine, Benny opened the box and dumped the contents on the bed. One by one he picked up the small bottles, reading each label as if it held a fond memory of another time before placing the bottles back into the box. "Valium, oxycodone, baclofen, ritalin, phenobarb...here's my bottles."

He picked up five empty vials and a piece of paper that had fallen to the bed when he turned the lockbox over. A slight sparkle appeared in Benny's eyes as he read over the recipe. "It appears I'm cooking up a little gamma g, liquid e...maybe some ecstasy for me." Benny licked his lips as a malicious grin took over his face. "I better get busy, I got work to do."

As the Police sang "I'll Be Watching You," Benny turned up the music, singing and swaggering to the hall closet.

"Oh, can't you see you belong to me.
How my poor heart aches with every breath
you take. Every move you make, every vow
you break, every smile you fake, every claim
you stake, I'll be watching you."

Getting on his hands and knees, he crawled deep into the back, shoving objects around until he found what he was looking for. He pulled out a large plastic storage container. Continuing to hum to the music, he placed it on the kitchen counter. He took the lid off and removed the contents one by one. "pH test strips, wheel cleaner, lye soap, alcohol, distilled water, and last, but not least, vinegar," arranging them shortest to tallest. Retrieving his ruler from the bedroom he aligned the ingredients on the kitchen counter. After he was satisfied with the lineup, he pulled the saucepan out by the handle and twirled it before placing it on the stove. He removed the last items: a pair of plastic goggles and elbow-length cleaning gloves. Standing in front of the foyer mirror and sipping his glass of wine, he gingerly positioned the goggles on his head. He tucked the few loose hairs behind his ears. Pleased with his appearance he picked up one glove at a time. Watching himself in the mirror he placed his hands in the gloves, stroking them up his arms.

When the government first outlawed GHB, Benny was extremely upset. He'd had to become resourceful, finding out how to get the ingredients and then learning how to make it. Once he found the recipe and saw how easy it was to get everything he needed, he started taking pleasure in being his own manufacturer. The first time he made it he enjoyed a sexual pleasure that was overwhelming. Over time he developed a ritual to make his lovely potion.

He opened another bottle of carmenere and cranked up his favorite playlist of music as much as he dared. He measured out the ingredients and heated them on the stove. While the toxic brew was coming to a boil, he reached into the bin. He pulled out the only picture he had of his mother and threw it to his feet. He stirred his pot of poison, feeling his cock harden. Looking at his mother's picture, he rubbed himself and worked on the zipper, excited for the release. The brew on the stove boiled faster and faster, but he was transfixed by his mother's picture.

He moaned low and long as his own brew reached orgasm.

"Only for you, mother, only for you."

And he exploded all over her wonderful face.

Chapter 2

Friday

No man is clever enough to know
all the evil he does.

Francois de La Rochefoucauld

"Damn it, shut up!" Benny rolled over, barely opening his eyes, and groped for his alarm. "Four thirty in the fucking morning. I gotta get a new job."

He sat on the side of his bed, holding his head, and wished he had remembered to take some aspirin last night to help with his hangover. As he remembered the activities of his night, his eyes widened. He shook his sleepiness off, and his scowl turned into a grin. With renewed vigor, he forgot all about his hangover.

He jumped up from his bed and scurried into the kitchen. He took his espresso machine and a coffee mug out of the cupboard above the counter. As the espresso brewed, he retrieved a ruler and a spoon from a drawer. He lined up his coffee cup, espresso maker, and spoon, measuring the distances between the objects. His smile broadened when he saw he placed them almost perfectly, having to move them just millimeters. Once he moved his coffee mug the necessary distance, he returned to his bedroom. He began to make his bed, pulling the sheets and comforter up from the bottom to the top, then stopped.

"I don't have time for this today, into the wash you go." He pulled the sheets and comforter off, rolling them into a ball before placing them in the hamper. Taking the pillowcases off the pillows, he placed them in the hamper as well. He positioned the pillows neatly at the head of the bed, using reference points on the headboard he had penciled there years ago when the bed was new. Grabbing a set of hospital scrubs and a clean towel from his closet, he walked into his bathroom to take a shower, closing and locking the door.

Showered, dressed, and ready to leave for work, he downed his double shot of espresso and rinsed his cup and spoon before placing them in the dishwasher. He methodically cleaned the espresso machine before placing it back in the cupboard. He looked at himself in the foyer mirror. He rearranged a few loose strands of hair behind his ears, and he gave himself a nod. Before leaving his apartment, he went back into the kitchen and glanced at the counter. Satisfied, he left, locking the two locks behind him.

In his car, he picked out one of his favorite Beatles CDs, singing loudly for anyone on the block to hear.

"I want you, I want you so bad, I want you, I want you so bad, it's driving me mad, it's driving me mad.

Duh, duh, duh, duh."

At an early age, Benny began to feel that all of the great rock stars were writing songs just for him. Meeting Rod Stewart, and then Maggie, cemented this idea in his head. Even before knowing Rod, he had tried to let John Lennon know how much he appreciated the music, and how much it meant to him. He had driven all the way to New York just to thank him. He would never forget that day.

He had followed John and Yoko from their recording studio home. As he walked toward John to thank him, a gun went off. He watched in horror as John fell to the ground, blood everywhere. Looking to see where the bullets had come from, he saw a man in the shadows. Benny recognized him from earlier in the day; the shooter had been lurking around John's building. Benny immediately realized it was he who had caused John's death. The news never did tell the whole story, but the shooter had been following him, not John. It made perfect sense. The shooter was jealous of Benny and the special relationship he had with the rock star. John Lennon had taken a bullet for Benny. He would always be grateful. For weeks he wrote letters to Yoko. He wanted her know he would always be indebted to her. After a year of no response, he realized she couldn't write back. She was concerned for his safety, of course, and contacting him would once again make him a target. Yes, he greatly appreciated Yoko and he sent her his thoughts almost daily.

Benny pulled his car into the hospital parking lot. If he tried to get in touch with Yoko now after so many years had passed, he wondered, would she think it safe to respond? That would definitely impress Maggie. Benny glanced at his watch, and seeing he was late for work, took the stairs two at a time. Work didn't turn him on as it used to, but it paid the bills.

On the surgical unit, he saw his assignment. *Great, an organ harvesting.* Benny thought these were painfully boring; after all, the patient was already dead. Brain dead. No excitement there. Already helpless and hopeless.

Another nurse anesthetist was looking at the assignments on the whiteboard as well. "I hear it's going to be a long one, too. They plan on taking every organ. Heart, lungs, kidneys, liver. Maybe even skin afterwards."

Benny looked at Jim, who kept talking.

"Very healthy guy, a young soldier. Just back from Afghanistan. That freak motorcycle accident yesterday? Yeah, incredibly sad."

Benny silently bet that the soldier's head didn't hurt nearly as bad as his did when he woke up this morning, cursing himself once again for still not taking any aspirin. Never really caring for Jim and not in the mood for this sappy talk, he looked straight into Jim's eyes.

"Well Jimbo, life's a bitch, and then you die." Benny turned to the anesthesia assistant standing next to him. "You getting my stuff ready? I want it done ASAP. I need some breakfast before my case gets going and that room's got to be ready to roll."

***

Benny couldn't help but obsess over the conversation he'd had with Maggie the night before. He was in the operating room with the harvesting, but his mind wasn't on it. His role was minimal anyway. Get the patient and keep him breathing. All of the organs had to stay pink and pretty until all the pieces and parts were plucked out and on ice. Once that occurred, the blood would be suctioned out, the oxygen turned off, and he'd be able to leave the room. Every once in a while he enjoyed watching the rest of the staff. The circulator and scrub technicians were usually in a flurry, getting the names of all of the harvesting staff, running for drugs, setting up equipment, and counting instruments. The nursing staff sometimes resembled chickens with their heads cut off, especially when there were new nurses working.

But today he just wasn't in to it. He couldn't get Maggie out of his mind. He needed a surefire way to win her back. Make her see she belonged to him. He knew he was going to have to get rid of the bastard who was tearing them apart. He had stayed up most of the night making GHB. It was a great drug for his purpose, anybody who took enough of it could literally choke on his own vomit. Benny thought GHB was the best drug ever made. You only needed a little to get wasted, and it was better than alcohol; nobody remembered a thing. Benny liked it because at higher doses he could render his prey helpless until he was done with them. What made it so perfect was that it was one of the few drugs that couldn't be picked up in toxicology reports. He had the means to kill this guy; he was stuck on the how and the when.

How am I gonna find this bastard? Gotta get to that psych unit. Figure out who he is…somehow get him to drink the stuff. Maggie sure did put me to a test. Once she sees me pull this off, she'll see me differently. Probably run into my arms and never let go. I'll have to teach her a lesson, though, for putting me through this. Get this guy to drink the stuff. And then make sure he's dead.

"Hey, Benny, are you with us?"

Benny looked up at one of the nurses.

"You have the chart? We need it. The harvesting people are on the phone to another hospital. We need to make sure the blood type is right, don't want to screw up like Duke did, you know."

Benny flipped the chart open to find the lab, but came across some neurological exams first. After glancing at them, he continued to look for the lab report that confirmed the blood type. "Here it is, B negative," and handed the chart over for the harvesting crew to confirm with the receiving hospital.

Benny looked down at the man on the OR table. He watched as the organs were slowly and meticulously cut out of the body. As he watched, a plan developed in his clever and cunning brain.

"Suction," the harvesting surgeon yelled out.

Transfixed, Benny stared as the surgeon's two assistants used a suction tip to slurp and suck the bloody watery mix out of the dead man's body.

***

Davis was dying. At least, he felt he was. Locked up in a godforsaken loony bin with drooling zombies. He needed to get out, mix a little business with pleasure. He had promised the ninety meetings in ninety days in his bullshit session with Andy Asshole—Andrew, whatever—and he made sure he said whatever it took to be a free bird by the night. His favorite hangout, Fantasy Fever, was having a T and A show he didn't want to miss. They always got girls who looked about twelve, his favorite age. He knew Fantasy Fever twat was legal, and with a little alcohol he could get hot and bothered enough to not care. He had to stay away from jail bait. Look clean.

He had turned over a new leaf, so to speak, and had worked hard to reach his new goal. He was now a bona fide informant, a snitch to the unsavory; but he preferred the term 'community service worker.' After all, he was doing the community a good service. For his payment, he held the golden ticket: cop connections. He saw how it worked on the street. If you're a squealer you get special treatment. Oh yeah, he had seen it, and now he was living it. Get out of going to jail and end up on the psycho ward instead; definitely better to be the squealer on the outside than the squealer on the inside. Yessiree, Bob, no more jail time for Davis. Before this managed care thing took over, he had always ended up on the psycho ward. That was the good life, when therapists dictated the treatment of a sexual deviant. But the tide had turned. He ended up doing prison time, had the pleasure of being Bubba's main squealer more than once. That was when Davy-boy decided it was time to turn the leaf. No more twelve-year-olds; get some cop protection and still have a little fun.

Davis was antsy to get back on the street. Three hots and a cot, the proverbial three day rest—called detoxification in medical terms—was about over. This place did beat the hell out of jail, and a couple of times a year he would check himself in when he was sick and tired of being sick and tired. In the good old days when rehabilitation was the going thing, the hospital kept him a couple of weeks before he was let loose. But in the last few years it wasn't much more than three or four days, and then they would call the damn cops, see if there was an outstanding warrant.

At first he fought getting out so early. After all it was cozy, and every once in a while he met some loser bitch who had a cute little girl at home. All he had to do was stick his hand down the crack whore's pants; he would get an invitation home every time. Those were the days. Now they barely kept you long enough to make any decent connections. And it was harder to get admitted. These days you practically had to sell yourself to the devil. Tell the nurses how much you hate yourself, what a miserable slug you are, and if you don't get help you're going to kill yourself. And now they even asked how you were planning to do yourself in.

He didn't actually have to answer that question this time. He vomited up blood on the nurse's paperwork and the game of twenty questions was over. And he even got a few extra days out of that, but he was ready to get the hell out of Dodge. He had people to see, things to do. Or was it people to do, things to see. Pussy to do, tits to see. He laughed at his own cleverness. He always impressed himself with how his mind worked, taking a simple and otherwise boring statement and making it nasty. Davis loved nasty. He was into his third day in the hospital, feeling good and ready for some nasty. Got food to stay on his stomach, shakes were gone, got a bath, a shave, and a few dollars from some of the whack jobs; promising to meet them on the outside and pay them back. Yep, the three-hots-and-a-cot club served him well, but he was ready to be gone.

Davis had just finished eating his lunch but was still hungry. The patient next to him had not touched his food.

"You not gonna eat that?" He pointed to the slab of meatloaf on his lunch mate's plate. The patient stared ahead, not paying Davis any attention.

"Not hungry, huh?" Davis stabbed at the meatloaf with his fork and took a bite. "Not too bad." He picked up the plate and scraped the rest of its contents onto his plate. "Thanks, dude. Can't leave this joint on a' empty stomach."

After he finished off his second helping, he placed his fork in the catatonic man's hand. "Thanks, zombie man. Now that I got me a full belly, I'm ready to take a nappy-poo." Davis stood up, rubbing his stomach. "Zombie man, your eyes are open but you act like you're dead to the world. You gotta teach me that trick. Pretty cool."

The other patients in the dayroom stopped eating their lunch to watch Davis. Encouraged by their sudden interest, he stood in front of the man waving his hands, trying to get him to blink. Not a move. Davis looked back at the man. He noted that the hand holding the fork had not moved. He had heard about these psychos; they could stay in one position forever. He took one of the patient's arms and positioned it over the man's head. The arm stayed. He took the other arm, extended it to the front, as a ballerina might hold her arm.

Davis leaned back, examining his work. He started chuckling. The fork was still in the patient's hand. It looked like he was getting ready to stab himself in his head. "Zombie man, you make my day. You gave me your lunch, and you make me laugh. Maybe I can pry open your mouth and you'll give me a blow job, too."

Davis flexed his knees, squatting up and down, grabbing at his crotch. The patients in the dayroom laughed at the scene as he continued with his gesturing, making sucking noises and rubbing himself in front of the catatonic patient. The mixture of Davis's laughter and sucking noises turned into gurgling. Spit and mucus blocked air from going in or out of his lungs. The more he tried to cough up the mucus, the more the mucus clogged up his windpipe. Grabbing at his throat and making guttural noises, Davis's face turned a dark red as he struggled to free the blockage from this throat.

The catatonic man stared past Davis, who kept trying to clear his throat. Finally, he coughed out a large chunk of phlegm right onto the catatonic patient's cheek. The patient didn't flinch, totally unaware of the possibility that Davis could have choked to death standing in front of him.

When Davis caught his breath he looked at his lunch mate with disdain. Davis's brush with the afterlife had not fazed the motionless man.

"You fucking retard," Davis said as he left the day-room, red-faced, clearing his throat, and breathing hard. Davis went to his room to lie down, his good mood gone.

I coulda choked out there. That fuckin' loser. Probably just fuckin' with me. This place is for crap. Where the hell is the staff, anyway? In the old days people cared about you. The staff was right there, waiting on you, hand and foot. You didn't have to take some fuckin' loser's lunch. There was always extra food and soda around; cookies, crackers, sandwiches even. These days you don't get shit.

Davis's mind wandered as he grew sleepy.

Sure do miss the good old days. No more gettin' to stay until the next meal and sure as hell don't get no group hugs when you walk out the door. And the worst of the bullshit—the stupid no-smoking policy. Whoever heard of a nonsmoking psycho ward? Instead, I get a patch. A fuckin' patch.

The first time Davis was offered a nicotine patch, he'd threatened God and everybody. In the past if he bullied staff enough, he could get what he wanted. This time was different.

"You damn asshole; I want a damn cigarette, not a damn fuckin' patch. I want one now. I'll tear this place up, you son-of-a-bitch nigger."

This time the staff member stood his ground, calm and matter-of-fact. The big black mental health worker stood in front of Davis, solid and cool as a cucumber. "Davis, my man, you do what you gotta do, and I'll do what I gotta do."

Reliving that incident took Davis back even further in time. A time that had seared his soul, branding him for eternity.

He was seven years old. He had been peeking through the crack of his mother's bedroom door, curious about the moaning and creaking that kept him awake at night. He saw "Uncle Joe" sucking on one of his mother's breasts with his hand between her legs. She was grabbing at his cock, rubbing it up and down.

Davis was mesmerized. He watched Uncle Joe straddle his mother's face. "Suck me, bitch," shoving his engorged cock into his mother's mouth. Davis watched as Uncle Joe pumped his cock in and out of his mother's throat. Uncle Joe started for his mother's crotch when he noticed Davis was watching through the cracked door.

"Well, well. Looky here." Uncle Joe dismounted Davis's mother and walked over to the door. "You wanna watch the show, Davey-boy? I'll give you a front row seat."

Davis stood there, with his hand in his pants, embarrassed.

"You gettin' off, boy? You gettin' hard, like Uncle Joe? You can suck me when your momma's done. Maybe I'll suck your little dick, too. You'll like it, Davey boy. It's good, real good. Here, just for you."

Uncle Joe knocked a bunch of magazines off a stool and placed it at the foot of the bed. Davis didn't want to sit. He was looking at his mother, hoping she would tell him to get out. But his mother was stoned.

"I said, sit down. You wanted to watch, hide behind the door, getting' your rocks off. Now it's time to learn. Now sit down, or I'll tie you down."

Uncle Joe got back on the bed. "Look, bitch, your little Davey-boy wants a show. Let's start with your ugly red cunt. Spread them legs and show your Davey-boy how you get yourself off."

Davis's mother looked at him and started to talk. "Joe, he's my boy. He's just a boy." Tears welled up in her eyes.

"Look, whore, he's asking for his momma's cunt. And if you want your next fix, you'll spread those damn legs." Joe shoved her legs apart, pushing his fingers in and out of his mother's vagina while sucking on one of her breasts. His mother responded, moaning and massaging her other breast, making her nipple hard. Then Joe slapped her across her face. Davis's mother let out a shriek.

Davis screamed out, "Leave her alone! Leave my mom alone! I'll kill you!"

"I know what you want to see, pig boy. You don't want to see some wrinkled old whore spread her legs. Hear that, wrinkled old whore? Your young, precious boy don't want to see your ugly whoreness. Go get Melissa out of bed. Let's see how much Davy-boy likes looking at some young pussy."

Davis's mom stared at him.

Uncle Joe pushed her off the bed. "Look, bitch, get me your daughter."

Dazed and drunk, Davis's mother left the room and came back with a scared and cold Melissa.

When Davis comprehended what Joe was planning he stood up and yelled at him. "Uncle Joe, I'll kill you. I swear, if you touch my sister, I'll kill you!"

"Davey, my man, you do what you gotta do, and I'll do what I gotta do."

Uncle Joe turned toward Melissa, pulling her nightgown to the floor.

"Davis...Davis! Time to get up. You got your discharge orders; it's time to hit the door. Davis! Get up, get moving. You're a free bird." Judy walked into Davis's room, jarring him from his hellish memories.

"Did you get to the discharge group while you were here? You were supposed to go to that group before you leave. You know the drill."

Davis stared at Judy, his mind sluggish from his journey into the past.

Judy went on, unaware of his childhood flashback. "We need to go over your aftercare plan. I sure hope you follow through this time. I see you in here way too often. You know what they say—'You always have another drunk in you, but you may not have another recovery.'"

"I know, I know, ninety meetings in ninety days. I think I'll go straight to an AA meeting from here. I'm going to try really hard this time, I promise." He swung his legs over the bed and sat up, saying the words he knew Judy wanted to hear. He shook himself, trying to shake off his nightmare memories.

He got off the bed and collected the only things he could call his own. "I get to keep this shit, right?"

He showed Judy what he had accumulated during his stay; a half of tube of toothpaste, three toothbrushes, two combs, and five small bars of soap.

"Looks like you went on a scavenger hunt while you were here." Judy was used to seeing patients take needed toiletries for the outside. "I don't care, keep it if you want. But back to your discharge plan...It's yourself you need to convince, not me. I'm not one of those therapists you have to suck up to."

Davis pulled clothes out of his dresser and shoved them into a plastic bag along with his collected finds.

Judy pulled his discharge papers from his chart and handed them to Davis. "Follow up with your medical doctor in two weeks. Here's a schedule of AA meetings. And the Salvation Army is expecting you to stay with them for a few nights, until a halfway house opens up."

Davis took the papers. Barely reading them, he shoved them in his bag.Judy stared at Davis. "You're going to die out there. You know that, right?"

"Don't worry 'bout me, Nurse Judy. I got those meetings memorized." He walked out his bedroom door to the main entrance of the unit with Judy trailing behind him.

"Can I help you?"

Benny was standing on the other side of the door when Judy opened it to let Davis out. "I'm...here to see a patient."

"I'll be with you in just a minute." Judy's attention was still on her patient. She paid little mind to Benny. "Davis, try to stay out of trouble and stay sober. I don't want to see you back here. However, I don't want to see you in the obits either."

Benny watched as Davis clicked his heels and saluted Judy. He slung the plastic bag full of hospital toiletries over his shoulder and walked away, wondering where he was going to get a cigarette and a ride to the closest liquor store.

Looking in Davis's direction, Judy mumbled, "Born behind the eight ball, and now he's living there. Might as well just shoot him."

"Shoot him? And you're a nurse?" Benny pretended to grab his heart. "He can't be that bad. After all, he's here for help."

"Yeah, right. Truth be told, he's a member of the three-hots-and-a-cot club."

Benny chuckled, "So you're going to put a bullet between his eyes for taking advantage of the system? You're sure hard-core. Glad to see we have caring and compassionate nurses working with the mentally ill."

"Mentally ill, my foot. He's a slimeball child perp who comes in here to hide out and dry out." Judy looked Benny in the eye. "I've come to the conclusion that the only way to rid this earth of that kind of scum is to put them six feet under. They sure don't respond to treatment. I hate to admit it, but I don't have much space in my heart for them."

"Well...Why don't you tell me how you really feel?" Benny tried to stay with the conversation but his mind was racing. *I bet this was the guy Maggie was talking about. It's gotta be. She didn't say there was more than one. He's gotta be the guy.*

Judy noticed Benny had on scrubs. "Hey, I shouldn't have gone on like that. What can I do for you? Are you here to do a medical consult?" She was hoping—praying, actually—that she hadn't just put her foot in her mouth. Over the years, she had learned the hard way that she had a way of speaking her mind that was not always positive or productive.

"Yes, I am a doctor. But I'll have to come back. I just remembered a meeting I should be at."

Benny turned to leave but couldn't. Judy had walked him through a door that was now locked. He turned back to her, and seeing keys in her hand, grabbed at them. But Judy was quicker than Benny, putting her hand with the keys behind her.

"Hey, you can't have my keys, doctor or no. If you want out, just say so."

But Benny ignored her and instead grabbed at Judy's shoulders, twisting her body around with such force that she lost her grip. The keys skidded across the floor, landing at the door. Losing her balance, Judy fell to the floor. Benny lunged for the keys.

"Give me back my keys! What's wrong with you? I'll call security!" Judy struggled to get up. Benny was through the door, dropping the keys behind him.

***

Benny practically sprinted to catch up with Davis. Not until he could see him in the distance waiting at the bus stop did he slow down. He was still breathing hard as he approached the bus stop.

"Gotta couple extra dollars on ya?"

Benny was more than happy to get closer. "Sure, I think I have an extra dollar or two." He pulled a five-dollar bill out of his wallet.

"Ain't you that guy that was at the front door of the psycho ward?"

"Yep. As a matter of fact, I am. Checking on a buddy of mine. Looks like he got discharged, though."

"You gotta smoke? Sure could use a smoke." Davis squinted at Benny. With the sun starting to go down behind Benny, it was right in his eyes.

"Don't have a smoke. Bad for you, you know." Benny studied Davis's wrinkled face. Davis was the kind of guy who always looked dirty, no matter how much soap he used. Hands and teeth stained from tobacco. Bald up top, with stringy hair, too long and dirty gray, hanging behind his ears and around his collar. Small eyes, pinched nose, stubble on his jaw line. Greasy, dirty, smelly.

"Yeah, yeah, yeah. What about a ride to the nearest gas station, or is that too 'enabling'?"

Why not? This was going to be easy. "Sure." Benny's mind was racing. He hadn't had a chance to think through his plan completely. "I'm parked in back. Let me get my car." Benny hurried away. He didn't want Davis to change his mind and get on the bus.

While Benny retrieved his car, he was thinking about what would have to happen to make his plan work—the ultimate plan to prove to Maggie how much he loved her. As it began to unfold in his mind, he came to see how clever it was. This revelation gave a surge of strength to his ego, as well as to his crotch. Arousal made him feel like a man. It used to be a rarity, but things seem to be changing. The tug in Benny's pants was getting so tight, he was afraid he might mess them up. But he had to be patient; he wanted to share it with Maggie. He wanted to share his brilliance and his passion with Maggie. He would have to time some things, make a few phone calls.

Davis was feeling frustrated. He needed a smoke, a drink, and a hot piece of flesh, Lord willing. While he waited for his new friend, Davis hoped a little pity would finance more than a pack of cigarettes.

Shit, maybe he's even a little kinky and would be interested in sharing some whore. Maybe he would even like some salami himself. Maybe the whore would make a great salami sandwich.

Davis giggled to himself. He could feel his salami getting hard just thinking about it. One thing Davis learned during his derelict existence is that kink crossed all walks of life. Davis was so pleased with the visual of the salami sandwich that he wasn't paying attention to the car pulling up to the curb. Nor did he see the car trying to get around Benny.

Andrew was irritated that some slob was slowing down traffic; he was ready to get home after a hellish week at work. It was Memorial Day weekend and he planned to enjoy all seventy-two hours of it. When he saw that it was because someone was trying to get Davis's attention, he became more curious than agitated. What was Davis doing out on Friday? Had Maggie changed her mind about discharging him? You can't trust those damn psychiatrists. They never do what they say. Hopefully it's an AA guy.

As Andrew passed the stopped car, he drove slow enough to get a good look at the guy who was motioning to Davis. The smirk on his face and the grin on Davis's told

Andrew they were up to no good. But what could Andrew do? Andrew's job was done, at least until Tuesday morning at nine.

"Come on, dude. What are you waiting for?" Benny yelled out the car window to Davis. Still grinning to himself and anxious for the fun to begin, Davis jumped into the car.

"My name's Benny. What's your pleasure?" Benny glanced over at Davis in the passenger seat, formulating his plans as he drove. Benny was going to need to get to his place with Davis in tow, or at least know where to find him later.

"Davis. Glad to know ya. For sure I need some smokes. And if you're willing, maybe take me up the road to Fantasy Fever. Ever heard of it?"

Benny's brain was working overtime. Fantasy Fever? Yeah, he had heard of it. One of his favorite haunts. Watching the whores sling their hips in his face, so close to his lips he could almost lick their crotch. And he had licked a few, licked them clean once GHB coursed through their veins. He had stayed away from that place since he and Maggie had started dating. She had touched his soul that immensely, that deeply. One day soon he would lick Maggie clean, maybe this weekend with her eyes wide open and in awe, maybe after seeing his brilliance. He was getting hard again. Benny glanced at Davis, hoping his face didn't give anything away. He had to play this right. Didn't want to scare off his prey.

Benny pulled into the gas station on the next corner.

"Here's your smoke stop and another twenty. Tell the clerk I need twenty in gas. I'll take you to Fantasy Fever. I might even buy us both a beer there, but I'll need to go by my place first. Only have a few dollars on me and I need to get a credit card."

"Sounds like a plan to me."

Davis jumped out of the car, not believing his good luck. Finished at the gas station, Benny and Davis drove quietly to Benny's home. Benny noted Davis lit up immediately, without the appropriate niceties of asking if he minded someone smoking in his car. *That's okay, dirt bag, smoke away; it won't be cancer killing you anyway.*

A few minutes later Benny pulled into his driveway. "Hang tight, I'll be right back." Benny turned his car off and jumped out almost in one motion. He was in his house before Davis had a chance to respond.

While Benny was gone, Davis lit up another cigarette. This was some ride, as he looked over the interior of the car. Leather interior, wood-grain dash, Alpine stereo system, built in GPS system. Davis wondered what this guy did, and who was he going to see at the loony bin, anyway. Nobody he had ever met at a nut ward had these kind of connections. No matter, Davis thought, as he took a long drag off of his cigarette, leaning his head back and watching smoke rings leave his lips; this was the life and he was going to enjoy it for as long as he could. Hell, if he played his cards right, maybe he'd get a chance to see the inside of this guy's pad, maybe hang out awhile.

Inside, Benny went straight to the lockbox under his bed to retrieve a key. He then went to his refrigerator to get his newly made stash of GHB. He had stored most of it in a large pickle jar, placing it in the back of the refrigerator for later use. The rest he stored in the small vials, taking great pains to use a ten-milliliter syringe to fill up them up.

They were in the refrigerator as well, but in a little wooden box behind the vegetable bin. He slid out the vegetable bin in order to get the stash. He pulled out the box he had had since childhood. It had been a present from a teacher—the only teacher who had asked about the sores on his hands, or seemed to notice when he was absent—the only person who had tried to give him hope.

Mrs. Riddle had given him the wooden box for his twelfth birthday. "Write your dreams down, Benny, and put them in this box. When you are out of hope, pull your dreams out of your box, and remember that life is not hopeless as long as you have your dreams."

As he opened his dream box, he realized her words had more meaning than he'd thought they ever would. His dream was to be with Maggie, and after he was finished tonight she would be free to be with him forever. Unlocking the safe box, he pulled out his stash, singing his jingle… "Gamma g, liquid e, gonna get some ecstasy just for me."

He grabbed three vials. *That's over thirty grams. More than enough.* He loved this drug. It had been his salvation. He had seen a dream come true many years ago—his mother's nightmare, but his dream.

He wasn't sure how much he would have to give Davis. He'd have to play it by ear. Alcohol would definitely speed things up. Benny knew that with two to four grams, Davis could end up in a coma, but he also knew that it could take as much as 120 grams to kill him. Davis wasn't a big guy, but on second thought, he grabbed a couple more vials. Surely, that would do the trick. He put a jacket on before he headed out toward the car, so he could tuck the vials in a pocket.

"All right, you ready to roll, see some good ol' American T and A?" Benny jumped into his car, started it up, and popped the Beatles' *Abbey Road* into the CD player. "Maxwell's Silver Hammer" played.

"Man, I love that song," yelled Davis, sitting straight up. He sang at the top of his lungs with Ringo. "Bang, bang, Maxwell's silver hammer came down upon her head. Bang, bang, Maxwell's silver hammer made sure she was dead."

There was Davis waving his grubby arms to the music, singing like there was no tomorrow. Benny looked ahead at the road. *Yeah. Bang! Bang!*

Benny pulled up to Fantasy Fever. Before he could put the car in park, Davis was swinging the door open to get out.

"Man, it's been too long! C'mon, Benny, we gotta get a good seat."

Benny looked around in the parking lot. He didn't think that was going to be much of a problem. Benny followed Davis into Fantasy Fever, immediately getting hit with the smell of stale cigarettes and beer. Until his eyes adjusted to the darkness, Benny had to squint in order to see Davis, who was at the bar, already ordering up a couple of beers.

"Follow me, Benny, I have a favorite table. You can see everything from there."

Benny, still squinting, looked toward the stage. There were three thin, scantily clad girls gyrating to "Miss You" by the Rolling Stones. While Benny knew the girls were over twenty-one, they looked to be about fourteen and barely into puberty. All three looked the same. Hair was long and stringy, none of them wore makeup, and their eyes seemed to emit a dull and lifeless ache. One of the girls started working the strip pole on the stage close to Davis's table.

Davis yelled out, "C'mon girl, show us what you got."

Davis turned toward Benny who was just getting to the table.

"See, Benny, this is the best table. Sure is gettin' hot in here, if ya know what I mean." He winked at Benny before turning back to the pole girl.

"Shake them titties, girl."

He was standing with one foot on his chair, holding his beer up above his head and singing to the music, "I've been walking in Central Park, singing after dark, people think I'm cra-azy. I've been stumbling on my feet, shuffling through the street, asking people, what's the matter with you, boy? Hey, can I get another beer over here?" Davis yelled to the bartender. "You mind, Benny-boy? You can afford another beer for ole' Davy, right? Hey, where's that beer? Make it two, one for my money man here."

Turning back to the girl on the stage Davis continued to croon, "Ahh, ahh, ahh, ahh, Lord, I miss you child, ahh, ahh, ahh." He chugged the backwash of his beer down, then started on the new one.

Benny turned his attention to the girl on the pole as she gyrated, rubbing her crotch against it. Her eyes were dull and glassy as her hips moved to the music, giving Davis what he wanted. Humping a pole was better than a beating or screwing their daddy.

"'I wanna kiss you all over, and over again.'" Davis cranked it up again when Exile's hit came on.

Benny wanted to tell him that the Rolling Stones and Exile wrote the songs they were hearing just for Maggie and him, but he knew he couldn't. He didn't want to be the cause of Mick or Jimmy ending up like John, shot to death. Benny just then realized it was Mike Chapman who wrote "I Wanna Kiss You All Over" for the Exiles, and it was Mark Chapman that shot John Lennon. Benny questioned the co-incidence; he could not believe that he had not thought of it until this minute. He was going to have to explore this and write to Yoko. She would want to know about this connection. But for now he needed to take care of Davis. He had to show Maggie he could take care of her and be her strength. *Yoko, I'm sorry but you will have to wait.*

"Benny, hey, Benny! Man this is great. I owe ya, I do."

"My pleasure Davis, I'm enjoying myself, too."

"Hey, bartender, we're ready for another round."

"Hey, man, I gotta take a piss, hold my spot."

Benny noticed the place was getting crowded and loud. All different walks of life looking for relief. From those that appeared mainstream: the white collar worker as well as the blue, to those who lived on the fringe: the drag queens and dykes. All looking to fill a void in their soul; needing to stop the black hole from rotting their gut. Their pain was glaring. His heart began to race. It was Maggie who satisfied his soul, who stopped the rotting in his gut; if he lost her he would become one of them. The thought nauseated him.

While Davis was in the bathroom, a waitress left two fresh beers on the table. Benny took a drink out of one. He took his vial of GHB out of his pocket and poured the potion into the beer. He placed that beer on Davis' side of the table and kept the untouched beer for himself. He looked up just in time to see Davis making his way toward the table.

"Hey, got you a fresh beer, Davis."

Benny picked up Davis's beer to hand it to him.

"A toast, Davis. What do you say?"

"A toast? I'm always for a toast." Davis looked around, the gyrating women on the stage catching his eyes.

"Let's toast to the Ts, what do you say?"

"The Ts?"

"Titties and twats, of course!" Davis busted out laughing.

"To titties and twats." Benny tapped his beer bottle with Davis's and watched him guzzle down the spiked drink.

Davis was in his element. He grabbed at one of the badly made-up transvestites sitting behind him. "Come on, honey, I don't care if you ain't got no twat. Let's dance."

He took her hand and moving to the music led her up to the dance floor. He shimmied into the middle of the group already there. "Hey, let's have a group dance! We can all dance together. Salami sandwiches for everyone!"

Davis moved from person to person, humping them like a dog in heat, flailing his arms above him when he wasn't grabbing the other dancers. He never remembered feeling so good. He saw Benny watching him.

"C'mon, Benny, join the party. I don't want to have all of the fun. You need to have a little. I'll gladly share, right, sweetie?"

Davis turned to swat one of his partners on her butt. He missed, tripped over someone's foot, and stumbled. He grabbed at the person closest to him to steady himself.

"Whoa...Hold still, baby, the room is spinning." Davis leaned on the person he had grabbed.

"Hey, man, you all right? You don't look so good."

"I don't feel so good, neither. I think I'm gonna puke. I gotta go puke." Davis tried to walk toward the bathroom, but the glaring lights hurt his eyes, and people obstructed the way.

"Hey, Davis. Hey, buddy. What's wrong? Let me help."

Davis looked for the person with the familiar voice. "Oh, man, Benny. I don't feel so good. I gotta go puke."

"C'mon Davey-boy, let's get you some fresh air. Sometimes pukin' is good for what ails you."

"You're my best bud, you know that, Benny? My best bud."

"Yeah. I know. Your best bud. Let's go."

Davis leaned toward Benny, falling into him. He clutched Benny's shoulders to steady himself. Benny grabbed Davis around the waist and Davis slung his right arm around Benny's neck. As Benny helped him toward the bathroom, Davis's legs gave way, and Benny had to tighten his grip around Davis's waist. Davis thought he saw them pass the men's bathroom, but he was too sick to care.

***

As Benny led Davis out the back door, two bikers walked in the front. Dressed in old leather jackets, faded blue jeans, and scuffed-up black boots, the unshaven faces of Fred and Tom fit in easily with the diverse patrons of Fantasy Fever. They found seats at the bar where they could watch the action on the stage as well as off. They had been hanging out at Fantasy Fever for months, fading easily into the woodwork. The barkeep gave them each a beer without asking for their order. Fred and Tom, sipping from their beer bottles, settled into the shadows of the night, searching for their connection. When they heard the siren of an ambulance approaching, they made eye contact with each other, but didn't move. Nothing could make them blow this undercover operation; they had worked too hard to become part of the city's slime, and tonight was supposed to be the payoff. Tom and Fred ended up waiting until the barkeep turned on the lights to clean up. Watching him wipe the sticky off the tables and chase the sleepy drunks out the door, Tom and Fred left wondering why Davis Melvin had stood them up.

***

Benny walked Davis out of Fantasy Fever into the back alley. A foul odor hit Benny full force. It was not only the smell of stale alcohol and cigarettes; he had gotten used to that in the club. As his eyes adjusted to the blackness of the night he was able to see bodies in motion on a decaying mattress partially hidden by a dumpster overflowing with rot. In another shadow two people were shooting each other up with crack. No one seemed to notice that Benny had laid Davis down, wrapped a tourniquet around his arm, found a vein, and injected Davis with more GHB.

"911, what's your emergency?"

"I found this guy, I don't think he's breathing, I think we need an ambulance."

"He's not breathing?"

"I don't think so."

"Did you check his pulse? Does he have a pulse?"

"I'll check it now … I'm not sure, if he has one, it's faint, maybe. I'm not sure if I'm doing it right. Can you just send an ambulance?"

"Okay, sir. What's your location?"

"I'm at the corner of Hay and Honeycutt. In the alley behind Fantasy Fever."

"Hay Street and Honeycutt. Okay, sir, someone is on the way. Do you know CPR?"

"Yes, yes I do."

"Good. You don't have to breathe him. You sure you can't rouse him?"

"I'll try again."

"Hey, dude, hey, get up, man, wake up." Benny said the words as he emptied Davis's pockets. "No, ma'am. He's not waking up."

"Okay. What's your name?"

Benny had pulled out Davis's wallet. He opened it and read the name on the ID.

"Davis. Davis Melvin." Benny wasn't sure if he wanted to be identified just yet.

"Okay, Davis. The ambulance is coming. I don't want you to hang up, but I do want you to start CPR. You know how, right?"

"Yeah, but no breathing, right?"

"Yeah, don't worry about that. I'll count with you if you want."

"Yeah, that would be good."

"One, two, three, four, five…"

While Benny and the operator counted in unison, instead of doing chest compressions Benny looked through Davis's wallet. Not much in it besides the ID card and a piece of paper with the name Gladys and a phone number.

"Twelve...thirteen...fourteen...you're doing good, Davis, nineteen, twenty, twenty-one, twenty-two..."

Benny continued to count with the operator, but had no intention of pounding on the man's chest. He had just given Davis enough GHB to put him in a deep sleep. He knew there was a risk that Davis could die in this back alley, but he doubted that would happen. He was the master of anesthesia, not just for work but for pleasure as well. Death was the plan in the long run. He thought about giving him more GHB now and that would be the end of it. But he wanted to show Maggie what he would do to protect her and how far he was willing to go to prove his love for her. And maybe most of all, he wanted Davis to suffer for being the stupid drunk that he was, tripping and landing right in the middle of Benny's life.

Benny crumpled up the piece of paper and threw it toward the dumpster. The moving shadows behind the dumpster caught his attention. The man was off of the mattress, zipping up his pants. His large shape intimidated the figure on the ground.

"Fifty dollars! You're not worth fifty fucking cents. Here's a buck. That's whatcha get outta me."

Benny saw the two crack heads move toward the man as he walked away.

"Hey, dude."

The man turned and faced the crack heads.

They nodded toward the girl on the mattress.

"You got a piece of that?"

"What about it? Want me to rate it for you? Not worth the dollar I gave her, that's for sure."

"Her price is fifty."

"So what? Go jerk yourself." The man turned to walked away.

"Her price is fifty and you need to pay the lady." The two pimps rushed the man. They slammed him against the dumpster and kicked him in the balls. As one of the pimps grabbed him, pinning him against the wall, the other pulled out a switchblade and nicked the man's neck.

"Empty your pockets or you'll be jerking off while I saw your head off your neck." The pimps carried the man back on top of the woman still on the mattress. "Empty your pockets over the lady here, and tell her she was worth every penny of fifty dollars and more. So much more that you're going to give her everything you got."

The man emptied his pockets the best he could, his whole body trembling with fear. Warm urine ran down his legs. He felt the cold blade under his ear. Hearing a siren scream in the night, he prayed for relief. The knife was so sharp he didn't feel more than a slight sting. Blood trickled down, blotting the man's shirt. Then it became a stream. The siren screamed louder, closer. The pimps continued to empty the man's pockets before throwing him into the garbage bin.

"C'mon bitch, we gotta get outta here."

One of the pimps grabbed the prostitute's arm to stand her up. The other snatched the money that had fallen to the ground. Together, the three ran into Fantasy Fever's back door, getting lost in the crowd.

Benny watched the side show with a cold detachment while counting with the 911 operator. He didn't need anything complicating his plan. He was glad to see that the siren had scared everyone off. The ambulance was for him, not for some horny bastard who couldn't save it till he got home. Benny decided that once he took care of Davis he'd call about the man in the garbage bin, if he thought about it.

One, two, three..."

The operator was still counting. Benny could hear the ambulance come to a screeching halt. Three medics ran into the alley with a defibrillator in tow.

"The ambulance is with you now, Davis. I'm hanging up."

Benny didn't bother to respond. He focused on the three medics coming his way.

"Hey, here I am. Glad you guys are here."

"Report says he's not breathing, and no pulse? Report says bystander doing CPR. That you?"

Benny nodded and watched as the three medics got to work. The one talking to Benny also assessed Davis's status and issued orders to the others.

"Lynn, get that AED hooked up, let's see what we got. Nick, get an IV going. I'll intubate."

Benny was impressed with what he saw. The lead medic grabbed an endotracheal tube from his toolbox, slid it down Davis's throat and hooked up an ambu bag to Davis in no time. The second and third medic ripped Davis's shirt away. Lynn opened up the AED, placed the pads and waited for directions from the machine. Nick tied a tourniquet around Davis's bicep and slapped at his arm to get a vein to rise. It only took a few minutes before the AED issued the directive, "Do not shock." Davis had a heart rhythm.

Of course he does, Benny thought.

"Looks like I got a vein, hanging normal saline." Nick taped the IV secure. "Anything else?"

"Give him a bolus of Narcan, just to be on the safe side."

"Lynn, do me a favor and take this ambu bag over so I can get some information."

Grabbing his pen and paper, he stood up and faced Benny. "Looks like you saved this man's life. Name's Steve. Tell me what you know."

***

On his way to the hospital Benny reflected on the story he had supplied to the medics. It was close to the truth. He had gone to Fantasy Fever to unwind after a hard day. Benny had decided to let them know he was a nurse anesthetist. It could work to his advantage and they just might recognize him. After all, he told the paramedics, while Fantasy Fever is scum city, it's a great place for a cold beer when you're trying to forget the life and death decisions of the day. Anyway, he was pretty much minding his own business. He had noticed him because the dude had been partying pretty hard. Drinking, dancing, grabbing at just about any he, she, or it walking by. Pretty annoying actually, and he was just about to deck him, he had told Steve, when he thought the guy was grabbing at him. But then he realized he had stumbled and was trying to steady himself. He'd said that maybe he drank too much and needed some fresh air—could he help him get outside? The next thing he knew he was doing CPR. Pretty benign story, Benny thought. Steve took the information down, loaded Davis in the ambulance, turned the siren on, and sped away to the only emergency room in the city.

Benny knew a lot of the ER personnel at the hospital. From rising through the ranks to working in the intensive care units and now in the operating room, his face was familiar. He was able to slip in and out of departments without question. He showed up in the ER while they were still working on Davis. The medics from the scene were already gone, off to save another poor soul, Benny surmised.

"Hi, Mallory, Stephanie, whatcha got here?"

Benny walked in on a nurse and a PA who were working on Davis.

Stephanie glanced at the door. "Hi, Benny, some drunk passed out, quit breathing, probably mixing up some drugs with his beer. He stinks to high heaven, that's for sure. What are you doing down here? Trying to drum up some business for the OR?"

Before Benny answered, Stephanie was back to business.

"Mallory, see if we have any lab work back. And while you're at it, find out why nobody's come to get this guy for his CT scan. I'm assuming it was ordered stat."

Mallory rolled her eyes. "Yeah, it was ordered stat. But you know how that goes."

"Unfortunately I do. Would you please let radiology know stat means stat. If there's a problem I want the phone."

Mallory shrugged her shoulders; she had been through this before. "Whatever you say, boss."

Mallory mockingly saluted Stephanie before leaving the room.

Benny watched as Stephanie began a systematic neurological examination on Davis.

"The OR is dead. Thought I'd come down here. See what's going on."

"I suppose." Stephanie was only half listening. She was preoccupied with why her patient's breathing was so weak.

"I don't get it. His EKG is not significant. Nothing significant from the NG tube but regular gastric contents. Don't have the drug screen back yet. They said they gave him some Narcan but it didn't help. Strange thing is, the medics who picked him up said somebody gave him CPR, a hospital employee even, basically saving his life, but there's no evidence. No broken ribs, nothing."

Stephanie opened Davis's eyes and flickered a light at his pupils, looking for a response. Then she balled up her fist and crammed it into Davis's chest. Nothing. Stephanie attempted to get some reaction from Davis with various pinches and prodding. She looked up at Benny, sighing and shaking her head. She was clearly baffled.

"Got the lab work, nothing really out of whack," Mallory said as she came back through the door.

Stephanie took the lab results from Mallory, looked them over, shaking her head again. "What about the CT scan?"

"They finally called. Said they were ready. Joni's coming from respiratory to help me get him there."

"I'll help, too. You could probably use an extra hand." Benny was more than happy to keep tabs on Davis's initial assessment.

"You know I'm always grateful for extra help. We're short tonight. Hell, we're short every night."

Mallory got Davis ready for the ride to radiology. EKG monitors, IVs, oxygen, all had to go. It was a major process. Joni came in to take care of the respirator.

When Mallory decided Davis was ready for transport, she checked with Joni.

"You good?"

Joni nodded in response.

"Okay, Benny, let's roll."

Stephanie, who had left the room to consult with one of the ER doctors, met them in the hallway.

"Mallory, there's orders in the chart to admit him to ICU. I've already called them. Give them a heads up about twenty minutes before the scan is over and they'll give you a room number."

Stephanie put the ER paperwork in a manila folder and placed it on Davis's legs. "You got it, boss."

Mallory, Benny, and Joni rolled Davis down the hallway toward radiology.

After the CT scan, Mallory, Joni, and Benny rolled Davis to the medical ICU unit. Mallory rattled off her report as the ICU nurses disconnected Davis from the ER's equipment and connected him to the equipment in the ICU room.

"Here's his record. The upshot is we don't know why he's like this. Found on the street. Drug screen negative, CT scan negative. Did have a positive alcohol level and there's a few tests still outstanding."

"Did he have surgery?" Melanie was puzzled, wondering why Benny was in the room. She never did like him and thought he was a little creepy, even though there was nothing she could pinpoint. Other people seemed to get along great with him and Melanie knew he was one of the best nurse anesthetists at the hospital. But she couldn't help it; she didn't like him at all.

"No. Couldn't sleep; just helping Mallory out in the ER." Melanie always put Benny on edge. Now he was going to have to deal with her. Talk about bad luck. "Melanie, I thought you worked for surgical ICU. You transfer over here?"

"Not hardly. Our census was down, and one of the nurses here called in sick. I'm just doing them a favor."

"Aren't you the good nurse." He was quietly relieved. He was also ready to get out of this room. He had a list of things he needed to do. The first one was to get some sleep. It was almost morning and the next forty-eight hours were going to be very busy. He wanted to get this show on the road.

"Mallory, if you're done with me, I think I'm going to skate."

"Yeah, sure, Benny. Thanks for your help. Any time you need something to do in the middle of the night, just let me know. I can always keep you busy."

"Great. I'll remember that. See ya."

He left the ICU while Melanie, Mallory, and Joni tended to Davis.

Before leaving the hospital he went to the operating room nurses' station. There he ran into the secretary watching a video on YouTube.

Glancing up just long enough to see that it was Benny, the secretary asked him, "What you doin' here?"

"Hey, Rita. A friend of mine got admitted to the hospital, just here late. Anything going on?" Benny scanned the secretary's desk searching for the rolodex.

"Naah, slow as snails. What's wrong with your friend?" Rita paid more attention to the YouTube video than to Benny.

He reached for the rolodex and flipped through the cards. "Hey, Rita, hand me that pen in front of you."

"Mm?"

He pointed to the pen.

"Here. What's wrong with your friend?" Video over, Rita wanted to know more about Benny's friend, but now he was busy scribbling down a number. "Benny, you must be getting deaf. I asked you what's wrong with your friend."

He handed the pen back to her.

"Oh, a little pneumonia, he'll be all right. Thanks, Rita, see ya." He tucked the number in his pocket and left the hospital.

Rita stood up and watched Benny walk away as a surgical technician came to the desk. She was about to take the rolodex off the counter and put it back near the phone.

"I thought I heard talking up here. Is there a case?"

"Naah. Just Benny. Looking for a number from the rolodex; probably for a doctor for his sick friend."

The surgical technician looked at the number Benny left exposed on the rolodex. "His friend needs a harvesting team?"

"Naah, that can't be right. Those cards must have moved. That don't make any sense. Here, look at this video I found on YouTube. It's a really good one."

Rita placed the rolodex near her phone. "Here, sit down so you can see this video. It's a hoot."

Rita and the surgical technician turned their attention to the computer, not giving Benny another thought.

***

Benny was tired; he felt it in his eyes, deep in his bones. He was on his way home to get some sleep. He knew he had given Davis enough GHB to keep him down for a good six hours, and since he was on a respirator he didn't have to worry about him dying either. He wanted to get at least four hours of sleep. This might be the only time to get it. He pulled his cell phone out along with the number he had found in the rolodex.

"Hello, this is the organ donor people? Uh, my uncle, he always…he's not doing good. He always talked about helping others if something bad happened to him. I don't think he's going to make it. I'm not sure if this is the right time, I feel kinda weird … Well, I'm not sure everything that's wrong. He's on a breathing machine at Sycamore Hills Hospital…His name? His name is Davis Melvin. Are you sure this is the right thing? I feel kind of creepy … Yeah, well, if it will help a lot of people … Yeah, he would want that … Okay, yeah, I feel a little better. Thanks. Okay, thanks, you too, bye."

Benny closed his phone. The pendulum was starting to swing and he knew there was no stopping it now.

Chapter 3
Saturday

What makes the pain we feel from
shame and jealousy so cutting
is that vanity can give us no assistance
in bearing them.

Francois de La Rochefoucauld

Kristin waited with nervous excitement at the airport terminal. She hadn't seen her brother since his wife's funeral. And now he was coming home to stay. The funeral had been so hard on everyone, so unexpected. Cancer was such a confounding disease. It seemed to have no limits on stealing life from the young. Kristin had thought that being a nurse would help her deal with death when it hit her own family, but when it robbed Eric of his wife, she could barely take it. The pain she saw in Eric's eyes was just too much.

Kris and Eric had always been close. She was two years older and often acted like a mother hen. Eric called her bossy growing up, and her mother would always tell her, "You act like his sister; I'll act like his mother." But their mother had also told them to be good to each other; and love each other. Friends may not always be around, so it would be important to be there for each other. Kris had come to learn just how true these words were.

"Hey, blue eyes!"

Kristin was caught off guard. Her mother called her blue eyes, but it was her brother's voice. She wiped her tears away, and looking up, she saw Eric.

"Hey, little bro!"

"Kris, you've got to get over that little bro thing, I've been taller than you for years, way taller." He responded good-naturedly by tousling the top of her head. He loomed over Kristin by a good six inches, and had since high school.

"You may be taller than me but you will always be my little brother!" Kris gave Eric a big hug.

"Let's get your bags; Mom can't wait to see you!"

They walked in silence, both happy to have the comfort of each other, knowing neither had to speak. The silence was not broken until they were in Kristin's car driving toward home.

"Eric, are you sure you want to move back home? I love the idea, but to quit your job, leave all of your friends? You and Katelyn were so happy in the mountains."

"You know Kris, when Kate first became sick our friends seemed to rally around us and really tried to support us. As the days and weeks wore on, one by one we saw them less and less. I don't blame them really, they have lives to live, children to take care of, but it seemed to sadden Kate. I hated seeing her like that; it hurt me to see her hurt. When she died, they all came back again, but not for long. They looked so helpless and guilty, like it was their fault that she died and they were still alive, enjoying themselves. It was hard on them and on me. I know they loved Kate, almost as much as I did. But it didn't seem to make it easier on any of us. I knew I would feel lonely, but I didn't like being alone.

I thought if I came home I wouldn't feel so all alone...things would be familiar."

As Kristin listened to her brother talk, she could feel the tears well up in her eyes, feeling the pain of her sister-in-law's death.

Eric went on, not noticing Kristin's glistening tears. "When Mom told me I was always welcome, even if it was to lick my wounds, it just sounded good." Eric looked over at Kristin.

"Hey. Hey, Kristin. Don't cry. I'm sorry."

"It's okay. I'll be okay."

Kristin sniffed and wiped her eyes with the back of her hand. She was glad she was driving and not able to take her eyes off the road. Looking at her brother at this point would reduce her to out-and-out wailing. He looked out the side window, not really seeing anything. Neither spoke for a few minutes, trying to get a handle on the pain searing their hearts.

Kristin was first to break the silence. She thought if she could bring up a different subject maybe the hurt could be tamped down, at least for a little while.

"So little bro, you looked into a job yet?"

Eric was happy to get his mind elsewhere. "As a matter of fact, on Tuesday I'm supposed to go to a job interview. I think it's just a formality. I did a phone interview about a week ago, thanks to Bear. I guess he still has some pretty good connections in the department here. So, what about you? Tell me what my favorite sister is up to."

"Ha-ha, you mean your only sister. You know, it's you, not me, who sounds more and more like Mom as we get older. Calling me blue eyes; your favorite sister. When we were little I would try to get her to tell me I was her favorite child, and she would say that I was her favorite daughter. I would say, 'Mom, I'm your only daughter.' She would just smile and say, 'Well, you are my favorite girl in the whole wide world,' and that would be the end of that. I guess I liked her answer so much I let her get away with not telling me I was her favorite child."

"Ah, always the analyst. I think you have more of a detective brain than I do."

"Having Bear for a stepdad doesn't hurt. Plus, being a psych nurse for so long I can't help it. I am happy in the operating room, though. You know, Eric, sometimes superficial is just that: superficial. It's actually a very comfortable place to be."

"Is that your final analysis, Dr. Freud?" Eric couldn't help but rib Kris; it was just too easy.

"All right, all right. Analysis paralysis. I guess I just can't help it, as I said." Kristin giggled at herself. "Okay, so where was I? Oh, yeah, a superficial place. Actually the OR is not at all superficial, but a lot of the people who work there are. I try not to dissect the people, but their personalities are so textbook, it helps me keep my psych skills up. Quite a narcissistic lot, they are, but I guess that goes with the territory. I don't feel as if I fit in there."

Kristin paused, thinking about what she had just said. "Does that mean I have a bigger or smaller ego?" Kristin looked at Eric for a response.

Eric just shook his head and burst out laughing.

Kristin reached over swatting Eric's head.

"Just call me Mrs. Freud." Kristin couldn't help but laugh at herself. "Anyway, I have to say I'm loving it. Surgery is just an incredible field. I am totally in awe of the sur-geons—the good ones, anyway."

"Well, please don't tell me about the bad ones...unless I need surgery, of course. How's good ol'...what's his name? Is there a name?" Eric peered over at Kristin to read her face.

"No, no name, nobody. You'd think I might meet someone in the OR, but as usual the good ones are mar-ried. So are the bad ones, when I think about it. There are a couple of single guys up there, but they are either creepy or gay. What about you? Are you ready to get back in the swing of things?"

"Not hardly. As I said, I'm still licking my wounds."

Kristin pulled into their mother's driveway. "Looks like we're home."

She shut off the car and looked over at Eric when she heard him sigh. She thought she saw a sense of peace over-come her brother. "You okay?"

"Never better, sis," Eric said, smiling to his favorite and only sister.

For the first time since Katelyn's funeral, the heavy load Eric carried in his heart and on his shoulders became a little lighter.

Kristin jumped out of the car and ran into the house to announce Eric's arrival.

"Mom, Bear, we're home! We're home." She held the door open for her brother, motioning him to get into the house. "C'mon, Eric, we'll get your luggage later."

Kristin and Eric's mom came running from the kitch-en. She called up the stairs to her husband. "Bear, Eric's home! Eric, I'm so glad you're here." Toni met Eric at the front door. She stood on her tiptoes to give her six-foot-two-inch son a kiss on the cheek.

Eric bent down, happy to accept her kiss and to hug her back. "It's good to be home, Mom, you don't know how much."

Feeling the tears well up in her eyes, Toni turned back toward the stairs. It was so hard to see her children in pain; she could feel it through and through. "Bear, did you hear me, Eric's home!"

"I'm coming, Toni, I'm coming. I was on the can. Can't a man get some privacy around here?" Bear gave his wife a playful swat on her behind as he passed her on the stairs, winking at Kristin.

"Bear, the kids." Toni blushed, trying to hide her approval of her husband's hands on her body.

"Woman, these kids have seen me pat you on the behind before. They might even see more if they keep watching." Bear continued to tease Toni, engulfing her slight frame in his massive physique.

"Oh, Bear, you're a silly old teddy bear." Toni returned his hug and not without returning the swat.

"I called you down to see Eric. Behave yourself."

Bear turned to Kristin and Eric. "You know, I usually have to tell your mom to behave."

Toni blushed again. A simple touch from her husband still excited her. She seemed to always want him, even after all of their years together. Toni decided to escape so she could compose herself.

"I'm going to the kitchen. Eric, I hope you're hungry."

"Maybe Eric's not, Mom, but I am. I'll come with you." Kristin giggled as she followed her mother to the back of the house.

"Hey, old man." Bear held his hand out to shake his stepson's hand but the two fell into a natural embrace, hugging and patting each other on the back. "How you holding up?"

"Okay, Bear. Sometimes I feel like I'm sucking wind, but I'm okay."

Bear knew what sucking wind felt like, and knew nothing made it better but the passage of time. "Come on, let's get your luggage. Then we'll grab something to eat. You hungry?"

"Maybe a little. Could use a beer, however."

"Got one of those, too."

Eric and Bear retrieved the luggage from the car. "You go on in the kitchen with your mom and I'll take the suitcases upstairs. She's been worried about you. She's really glad you decided to come home. I am, too."

"Thanks, Bear. You know, I always wanted a relationship like the one you and mom have. I thought I was going to have that with Katelyn."

Both Eric and Bear had tears in their eyes.

"Eric, I know the pain you're feeling is almost more than you can handle. Just try to take it one day at a time. For what it's worth, if you remember correctly it took both your mother and me a couple of times before we got to hold on to the magic."

"Yeah, now that you mention it, I do." Eric gave his stepfather a gentle nudge. "So there's still hope, huh?"

"You may not feel like it now. But with time you will, son. Now go see your mom and get that beer. They should be ice cold."

Kristin and Toni were laying out lunch when Eric walked into the kitchen.

"There you are. I was just telling Mom that you have an interview this week with the police department."

"Yeah," Eric replied, pulling a cold beer from the refrigerator. "The face-to-face interview's on Tuesday. Already had a phone interview, so I'm hoping Tuesday's just a formality." Eric popped the top off his favorite beer, Samuel Adams, and took a big gulp. "I'm sure it helps to have Bear as my stepdad. Shoot, it's probably because of him I'm a detective anyway."

Even though Toni discouraged preferential treatment because of connections, she was grateful for this one. She knew that Eric had the credentials to land this job without Bear, but having a foot in the door helped to ease the worry. And she knew Eric would jump into this job with both feet; hopefully it would give him a place to channel his pain. "Eric, we've got hoagie rolls, roast beef, ham, provolone, swiss, colby. What's your pleasure?"

"Mom, you sit down and relax. Kristin will get something for me if I need it." Eric winked at his mother.

"Hey, thanks, little bro." Kristin reached for plates from the cupboard.

"But I will. Mom, you just enjoy Eric being home. Let's see if I can get this right. Everything except swiss cheese, and no tomatoes. Plus, a lot of mayo. Still right?"

"Yep, and heavy on the roast beef. All of a sudden I'm starving." Eric finished up his beer and reached for another.

"Grab two while you're in there." Bear walked into the kitchen. "I could use a cold one myself."

***

Benny set his alarm for nine in the morning. He didn't dare sleep any longer. Davis would need more GHB for one thing. Benny hoped he would be able to give Davis something to paralyze him until the harvesting, but if not the GHB would have to do. After a quick shower and throwing on a pair of scrubs, he reached under his bed and pulled out his lockbox. He took three syringes and needles out and put them in his breast pocket. He pulled out a bottle of Ritalin, and popped a couple without using anything to wash them down. After getting the key for the dream box, he put the lockbox back under the bed, went to the refrigerator, and grabbed a couple of vials of GHB. He took the syringes and needles out of his pocket and drew up ten milliliters of GHB in each syringe. He put a short white lab coat on from the hall closet, put the syringes in his pocket, jumped in his car, and sped toward the hospital.

At the hospital his first stop was the medical records department. He needed to retrieve some paperwork from the harvesting he had witnessed on Friday morning. Because the medical records department had become so restricted over the years in an effort to protect privacy, Benny had to punch a code at the entrance in order to gain access. He looked around to see a few transcriptionists typing away, not noticing he had come through the door. He could barely hear a radio playing in the background. On a regular workday, the medical records department would be in constant motion. Charts stacked on every desk, in every bookcase. Some to be copied, others reviewed, some to be taken apart, or put back together and then placed in a different stack. The noise level seemed to match the amount of clutter; computers buzzing, people chatting, radios playing. Since it was Saturday it was the quiet that was deafening. Benny walked to the physicians' workroom. On any given day and at any time of the day, there could be two or three people, usually doctors or physician assistants, sifting through stacks of delinquent charts, dictating, signing, or dating their work.

Today, it was a flunky hospitalist and a nurse practitioner with patients' charts that were stacked three feet high. Benny didn't know either of them but had seen them around, and nodded his head at them when they looked his way. No bother there. He went back out to where the transcriptionists were keying the dictation in their ears.

"Hey, ladies." Benny touched the closest one on her shoulder.

She jumped. "Sweetie, don't scare me like that! You're gonna give me a heart attack!" Candy fanned herself for effect.

"Sorry. Didn't mean to scare you."

Over her initial fright, Candy quickly sized Benny up. This fella was kinda cute. Candy had not worked at the hospital very long before she started hearing the latest gossip about the hospital romances. Some of them were just like the stories she watched on TV. A doctor having an affair with a nobody girl. But the nobody girl listened to her doctor, loved her doctor, put him on a pedestal. And then he would love her back. He would dump the snotty wife and love the nobody girl forever.

Candy had become so obsessed with the hospital gossip that the lies became her truths. She finally understood her destiny. She tried to explain it to her boyfriend when she broke up with him. After all, he lived in a trailer park. Surely he saw that she deserved more than that.

This fella just might be the one, Candy thought.

She gave Benny the once-over.

"That's okay, sweetie. What can I do for you? Or should I say, what can I do to you?" Candy eyed Benny up and down, giggling at her own brazen behavior.

The other typist, at first startled by Candy's outcry, went back to her typing. She had seen Candy "at work" many times before and had become bored by Candy's sad attempts to snag a man.

Benny was only slightly amused by Candy. *What a slut. I should tell her to go hang out at Fantasy Fever with all the other needy whores.* "I need a chart from yesterday's discharges. I work in the OR."

"Hot damn, sugar pants, you a surgeon?" Candy thought she had hit pay dirt. "Come on this way, I'll find you that chart." Candy walked Benny toward a pushcart that resembled a large grocery cart crammed full of medical records. Benny immediately started digging through the pile of charts. "This part ain't my usual department, but I'll help you find what you're looking for. Whatcha- doing here on a Saturday morning, anyway? Ain't you got a sexy wife to keep you home and horny?" Candy leaned across the pushcart toward Benny. It gave him a full view of puffy pale breasts busting from her Wonderbra.

Benny was disgusted, but he needed that chart. Benny grabbed Candy by her shoulders. "What's your name?"

"Candy, sugar pants, what's yours?"

"Benny." Staring at Candy's mountainous cleavage, then into Candy's eyes, he continued, "Those are the puffiest, tastiest looking pieces of Candy that I have seen in a while. And I would love a taste but I've got to get my work done."

Candy could feel her heart starting to beat faster. He wanted her, she could feel it. She knew she could get her a doctor. Maybe he'll even take me here, right now. She had heard the stories. They get all hot and bothered at work, wanting to share their love juices with everybody, not caring about waiting until they get home. Then she would be in the gossip, just like the stories on TV.

"You sure you don't want a taste now? My candy's awfully sweet." Candy moved around the cart to get closer to Benny. She had moved so close to him, her pushed-up miracle breasts hampered his arms from moving freely.

"You're definitely tempting, but I've got things to do." Benny was getting testy, starting to lose his cool. He pushed Candy away and focused on finding the record he needed.

Candy watched him for a few seconds. She wasn't sure what to do next. Doctors were definitely strange, but she was ready to listen, put him on a pedestal, be his nobody girl. But this was going to take more effort than she thought. "Benny, honey, I gotta get back to work. Come see me at my desk when you're done. I'll give you my phone number for later. Okay, sweetie? Okay?"

Candy had to nudge Benny to get him to look at her. When he barely looked at her, Candy went back to her desk, wondering how something that looked so promising could end so quickly.

Benny was deep in thought, wishing he had grabbed the paperwork on Friday when he had the chance. It would have helped, too, if he could remember the name of poor slob who had been gutted. He kept searching through the mountain of records until he found the one he wanted.

He looked around him to see if anyone was watching. Just to make sure, he sat down in the nearest cubicle where he could look at the record without being observed. Flipping it open, he combed through the different sections looking for the tests he needed. It was getting harder and harder to locate specific paperwork in the records these days. Now that the hospital had to tighten their financial belt, all the color coded forms were being replaced by white copies. Finally Benny found what he was looking for. "Apnea test, EEG. Here's the Glasgow. Hmm...should already have a Glasgow, but just in case. Maybe the lab, too."

He removed the paperwork from the record, rolled it up, and put it in a pocket. He walked to the cart where he had found the record. Before returning it he looked at all the different stacks of records. Most of the stacks were labeled, in some form or fashion, above or below them, dictating where they needed to be next. Benny walked to the bookcase labeled "Ready for Microfiche" and shoved the record to the bottom of the pile. He left the medical records department the same way he came in, forgetting all about Candy and her puffy white wonder breasts. Not waiting for the elevator, Benny bounded up the stairs two at a time toward Davis's nursing unit. As Benny walked through the doors of the intensive care unit he was hit with noise and commotion. The chatter came from everywhere: relatives visiting the patients or talking with staff; doctors asking for reports; respiratory, lab, and housekeeping staff waylaying their favorite nurse to gab about the shoddy work done by their co-workers. All of the televisions were on and blaring. Machines beeped, swooshed, or sucked. The hallway was an obstacle course of an assortment of rolling carts, each with its own purpose. A couple held breakfast trays, others were dirty-linen hampers, and in front of every room was a nurses' portable workstation. He recognized the craziness on the ICU unit immediately. The more seasoned staff had a name for this controlled chaos: ICU psychosis. It was always a harbinger of impending death—even more than a full moon—some nurses swore.

Benny went to Davis's room. It was empty except for the patient he had left just a few hours earlier. There he was, a tube sticking out of his mouth, connected to a respirator. The rhythmic machine swooshed, pushing oxygen into his lungs, and then swooshed again, pulling carbon dioxide out. Benny pulled a syringe of GHB out of his pocket and immediately gave Davis a bolus through his IV. Just as he turned around to look for the chart a nurse came in the room. Benny was grateful to see a nurse who he knew trusted him.

"Hey, Benny. You know this guy?"

"Lee. Not really. I was with the ER nurse last night when she brought him up. Just helping out. You guys know any more?"

"Sure don't. Tests aren't conclusive. I do know the vultures are already circling. They said someone called the donor hotline, said this guy was a possible donor. There's a few more tests that need to be done, but it doesn't look good either way." Lee was hanging a new bag of IV fluids, documenting vital signs.

"Those harvesting teams, they give me a creepy feeling. They can practically smell warm blood in a dead body."

"Yeah, we did a harvesting just yesterday, seems we're seeing them more often lately. Hey, you mind if I look at the chart? I couldn't sleep last night and ended up helping out. This case just got my curiosity. No relatives?"

Lee handed Benny the record. "None on my shift. But I heard it was a relative that called the harvesting team. Tell me if you see something of interest, maybe I missed something. I'll be at the nurses' station for a minute if you need me. Need to get some paperwork for his chart."

Benny looked through the record. They had continued the neurological exams, as he thought they would. No apnea tests yet. He was coming back, anyway, to give him another dose of GHB. He'd slip the tests in then, and the EEG. From Davis's chart Benny took out a sheet of labels with Davis's name and his medical record number printed on them and slid it into his pocket. Leaving Davis's room, Benny dropped the chart on Lee's workstation. He saw her kneeling on the floor by a meal tray rolling cart.

"I didn't see anything, Lee. See ya."

Lee looked Benny's way, nodding. She had stooped down to the floor, cleaning up an overturned milk carton while a housekeeper sat at the nurses' station reading the local paper.

Benny went to the hospital cafeteria to get something to eat. It was relatively quiet. After breakfast time but before lunch. He grabbed a sandwich and a bottle of water from the quick service line and found a table tucked away in a corner. He unwrapped his sandwich only halfway so he wouldn't have to touch it with his own hands while he ate. Even though he washed his hands before he came into the cafeteria, he still had to touch things between washing his hands and the handling of his sandwich.

Once he took a bite he realized how hungry he was, and the sandwich was gone in no time. Then he gulped down some of his water. He wiped the table down and made sure no crumbs or drops of water were left behind, pulled the confiscated papers out, and went to work on the needed modifications. He glanced at the clock on the wall. He didn't need to give Davis more GHB until the change of shift. He'd wait until then to get this paperwork back in his chart. Benny was hoping Melanie would not be there; she could definitely make things more difficult. Seeing he had a couple hours of free time, Benny decided it would be a good idea to get a nap. He would have to be up off and on throughout the night and had to work on Sunday. What he wanted to do was call Maggie; hear her voice, caress her soft skin. But he vowed to deny himself. This was to be his sacrifice until he could adequately demonstrate his love to her. Hopefully, if everything went as planned, he would soon be able to go to her and show her proof of his love. *Soon, Maggie, my love, my life; very soon.* Benny placed his paperwork in his lab coat pocket and walked out of the cafeteria.

"Sugar pants! Hey, you were gonna come by my desk and get my number." Candy was coming into the cafeteria for her morning break and ran into Benny on his way out the door. Benny was caught off guard, still with Maggie on his mind.

"Excuse me?"

"Benny, honey. It's me, sweet Candy." Candy licked her forefinger, letting her finger linger on her bottom lip for just a second.

"You remember my candy." Candy challenged him to remember her from the morning. She then started to lightly caress one of her own breasts.

Benny's memory of the morning came back to him. *What a whore.* "Oh, yeah. So thanks for helping me. See ya."

"Wait, sugar pants. You didn't get my number, and I gotta few minutes now." Candy was thinking hard. She needed to keep him interested. She was getting excited again, like this morning. She could feel her nipples harden under her blouse. "Hey, maybe you could show me the OR if you got the time, if you know what I mean." Candy could feel the pulse in her groin. It had been forever since she had been touched, since she'd dumped her boyfriend from the trailer park.

Benny was reminded of the trash from Fantasy Fever. It had been a while since he had been with a woman the only way he could. He had plenty of GHB to go around. He looked at Candy. What a fat hog. But he was wound awfully tight. A little release might be good. He doubted if he could nap anyway.

"I tell you what. Can't go to the main OR, surgery going on. But the day surgery unit is closed; no surgery there. I'll be able to show you all kinds of stuff. Let me get a Coke before we go, I'm thinking I might get a little thirsty."

"You kidding? Really?" Candy felt her crotch tingling; she wanted to rub it. She waited outside the cafeteria door while Benny paid for his soda. This was going to be hot. Just like in the stories on TV. This was off limits, forbidden. Next week she would be the queen of the hospital gossip. They'd be talking about how Benny fell in love with Candy, she would be his nobody girl. Then she would be somebody. All the other girls would look at her and be jealous. She knew it, her destiny was starting today.

"Let's go, sweet Candy. I'll show you some of the toys they have; maybe they were named after you. Ever heard of candy-cane stirrups? They can be all kinds of fun. Are you all kinds of fun, Miss Candy?" Benny smiled at her while they walked down the hallway.

Candy was so excited she wasn't even sure what he had said. The halls were empty. Their footsteps echoed up and down the hallway. Candy just knew Benny could hear her heartbeat; she could definitely feel the pounding. Even though the day surgery department was a Monday through Friday operation, it was never locked.

Benny ushered Candy through the maze of different rooms: the preoperative room, a supply room, a utility room, deeper and deeper into the maze, passing a couple of the operating rooms. There were no windows to see the outside world.

Candy heard a low howling of what she thought was the wind. It made her feel a little apprehensive. "Sugar pants, this sure is a creepy feely place. It's too quiet."

Benny didn't respond. He opened a door and gently guided her through it.

The quietness made her nervous. She started talking just to make noise. "Are we going to have a storm today? It sounds like the wind is blowing." Candy looked to Benny for comfort. "You're my strong man though, aren't ya, sugar pants? You'll help me feel safe, won't ya?"

Candy started for Benny as she eyed the operating-room bed. He had put his soda down on a small metal table and had his back toward Candy. He took a drink of the soda before pulling the small vial out of his pocket and poured some of the contents into the cup.

As Candy nestled up to Benny's back, he turned to face her. "Here, Candy, have a drink. Don't want you to get thirsty during the tour."

Candy took the cup from Benny. "I am a little thirsty."

He slowly backed her up until she was stopped by the bed. "Take another drink, Candy." Benny gripped her hand that held the drink, guiding it to her lips.

"My man is taking care of me. Sugar pants, what's your last name anyway? Dr. Who? Just wait till the girls hear about my man. They'll be so jealous."

She sipped another drink before he took the drink away.

"Let's get down to business, Dr. Who."

Giggling, Candy sat herself on the bed. She pulled Benny in between her legs and massaged Benny's thighs. She was feeling dreamy.

"Let me help you lay down. Time for me to taste some of your sweet candy."

She watched while he took two long metal poles that looked like candy canes off a hook from the wall. She watched him fasten one to each side of the bed. He put arm boards on each side of the bed as well. "Whatcha doin', Dr. Who? C'mon, sugar pants, c'mon, Dr. Who, have some a my sweet candy." She tried to get up, but the room was dizzy, and she fell back, almost falling off the bed.

"Whoa, Candy. Here, let's get something to help you stay on that bed." Benny helped Candy lie down. He reached into a drawer close to the head of the bed, pulling out two long soft ties: arm restraints. He tied each of Candy's arms to an arm board. Candy was so drugged, she could only watch. He then walked to the end of the bed. He picked up her right leg first, taking her shoe off and placing her foot in the stirrup. He then did the same to her left. Using the remote, he pivoted the end of the bed so that her bottom was at the edge and tilted toward the ceiling. She made a vain attempt to pick her head up to see what was happening. As he pulled her pants down toward her ankles, she caught his glare. His eyes pierced her soul with disgust. Terror set into Candy's being. For a split second, she was fully aware that she had met the devil. She tried to scream...right before she passed out.

After Benny had his fill of Candy he cleaned up the semen that ended up on the floor; he had no desire to leave a signature. He couldn't decide if he should leave Candy on the bed or try to move her. She wouldn't remember too much. He looked at his watch. It was about time for him to get back to the ICU; he needed to get that paperwork in Davis's chart before the second shift came in. He also needed to give Davis more GHB. He opted to leave her where she was. She's a nobody, he reasoned, and she would probably be too embarrassed to tell anyone, anyway. He looked at Candy's fat, pasty thighs hiked up in those candy-cane stirrups. She definitely gave new meaning to the term "hog-tied." As he left the room, he turned off the lights and closed the door; not giving sweet Candy, the nobody girl, a second thought.

Before Benny made it to the ICU unit he gave the harvesting team another call. "Yeah. I called about my uncle yesterday, Melvin Davis ... You did call? I think those tests were done today ... Yeah, I just hate to see him suffer, that's all. And he could be saving so many people. That's what he'd want, ya know. That's all. Okay, okay. No, that's all. Bye."

The vultures were starting to get nosy. Asking too many questions.

Benny made the trek up to the ICU and went directly into Davis's room. Lee was hanging a new IV bag.

"Back so soon?" Lee was surprised to see Benny back at all.

"Yeah, I guess I'm having trouble letting go. Any change?"

"Not really."

"Care if I look at the chart?"

"Be my guest. It's about time for me to go, anyway. I need to go give the report. See ya."

"Who's relieving you?"

Benny called the question to Lee, but she didn't hear him.

The clamor on the unit was still at a vigorous pitch. Since Lee was gone, he wanted to give Davis more GHB. Maybe this would be the last. He could give him a little extra; too bad he couldn't make it a drip. *Why not?* He just needed to get it into the bag before anybody came in. The nurses were reporting off to each other, he should have the time.

Benny stood by the IV and peered out the door. From this angle no one could really see him. He pulled the drug-filled syringe out of his pocket, grabbed a needle from the nursing supplies in the room, and quickly injected most of the drug into the IV bag Lee had just hung. *This is perfect*, Benny thought. This should get Davis through the night without Benny having to come back. Benny was very pleased with this turn of events. The newly concocted GHB drip would definitely make the next twelve hours easier. He settled in with the record. He pulled the paperwork, which he had confiscated earlier in the morning, out of his pocket and put it in the chart. He was extremely proud of himself. Getting that paperwork in the chart could have been a problem. He would definitely be able to get some sleep now, which he needed badly. The Ritalin was wearing off and his eyes were getting tired. Benny stood over Davis's bed staring at the lifeless body. The repetitive swooshing of the ventilator was taking a toll on Benny, putting his brain in a dull haze.

"What are you doing here?" Melanie's harsh tone pierced Benny's trance.

Benny jumped. *Great.* "Just seeing how he's doing. How are you doing this fine evening, Melanie?"

Ignoring Benny, Melanie walked past him and reached for Davis's medical record. "There it is."

At that same time, another person walked in the door. "Melanie, I have the harvesting team on the phone. They want to know if the apnea test has been done yet."

"I don't think so, Iris. Lee didn't say anything about it when she gave the report."

"Can I see it?"

Iris didn't wait for Melanie's response. She took the record out of Melanie's hands. "I'll have it at the nurses' station." Iris left the room.

Melanie faced Benny. "Why did you say you were here?"

Benny decided it was time to go. "No reason. Leaving now."

Bingo! Benny left the ICU as Iris spoke on the phone to the harvesting team.

"Apnea test?" he overheard Iris saying. "It's here now. And that completes the paperwork."

Benny would be able to get some real sleep now. Davis was on a GHB drip. The harvesting team would be ready first thing in the morning. By tomorrow night Maggie would be his.

At home, Benny realized how hungry he was. He wanted a big fat porterhouse. He pulled one out of the refrigerator and tossed it on his indoor grill. Five minutes on one side, five on the other. A dash of salt. While it was browning, Benny opened a bag of salad and dumped it in a bowl. Washed and cut a tomato and dropped it on the lettuce. Pulled a wine glass from the cupboard and popped the cork on a bottle of carmenere. Before sitting down, Benny turned on the Police. He listened to "Every Breath You Take" as he relished the taste of blood from his steak mixing with the carmenere in his mouth.

***

Around midnight, long after Benny had fallen asleep, Candy woke up in the dark. At first she was disoriented and confused, but as she began to remember her day, tears welled up in her eyes. The tears continued down her face as she struggled to free herself from her bondage and pull her panties and slacks up from around her ankles. Her rectum hurt so bad she could barely walk. Once she comprehended what must have happened to her, she threw up all over the floor. Still confused, and now scared, she stumbled around in the darkness until she found her way out. As she ran down the hallway toward the medical records department the soreness of her rectum made her cry even more. She was praying she would not run into anybody before she got home. Hobbling to her car, she decided she didn't want to work in the medical records department after all. She would just be sick for a while and then quit. And she would never, ever mention to anyone what had happened. Maybe she didn't want to be some doctor's nobody girl after all. On the way home Candy had to pull over on the side of the road to throw up again.

Chapter 4
Sunday

Those who are incapable of committing
great crimes do not
readily suspect them in others.

Francois de La Rochefoucauld

Benny woke up easily to go to work. His body was electric, full of energy. If all went well, this would be the day he would show Maggie just how much he loved her. Just thinking about it made the gaping hole in his gut feel smaller. He took a hot shower, threw on a pair of scrubs, shaved, tossed back a cup of coffee, and drove to the hospital. Before he left, he made sure he had a couple of syringes full of GHB in case he needed them. Once he got to the OR, he saw the charge nurse writing the assignments on the white board.

"Good morning, Benny. So far we have two hip fractures, an amputation, a clotted AV graft, and a tubal. What's your pleasure?"

Benny studied the board. *Where's the harvesting?* "Is that the schedule?"

"Hey, now, don't be wishing a bad day on us. Five surgeries to start a Sunday is enough."

"Who are the docs?"

"Zollner has the fractures, the amputations are Mc-Ilveen's, Pruitt has the clot, and Hansen has the tubal. The schedule has Zollner and Hansen starting at seven thirty. Paula's on the phone now to see if she can get McIlveen or Pruitt in at seven thirty so we can run three rooms."

"Good luck with that. Pruitt maybe. But you know McIlveen. The world revolves around his belly button, not vice versa."

Benny walked behind the nurses' station to look at the schedule. He was hoping Davis's harvesting was just overlooked. If it didn't happen today it would make things so much more complicated. Benny was getting tired of it all and ready to be done with it. Plus, if it didn't happen soon he was going to have to get more drugs into Davis's system. He was taking a chance as it was, putting the GHB in an IV bag. While he was looking at the surgery schedule for the day and for Monday as well, the phone rang. When he realized the secretary was not going to answer it, Benny picked up the phone. The caller wanted the charge nurse. He put the call on hold and walked back to where the charge nurse, and now the anesthesiologist, were making assignments on the big white board.

"Rhonda, call for you."

Motioning to the white board and talking to the anesthesiologist, Benny said, "Put me wherever. I'm going to get some breakfast."

Once inside the stairwell, instead of going downstairs toward the cafeteria, Benny went up the stairs to the ICU. He needed to see what was going on with Davis. His good mood had turned soured in a matter of minutes. He was getting nervous about his plan. Davis wasn't on the schedule for Monday, either. Harvesting teams never put off a surgery. Benny likened them to sharks circling at the first smell of blood; then once the body was on the operating room table the feeding frenzy continued until the patient was ashen from the blood being sucked down the drain. When Benny left Davis the night before, the sharks were circling. He was sure all of the paperwork was there. He might have to re-think his plans for Davis. What if he had awakened during the night? Benny was sure he gave him enough GHB, even if it was in a drip. Benny got to the ICU and from the hall-way saw Lee in Davis's room. But he couldn't see Davis. Lee was blocking his view. He was going to have to walk all the way into the room. What if he was awake? Benny could feel the gaping hole in his gut widen. No! That would not work. Benny took a deep breath before going into Davis's room.

"Hi, Lee." Benny walked around her.

There Davis lay, in the same coma like state he was in when Benny left him yesterday. Benny let out a large sigh.

"Hi yourself, Benny. You all right?"

"Yeah, I'm fine. Guess I was holding my breath, get-ting up those stairs."

Benny eyed the IV bag, which was almost empty. "No better, huh?"

"Naah. Got a call from the harvesting folks. They want to do it today."

"Really? It wasn't on the schedule when I was down there."

"They just called, not five minutes ago. They're prob-ably talking to the OR now. You guys have enough folks to do it today?"

Benny tried to hide his relief. "I think so."

"He was your friend, wasn't he?"

"Not really my friend, just some poor fool I happened to run into."

Benny guessed he only had a few hours before the GHB would begin to wear off. He was going to have to make things happen, one way or the other. Benny turned to go back to the OR. He knew that nobody would want to do the harvesting on Sunday, but he also knew that the harvesting team usually got their way.

"Hey, Benny," Lee called out to him as he walked away. "Did you want something?" She was replacing Davis's empty bag of saline with a new one.

"Not anymore, Lee. Thanks. See ya."

The anesthesiologist, Rhonda, and Paula were discussing the harvesting at the nurses' station. Some of the other staff scheduled to work that day were listening in on the conversation.

"Zollner can follow himself; Pruitt said he could come in around eight. McIlveen said he'd get here eventually, said he was up all night. And Hansen will be here at seven thirty. The harvesting team said they would be here around ten. We should only have McIlveen going if no one adds anything. It should be okay."

Rhonda looked at the nurses and scrub techs standing around.

"Kristin, you, Tommie, and Blanche will have Hansen in room three. The harvesting can follow."

Before Kristin could answer, Benny interrupted, "Hey, Rhonda."

Rhonda looked up from her assignment sheet. She tried to hide her irritation. Why did these nurse anesthetists always think it was about them? "Yeah, Benny."

"Put my name up there with Hansen's case, will ya?"

Even though the anesthesiologist would be by any minute to assign the nurse anesthetists, Rhonda responded by picking up a marker and adding Benny's name to the case. This was a small irritation for her, and she knew there were always bigger battles to be fought. Rhonda looked to Kristin. "You good? If I hear that the harvesting team will be later than ten, I'll let you know. Otherwise, that's what we'll plan on. Hansen should be in and out pretty quick."

Kristin nodded to Rhonda before leaving to get her room ready. If she was lucky she could get her part done before Dr. Hansen arrived and she could steal a quick cup of coffee. She would enjoy the first case. Dr. Hansen was easy to work with and rarely in a bad mood. Kristin liked working with Tommie and Blanche, too. They were hard workers, taking responsibility to make sure everything was right for the surgeon as well as for the patient. Kristin was still amazed at how the same surgery could be so different depending on the staff involved. But she definitely was not looking forward to the harvesting. It was not one of her favorite surgeries. She had only been involved in a few of them. They were eerie and hectic. And she wasn't particularly happy about having Benny as the nurse anesthetist. He was probably one of the best in the business, but he was not very nice to her. She seemed to get on his nerves, for no reason that she could see. She had also noticed he was much friendlier to other nurses. She wondered why, but never wondered enough to ask him.

Together with Tommie and Blanche, Kristin helped prepare the operating room for their first case of the day. As Kristin predicted, the first case went off without a hitch. Dr. Hansen was on time and was his usual friendly self. His patient had just given birth to her third child and she and her husband had decided three was a charm, especially since their third was a boy, after two girls. Right before the surgery the husband joked that at least now he would have someone on his side. Even Benny was on his good behavior.

After the first case, Tommie and Blanche prepared for the harvest. Kristin finished her notes from the tubal ligation.

"If you guys want, go ahead and take a break after you check your trays. I'll go hunt down the slush and some of the other equipment."

"You think it's still on for ten?" Blanche wanted to get some breakfast in case she didn't get a chance to eat lunch. Some days were like that in the OR. You'd better eat if you got the chance. Hell could break out at any moment.

"I doubt it." Kristin looked at her watch. "It's close to nine thirty now. You know those teams usually run late. But the slush can start thawing. I'll check with Rhonda on the time. I hope they are running behind. I wouldn't mind a cup of coffee myself."

"Sounds good to me," Tommie spoke, with Blanche nodding in agreement. Tommie and Blanche were pulling the sterile instrument trays out of the case cart, making sure they had them all. "What all they taking? You know, Kris?"

"I think it's going to be pretty much everything, at least the major organs."

"We'd better get the thoracic saw tray. It's not here. Looks like we have most everything else." Blanche left the room for the needed tray.

"After our break, we'll double-check everything and start opening. If you need us to help get any other equipment let us know. It's been a while since I've done one but I know we need like two of everything. A boat-load of stuff."

"Yeah, I think you're right, Tommie. I'm about done with my notes. I'm going to take a fast break."

Blanche came back in the room with the needed tray. "Rhonda was just in sterile core. She said the harvesting team shouldn't be here till close to twelve. She said to go ahead and get the room ready except to open the instruments and then eat lunch at ten thirty."

"Sounds good to me. Let's go get a cup of coffee, Blanche." Tommie turned to Kristin, who was still on the computer. "Kris, we'll meet you back here in a few minutes."

Kristin waved them off as they left the room. She realized she hadn't checked her e-mail in a while, and this would be a good time to get it done. While looking at her mail, which she surmised was mostly junk, Benny came into the room. Kristin didn't acknowledge him. She had been on the receiving end of Benny's strange mood swings more than once. It taught her to refrain from encouraging interaction with him. Psychiatry had prepared her well for the OR. The place seemed to crawl with personality disorders. She had come to the conclusion that Benny was a bit of a sociopath. He could be very cold at times, and then at the drop of a hat be incredibly charming. It was very unsettling for her.

"So, I hear the harvesting is on for twelve." Benny was looking over his anesthesia equipment. "Will you be going with me to get the patient?"

"I suppose. I'm sure Rhonda will let me know one way or the other."

"What's this guy's name, anyway? Davis what?" Benny wanted to engage her in conversation. He also liked making the nurses work a little extra, just for him.

"I don't know." Kristin was not going to bite. When she first started working in the operating room, she jumped to meet everyone's needs. As her knowledge grew of the OR dramas that often unfolded, she came to the conclusion that it was usually for one of two reasons various OR staff would ask her to do something. Either they were lazy and wanted someone else to pick up their slack, or worse, they felt the need to act superior by dictating demands. With Benny, it could be either way.

"Look. Just look in the computer. How hard can it be?" Benny's demeanor had changed from his pleasant self to his hateful self.

"I will when I'm finished. I'm doing something else right now." Kristin also knew that with Benny it didn't matter if she helped him out or not. When she was new and tried to be helpful, he still belittled her with his pompous arrogance. She learned to deal with Benny the same way she learned to deal with psych patients with pervasive personality disorders. No power struggles, no feeding into their needy victim role-playing, and no compromising of her own value system. Except for when it came to caring for her patients, Kristin was true to herself first. She learned it was the only way to survive in the OR.

"Oh, forget it, I'll find it myself." Benny slammed one of the drawers shut in his supply cart before leaving the room. The noise startled Kristin, but she ignored Benny's outburst. She willed herself to stay focused on the computer. Kristin could feel his glare on her back.

Benny walked to the charge nurse's desk.

"You need to do something about Kristin. She has a bad attitude."

"Really? Kristin? One of my best employees? A bad attitude? Oh, well." Rhonda was wise to the games played in the OR and wasn't in the mood.

Benny scowled at Rhonda. "You nurses are all alike. No wonder this place it going to hell in a hand-basket."

Rhonda took a deep breath in and out. "Look, Benny. I'm not going to take the bait."

Before Benny could respond, Rhonda picked up the ringing phone on the desk.

"You'll be here in forty-five minutes? What happened to twelve? Okay. Yeah, we can be ready."

Continuing to ignore Benny, Rhonda spoke into the loudspeaker's microphone. "Kristin, Tommie, Blanche, call the front desk."

Kristin had come up from behind. "What's up?"

"The harvesting team just called, they'll be here in about forty-five minutes instead of noon. Get Tommie and Blanche; make sure that room is ready. As soon as they get here, we'll go get the patient."

"Man, I thought we were going to get a decent lunch. Crap. I'll tell Blanche and Tommie." Kristin walked toward the break room to give the scrub technicians the news.

As Kristin walked away, Rhonda yelled out to her but was looking at Benny, "Oh, yeah, and Benny here, thinks you are a pain in the ass." Rhonda couldn't help but crack a smile. She knew she would be pissing off Benny, but she just didn't care. Life was too short to get her panties in a wad over the likes of Benny. He was a jerk, and Rhonda knew it.

"You're a shit." Benny said it staring directly at Rhonda; his cocky, inflated sense of self-worth popped, just like a balloon meeting a straight pin. At that moment Benny hated Rhonda, and Kristin, too. Maybe once he took care of Davis, he would give them some special attention, the kind of attention his mother got.

He had wanted to alienate Kristin before the harvesting, to create an adverse atmosphere. Rhonda turned his complaints into a joke, minimizing his advantage. Kristin would be on her game, something he wanted to prevent. Benny had watched her work in the past, as he watched all of the OR staff. He had made it a point to learn how each staff person dealt with criticisms as well as compliments. When he was bored at work and wanted to humor himself, this knowledge came in handy for a friendly game of cat and mouse. Benny had learned that when Kristin was in adverse situations she had a tendency to shut down, be less interactive with everyone around her. A type of self-preservation, Benny assumed. She also had a tendency to make mistakes when she was in that mode. Otherwise, she was too good a nurse, too thorough when it came to doing her job, such as reviewing paperwork in the chart. Benny didn't need that today. He needed this harvesting to be completed without a hitch. Rhonda's words soured Benny's mood. "Look, I don't want to work with her. Don't you have another nurse?"

"No, Benny, I don't. I'll go up and get the patient with you if that will make you feel better. Kristin can stay down here and finish getting the room ready. I want them to get lunch before the case anyway. It looks like it will be long one, and I don't know if I'll be able to break them for lunch later. The list of cases we have to do today is growing."

Benny gave Rhonda a tense smile. "Fine. I'm going to grab a cup of coffee. Call me when it's time to go."

Benny left Rhonda at the nurses' station. While he didn't show it, he was actually pleased that she would be going with him to get Davis. She wasn't nearly as efficient as Kristin and once they got into the OR with Davis, Kristin would not have a chance to review the record in great detail.

Rhonda shook her head as she watched Benny get on the elevator. "Kristin, call the front desk. Kristin, call the front desk." Rhonda used the overhead microphone.

The phone rang immediately.

"Kris, make sure you and your crew eat lunch before this case. I'll go with Benny to get the patient when it's time. You can stay and get the room ready. Yeah, I think Benny is a jerk, too." She put the phone down as Paula came back from her break.

"Paula, I'm going to grab something to eat. If the harvesting team shows up, give me a call. I told Benny I'd go with him to get the patient."

"Sure thing. No new cases?" Paula looked at the case list for the day. "Never mind. Do I need to order these case carts?"

"I got the gallbladder in but not the declot. I told both surgeons they should be able to do their cases around one or two."

"What about McIlveen?"

"Haven't heard from him. Try calling him again. He needs to get in here or he's going to get bumped. Anesthesia has already approved it."

"Got it. One of my favorite things to do is tell some of these lazy-ass uppity surgeons to get their lazy-ass uppity selves in here."

Rhonda couldn't help but laugh at Paula. She knew the feeling. "Not quite that way, I hope."

"Don't I wish. Lazy-ass uppity surgeons," Paula mumbled, as she dialed a number on the phone, logged back into her computer, and pulled out a book to read all at the same time. Working in the OR made Paula extremely efficient at multitasking.

Kristin, Blanche, and Tommie had decided to eat before getting the room ready. If the room was ready but the harvesting team had yet to arrive, they would have to take turns staying in the room since all of the sterile supplies would be opened. Kristin and Tommie were working on the slush when the phone call came. Blanche was wearing a sterile gown and gloves, getting the back tables set up with the needed instruments.

Kristin picked up the phone, listened to Paula on the other end and hung up.

"They're here. Rhonda and Benny went to get the patient."

"I'm ready to count if you are, Kris. Then I need to break scrub so I can go to the bathroom."

"Sure, Blanche. I'll get the count sheets." Kristin gathered up the papers with the inventory of instruments listed from each tray.

"While you guys count, I'll go pee. I don't want to have to go in the middle of the case. Can you think of anything else we might need that I can bring back?"

Kristin looked around, doing a quick inventory in her brain. "I think this is it. I'm sure if they need anything else, they'll let us know."

"Yes, we will."

"Looks like you have everything, including the kitchen sink."

"I'll take a beer!"

In walked three men and a woman, laughing and talking all at once. Except for the frames of their bodies and the hats on their heads, they pretty much looked alike. Kristin could not tell for sure who said what or who was who. Kristin saw more commotion out of the room's window at the scrub sinks. Three more people were in the hallway washing their hands, chatting with each other. All of a sudden the OR room was packed with people and noise. Kristin had only done a few organ harvestings and she found it curious that these harvesters were such a jovial bunch. They reminded her of the characters in *A Christmas Carol* who were all too happily gambling over Scrooge's belongings during the Ghost of Christmas Future's visit. Kind of ghoulish, Kristin thought.

Kristin immediately introduced herself. "I'm Kristin, the circulator. This is Blanche, your scrub. And the person who just left is Tommie. She'll help me circulate. Blanche and I were just counting the instruments. We'll be finished in just a minute."

"Nice to meet you Kristin, Blanche. I'm Dr. Roberts; the one requesting a beer here is Dr. Salgado, and this is our PA, Allison Conway. Allison, look over their wares and see if there is anything worth pocketing." Dr. Roberts and Dr. Salgado chuckled to themselves.

Allison rolled her eyes. "Ignore them. I do."

Kristin couldn't help but giggle. The third man had been going in and out of the OR, but finally came over to Kristin.

"Hi, I'm the donor coordinator, Mike Brown. I'll write everybody's name over...there." Mike looked around the room until he saw the white board on the wall. "The folks outside the room washing their hands are Doctors Ford, Campbell, and Shah. They are getting the liver and kidneys. Those guys," pointing to the three people who had walked in with Mike but had walked back out to wash their hands, "are Doctors Roberts and Salgado. Allison is their physician assistant. They're getting the heart and lungs. They'll go first, of course. Once they're done, they'll leave with those organs. Then the liver and kidney guys will finish up. I'll stay until it's all over."

Kristin and Blanche finished their counting. It was so noisy, Kristin had trouble thinking clearly. When Tommie got back, Blanche left the room to go to the bathroom. She was happy to get away from the noise for a minute. Once the harvesting started it would be unbearably quiet. Blanche knew she would want to get away from that eerie quietness as well. Harvestings were not her favorite. She couldn't help but wonder if the patients were really brain-dead, as they were supposed to be.

Kristin decided it was a good time for her to get to the bathroom as well, since the patient wasn't in the room yet.

"Mike, I'll be right back. Is there anything you need before I leave?"

"Not this minute. But I will need some drugs. I'll get the list ready for you while you're gone."

"Okay. Tommie's here if you need anything else before I get back."

"Great, thanks." Mike went back out into the hallway where he had placed a couple of crates full of supplies.

Kristin went to the locker room. She also went by the break room and grabbed a sip of her coffee before the craziness began. As Kristin walked back to the operating room, she saw Rhonda and Benny coming off of the elevators with her patient. She took a shortcut through the nurses' station so she would get to the room before they did. She met Tommie in the sterile core. Tommie motioned to her that she was going to the bathroom. Kristin nodded as they passed each other. She opened the door to the operating room and walked into an atmosphere full of energy. Blanche was already back and scrubbed in. Nursing assistants stood around waiting to help move the patient onto the OR table. The heart and lung surgeons were in line to get their sterile gowns and gloves on. Someone had turned on the radio; music was blaring.

A couple of the harvesting team members sang along with Sonny and Cher, "...and the beat goes on, and the beat goes on."

Kristin walked straight to the main doors of the operating room to help hold them open for Rhonda and Benny. As Kristin pulled the doors open, in rolled Davis.

"Drums keep-a-pounding-a rhythm to the brain."

Not this brain, Kristin thought, as she helped direct Davis's bed into the room.

"la de da de de...la de da de da..."

More noise. Davis was hooked up to a monitor assessing his heart rhythm. The beeping added to the noise level. Benny was pumping oxygen into him with an ambu bag. Simultaneously with Kristin, the nursing assistants converged on Davis.

"Let's get him lined up with the bed. Watch the IV." Benny was quick to claim the authoritative position. "Move the OR bed over, I want to hook him up to the ventilator before we move him."

One of the assistants grabbed the remote for the OR bed and unlocked it. Once moved and relocked, they pushed Davis's bed closer to Benny. He connected the tube sticking out of Davis's mouth to the ventilator. With his hands free, he took Davis off the portable EKG monitor, hooking him up to his own.

"Kristin, did you call Moore? Let her know we're in the room?"

"Doing it now," Kristin yelled out above the noise, walking to the phone. As she dialed the anesthesiologist's pager, Mike handed her a list of drugs.

"Thirty thousand units of heparin, one gram Solu-Medrol, and Regitine fifteen milligrams?" Kristin looked to Mike for confirmation.

"Right."

"Kristin, I'll go get that for you." Rhonda had walked over to where Kristin and Mike were standing.

"That would be great, Rhonda. Thanks."

"Okay, everybody ready?" Benny asked the crew.

"Yeah." Everyone answered back in unison.

"Is that Foley between the beds?" Benny's question got Kristin's attention.

"Shit," someone said.

"That wouldn't feel too good."

"How would he know?" giggled a young nursing assistant who was new to the OR and not really sure what was happening. She had entered the room because of all the commotion, tagging along with the other nursing assistants.

Everyone moaned.

"Should she be in here?" Benny bellowed.

Behind her mask, the new nursing assistant could feel her face heat up, turning beet red. Her eyes began to well up. She backed away, bumping into Kristin. Everyone else worked to get the urine bag out from between the two beds.

"Ignore him, he's a jerk." Kristin put her arm around the new assistant's shoulder and whispered in her ear. "C'mon, you can help." Kristin felt Tameka's resistance. "C'mom, now. You gotta have thick skin in this business. Help me out. We'll take his feet."

Benny was at the head of the bed, supporting Davis's head and breathing tube. "Ready, on three…one, two, *three*."

In one swift motion, the staff closer to Davis rolled him onto his side. The staff on the opposite side of the OR bed slid a towel-covered rolling board under Davis. In what seemed to be an effortless transfer, the staff on the opposite side of the OR bed pulled on the towel he was lying on while Benny continued to support his head and Kristin and Tameka supported his legs. The staff that had been closer to Davis pushed him away from them and toward the OR bed. Once on the bed, the roller board was retrieved as the staff now closer to Davis rolled him toward them and up on his side.

Once the board was out from under Davis, Tameka and one of the other nursing assistants were quick to take

Davis's bed out of the room. Tameka wanted to get out of the room and away from Benny as soon as possible. She had been singled out for ridicule and had no desire for more.

Kristin busied herself making sure Davis was properly positioned on the bed. She looked around the room for a nursing assistant to help. As she placed the arm boards on the bed, she bent down to hiss at Benny, "You've chased away some of my help. Thanks a lot."

"She'll get over it. Besides, if you did your work instead of running your mouth as you're doing right now, you'd be done." Benny turned his back to her.

Kristin was furious. She stopped what she was doing and walked behind the anesthesia machine to face Benny. For a second or two she watched him pull out some drugs from his medication cabinet, thinking twice about what she wanted to say, then said it anyway. "You're an ass."

"Get to work. I'm busy." Benny stayed focused on his activity, barely giving Kristin attention. He needed to get some medication into Davis before Davis entered into an arousal state. That would be very bad.

Before Kristin could go on, Rhonda came back in the room.

"Here's the medications you need."

"Thanks." Kristin took the drugs and looked about the room for Mike. Not seeing him, she walked with Rhonda to the scrub sinks. Mike was busy pulling out multiple sizes of containers.

"Here, Mike, here's your meds."

"Rhonda, Benny was a jerk to Tameka. Go check on her for me. Tell her..."

"That Benny's a jerk?"

"Yeah, and that I told him so."

"My pleasure." Rhonda gave Kristin a wink and a nod, and left them to check on Tameka.

Kristin turned to Mike. "You need some help with any of that?"

"I can get it if you hold the door open for me."

Kristin obliged, and together they went back into the room.

"Kristin, I got the prep ready, you want me to do it?" Tommie stood next to the draped and sterile prep stand. On sterile towels sat a bowl of multiple gauzes soaking in a brown-colored cleansing solution as well as extra sterile towels for drying.

"That would be great, Tommie, thanks."

While Tommie washed Davis from his neck to his thighs, Kristin looked around for his record. "Anybody see the record?" It was still so noisy, she practically had to yell.

"Here, I have it. Sorry. Just looking over the paperwork." Mike held the chart up for Kristin. "You can have it."

Kristin walked to Mike. "Thanks. You sure? I just want to look at the paperwork myself."

She took the chart from Mike and looked for the consents. She wanted to make sure they were in order before the first cut. Rhonda would have checked prior to bringing the patient down, but it was still Kristin's responsibility to do it one more time, right before the first incision. She was grateful someone had turned down the radio. Between the chatter, the beeping of the machines, the moving of equipment, and the stress of this procedure, Kristin's head had started to hurt. She glanced over at Benny, wondering how he could be so unfeeling. *He's gotta be a sociopath, there's no other way.*

"Kris, hey, Kristin! Time to do the time out." Blanche called out to her. The two surgeons looked at Kristin to get the ball rolling. Tommie had not quite finished the first washing of Davis's body.

"Not quite ready. People still moving around. You got a surgeon there who still needs to prep. Nobody can move when we do the time out, Blanche. You know that."

"Hand me that paint, Blanche, so we can get on with it."

"Yes, sir!" Blanche retrieved two sponge sticks and a small medicine cup full of brown fluid from her sterile field and handed them to Dr. Roberts. He dipped a sponge stick in the brown antiseptic and stood behind Tommie. She barely had time to pull off the sterile blue towels she used to dry Davis's body before the surgeon started to paint the chest. He used up and down strokes on Davis's torso, moving outward until the brown liquid covered him from throat to groin and from side to side. He held out the used sponge stick for Kristin to take it.

"Here ya go," Roberts gingerly handed the instrument to Kristin so he would not contaminate himself. After she took it from him, he repeated the process with the second sponge stick. Kristin dropped the sponge into a kick bucket on the floor and placed the sponge stick inside the case cart. She walked back to Dr. Roberts as he finished up Davis's chest with the second painting. She took the second stick from him, and careful not to touch his gloved hand, held out her other hand, palm up. Dr. Roberts placed the almost empty cup of antiseptic liquid on top of her open hand.

As Kristin backed away from the sterile field, Blanche initiated another flurry of action.

"Here, doc, grab this." Blanche directed the heart and lung surgeons to help her place sterile drapes on Davis. Kristin chuckled to herself. Blanche never met a surgeon she couldn't supervise. Every OR needed someone like Blanche. No pretense, no self-esteem issues, skin thick as a snake's. The surgical team threw the excess paper off and away from the sterile field they were quickly creating. Tommie and Kristin tried to catch the paper as it spiraled toward the floor. Once the sterile field was created, Blanche and Allison pulled up the tables that held all of the sterile instruments. As Tommie and Kristin scurried around the OR table connecting all of the devices the team would need, the anesthesiologist, Dr. Moore, walked into the room.

"Benny, everything good?"

"Yeah, no problems." Benny barely looked her way.

She introduced herself to the cardiothoracic harvesting team. "Dr. Moore, anesthesia. Let me know if you need anything."

"Cold beer, I'll take a cold beer." Dr. Salgado smiled at Dr. Moore, even though no one could see under his mask.

"I'll get a six pack and we'll share." Dr. Moore nodded to Salgado and laughed with everyone else. Dr. Salgado nodded back. "I'm Salgado, but you're going to need more than a six-pack."

If Kristin heard the line "I'll take a cold beer" once in the OR, she'd heard it a million times. And everybody always responded with a laugh. It was the kind of work that warranted a cold beer; at least one and usually more. Dr. Moore caught Kristin's eye before she walked out the door.

"Kristin, call if you need me."

"Okay, thanks." Kristin and Tommie had just completed attaching all of the needed cables and suctioning devices the surgeons had thrown off. Kristin went back to the chart, flipping it open to the consents.

"Okay, everybody. Now we are ready for the time out." She looked up to the crew making sure she had everyone's attention. "Patient's name is Davis Melvin; date of birth is January 12, 1964. The first consent states we are procuring the heart and lungs, and the second consent states we are procuring the kidneys, liver and pancreas. No allergies, position is supine, no x-rays, no implants. Safety strap on, instruments sterile per the indicators. Fire risk, two. Everybody concur?"

From around the room there was a resounding *yes*.

As the surgeons busied themselves with the task at hand the room settled down. The sounds of the respirator and EKG monitor continued in a uniform manner. Benny was playing quiet but eerie music from his iPod. Tommie stood by the scrub table in case Blanche needed her. Conversation bounced between upcoming vacations and politics.

"Had a chance to go to Dubai last year. Now I know what those Arabs are doing with all our gas money. The architecture is unbelievable."

"Bovie."

"Is it pretty, Doc?" Blanche was always quick to engage in conversation as she handed over the electrical cautery knife. "I've been to New York City. Is it like New York City?"

Dr. Roberts laughed. "Suction that, Sal."

His partner was ready with the suction and a sponge.

Dr. Roberts continued to work. "No Blanche, it's nothing like New York. Dubai is a different world. It's really quite bizarre, when you think about it. It's in the middle of the poorest of countries. People are starving in every direction. It looks like a mirage that only really good drugs can dream up. Like the Emerald City must have looked to Dorothy in *The Wizard of Oz* and then some. And what's more bizarre is they built this gigantic ski resort. In the middle of a frigging desert."

"Allison, hand me that retractor."

"Get outta town! Really?" Blanche couldn't believe it. She looked to Allison. "Really?"

"Really." Allison confirmed the surgeon's story.

Kristin was only half-listening. With Tommie in the room Kristin hoped she would get most of her notes completed before the case was over. Tommie could get any extra supplies the team might need. As she typed her notes, Kristin realized she didn't note what time the patient had come into the room or the time the surgery started. She would have to get the information from Benny's paperwork. Since she was not in the mood to address him, she walked behind him to see his paperwork over his shoulder. He was reading a magazine. His paperwork was lying on his desk next to a couple of syringes and a vial of medicine. Scanning the paperwork, she couldn't find the times she needed. She knew it would be useless to ask, so she started to walk back to her computer.

"What do you want?" Benny's question made her jump.

"I thought maybe you wrote the times I need on your paperwork. No bother, I'll come up with something."

"When you do, let me know."

"Sure." Kristin wanted her interactions with Benny short and sweet. As she turned to walk back to her computer something caught the corner of her eye. She looked toward the movement. It was Davis. All she could see was his head, the side of his face. His eyes were taped shut. He had a breathing tube down his throat. Kristin looked at his face. *Was he grimacing, or trying to? Had to be involuntary movements. Right?*

Kristin gave herself a shake; chastised herself for having such a vivid imagination. Had it been any other anesthetist, she would have asked about that grimace, but asking Benny was definitely out. Who knew what kind of answer he would give her anyway? Back at the computer she turned her attention back to her notes, making an educated guess about the times she needed. Finally settling into typing her notes, which was the most mundane part of her job, her brain was able to relax. She overheard one of the surgeons say something work related. Her ears instinctively became more focused on the talk.

"How's that slush coming?"

"Great, Doc. Whenever you're ready."

"Send it up."

Blanche filled two bowls from her back field full of a frozen slushy mix. One of the surgeons poured the slush into Davis's body, packing the mixture around Davis's heart, and sending the empty bowl back to the PA for more. The other surgeon started sucking out what was melting because of Davis's warm body.

"Keep it up! We need to cool these organs down now. I need a lot more than that."

"I'm coming, I'm coming!" Blanche shot back.

Allison retrieved the bigger basin from the back table, loaded it with slush, and handed it to Roberts.

"That's what I'm talking about!" Roberts took the slush and packed it into the cavities of Davis's body. Kristin watched as steam rose from the man's filleted body.

Blanche was not about to be outdone. "I can do that, Doc!" She grabbed the other large basin and scooped up the slush, waiting for Roberts to take it from her. "Why didn't you say so?"

Roberts, Salgado, and Allison worked intensely, focused on their task at hand, packing the frozen slush in, sucking the melted pink-tinged fluid out.

Kristin got out of her chair to watch. It was too surreal, as if time were standing still while this so-called modern medical miracle took place. Cutting the heart out of a man to save the life of another. What a strange sight to watch. She noticed that even Benny was captivated by the activity. He was at the head of the bed, standing and watching every move. *Maybe he does have feelings*, Kristin thought to herself. *He sure is getting caught up in all the action.* Even though Kristin could only see his eyes, she could tell he was engrossed with Dr. Salgado sucking the melted pink slush out of Davis's body.

"Benny, we're ready for 30,000 units of heparin, please. And let me know when three minutes are up."

"Sure thing."

Kristin continued to watch, mesmerized by the howling sounds of the suctioning, the respirator breathing in and out, the steady beeping of the heart monitor, Enya singing from Benny's iPod.

"Okay. Three minutes." Benny called out, watching the quick work of the surgeons.

"Clamping aorta," Roberts yelled out. Allison and Salgado continued to work with the slush, while Roberts started cutting the heart away from the body.

Roberts turned to Benny. "Ready for a cup of coffee?"

Benny had been lost in the moment. "Huh?"

"The respirator. Turn it off. IVs, too. Your part's done. But you're more than welcome to stay and watch, of course."

"Oh, yeah," Benny hit a button on his machine. The beeping stopped. The sounds of respiration stopped. Benny felt the hardness in his pants. He had to look down, make sure he didn't make a mess. Relieved to find his pants still dry, he answered the surgeon.

"No thanks, Doc. You've seen one, you've seen them all. If you know what I mean."

"Yeah. Actually, I do know what you mean. We're about finished ourselves."

Before Roberts's team completed the dissection of Davis's heart they inspected it. "All four chambers look good, free of gross malformations, no ischemia present."

Mike was on the phone to the recipient's surgery team. "Okay, let's review the info. Got a male heart, type O positive blood, ready to put it on ice. Everything looks good, heart looks healthy ... Yep, tell the recipient to come on down."

"Here you go, Allison. Pass that off to Mike when he's ready."

Allison held out a sterile basin for the heart and immediately passed it off to Mike. He placed the heart in the prepared ice-filled cooler. Before Kristin realized what was happening, the two heart surgeons and Allison were out of their sterile gowns and on their way out the door. Allison took the cooler with the freshly plucked heart from Mike and stopped to bid Kristin farewell.

"Sorry for not staying for the grand finale but we have a plane to catch and a life to save. Thanks for your hospitality. We owe you more than a beer."

"Sure, Allison. No problem. One day I'll take you up on that beer." Kristin knew Allison wouldn't take her seriously, that it was all a part of the OR jargon. "It was good working with everybody, see you next time."

With the heart team gone, Blanche and Tommie helped the next team of surgeons take their places alongside the OR bed. All was ready for part two of the harvesting.

Benny had left the room as well. He saw all he needed to see; Davis's life literally sucked out of him. He had no desire to see the rest of the gutting process. He wanted to plan his evening with Maggie. Just thinking of sharing his news with her made Benny giddy with excitement. He would have her in his arms tonight, forever. And maybe he would share more than his news with her. Maybe he would be able to share his full, hard cock with her as well.

Benny was in the main hallway looking at the assignment board with Rhonda. "The heart team is gone. The poor slob is about gutted. What else is going on?" Benny had taken off his face mask.

Rhonda opted to ignore Benny's crass comment. "Mc-Ilveen finally decided to grace us with his presence. The gallbladder had to be put on for Monday, needs cardiac clearance. The declot ate a full breakfast at nine, so we can't do that until five. That might end up on Monday's schedule, too. So it looks like we just need to finish the harvesting and McIlveen. As long as no one adds anything else, of course."

"Cool. I'm outta here."

"You'd better check with Moore first."

"Yeah, yeah." Benny scowled at Rhonda as he walked toward the anesthesia break room. But he knew Rhonda was right. He would have to clear it with Moore first.

"I'm done with the harvesting. Any chance I can get out of here?"

Moore was in the break room eating lunch and watching the news on the TV. "Have you checked with Rhonda? Nothing else going on?"

"Just McIlveen."

"You got a hot date or something? You never ask to leave early."

The question irritated Benny. "What's up with the twenty questions? Yes or no?"

Dr. Moore was taken aback. "Whoa there, Benny, save your attitude for the nurses. You need to have it in check when you're talking to me." Dr. Moore had already heard of his ugliness to Kristin and Tameka from Rhonda. Dr. Moore allowed Benny to get away with his behavior toward the nurses, partly because it helped them to grow thick skin, which they needed if they were going to survive in the OR, and partly because Benny was one of the best anesthetists she had ever seen.

Bennie didn't respond.

"Didn't know I hit a nerve. Yeah, go on if you want. We should be okay."

"Good. See ya," and Benny was gone.

Back in the harvesting, the liver and kidney team were making a startling discovery.

"This liver is cirrhosed."

"What?" Kristin thought she heard the surgeon say the patient's liver was bad. She had been getting the paperwork in order for the morgue and not paying attention to the surgery.

"This man's liver is diseased. I thought his liver panel was clean."

Kristin could tell Dr. Ford was not a happy man. "Let me look at the lab." Kristin hated an unhappy surgeon. Kristin had learned that if the surgeon was unhappy, she too, would soon be unhappy. She found the lab work as well as the other tests that brought Davis Melvin to this end. "His AST and ALT are both under thirty, the bilirubin within normal limits, too."

"This is not a liver with an AST and ALT under thirty, or a normal bilirubin!" Dr. Ford looked at Kristin for answers.

Kristin scanned through the different sections of the record hoping to find something, anything that would explain the cirrhotic liver. Something did catch her eye, and it stopped her cold.

"Oh my God."

Tommie looked over at her. "What is it?"

"I'm not sure, Tommie, come look." Kristin looked at the sheets in her hand, turning them over to look at both sides, and again going through the chart.

Tommie took the loose papers from Kristin's hand to see what had caused the upset. At first she didn't see it. "Where?"

"Look." Kristin pointed to the bottom of the papers where labels with the patient's identifying information belong. "Now, look at this one." Kristin pointed to another page. The patient name on the other sheets didn't match.

Tommie compared the name, Social Security number and the birthday. Nothing the same. "Oh, my gosh! I think we did this guy the other day."

Tommie asked Blanche, "You remember that harvesting we did the other day?"

"I sure do. Some young GI who had a bit of bad luck. Motorcycle accident. Beautiful body; brain, total mush."

Tommie looked at the birthdates. "Heck, there's a twenty-year difference here."

"Surely, there's been a mistake. Let me call Rhonda." Kristin walked to the phone to call the front desk.

"Close this man up. We don't even know who we have here. This is totally unacceptable. I will be talking with the administrator of this facility immediately." Dr. Ford broke scrub, throwing his bloodied gloves and gown to the floor. The other two surgeons quickly sutured Davis Melvin's torso.

Before walking out, Dr. Ford stopped right in front of Kristin. "You need to call that heart team immediately. There's a man on a table somewhere who is getting ready to die."

Kristin felt an empty pit in her stomach. Hearing Rhonda pick up on the other end of the phone, Kristin informed her, "Rhonda, we're gonna have a bad day. We need to get that heart team on the phone. We don't know whose heart they have. And might as well get the administrator on call on the phone, too. This doesn't look so good."

***

Kristin had not seen Judy in almost a year. Ever since she left the psych unit and transferred to the operating room, it seemed there never was enough time for all of the things she wanted to do. Kristin needed to tell Judy about all the crazy stuff she saw in the OR. She needed to unload. There was no one to talk to in the OR; no one she felt she could trust. When Kristin first transferred there she felt like a fish out of water. A lot of people warned her it would be hard, transferring from psychiatric nursing to the operating room. But Kristin had been a psych nurse for over ten years, and as much as she liked it, she wanted to see another side of nursing. She definitely got more than she bargained for. Had it not been for the operating room school the hospital offered, she never would have transferred. It was one of the hardest things she had ever done—not just because of everything she had to learn, but the staff seemed so unforgiving. Kristin thought for sure that it must have been the OR that first honed the mentality of "nurses eating their own." Early on in the OR school Kristin decided she was going to stick it out. On one of her more dreadful days, she came to the conclusion that she did not transfer to the OR because of the staff there, and she was not going to leave because of them either.

Over a year later, she was finally coming into her own. But she still felt like a loner there, and it would be good to see a friendly face.

If she was honest with herself, she would have admitted she had to get off the psychiatric nursing unit to get away from Zach. Dr. Zach Newton. She didn't want to love him; she had tried hard to stay away, but anytime they were in a room together the chemistry was overwhelming. At first she thought it was one-sided, that only she could feel the electricity. Kristin paid attention to how he treated the other staff, if his eyes met their eyes with the same sparkle. He was always kind, but it appeared he gave her the extra attention. He was also married. And Kristin had to get away. Kristin was thinking of their last discussion together as she checked her makeup in the mirror. They had run into each other at the hospital cafeteria a few weeks ago. Zach and his wife were getting ready to go on a vacation to some stupid island.

"Sounds just peachy!" Kristin couldn't believe what had tripped off her lips. Zach just laughed, eyes sparkling, flirting with her soul.

"You could say that. I'll tell you what; I'll drink a fuzzy navel while I'm down there, in your honor."

"Great...just great," half-aloud, half mumbling to herself. Kristin felt uncomfortable, her eyes darting away. She wanted to hide her nervousness, her despair. "Hey, Zach—I mean Dr. Newton—it's really good to see you, really. But I've got to get back to work. Thirty-minute lunches go by fast, especially when you're in the cafeteria line for almost fifteen."

"It's good seeing you, too." Zach didn't want to let her go. He had felt the chemistry from the beginning and had tried to ignore it. Just temptation, he reasoned. Being a psychiatrist, he understood the human condition, married or not. Attraction to other people was just a part of life. He knew it was up to him to keep his marriage safe. And in his mind he had done his ever-loving best. But it was not enough; his marriage was failing, spiraling out of control. Going out of town for this vacation with his wife was their swan song. It hadn't been booked that way, but he knew it, and he was thinking his wife probably sensed it as well.

"Did I ever tell you how impressed I am that you went from psychiatric nursing to the operating room? How they treating you?"

Kristin looked back at Zach. She felt absolute peace whenever their eyes met. "Pretty good, I guess. Some days are better than others, but I'm getting there. Look, Zach, um, Dr. Newton, I would like to stay and talk, but really, I have to get back to work. It's good seeing you, really." Kristin knew she was fumbling around for words; trying to keep it professional. But she couldn't help it, and she had to get away. Kristin didn't wait for Zach's response, she couldn't. Kristin turned from Zach and walked back to her unit.

Zach wanted to reach out to Kristin. He wanted to stop her from leaving but hesitated. He knew how she felt, and he knew it wasn't fair. They had had that discussion before. Zach knew he had decisions to make. What Kristin didn't know was that once she had left the psychiatric unit to work in the OR, he missed her more each day; he found he missed her madly. When he finally dared to look into his soul for the truth he knew he loved being with her. This unexpected insight made what should have been a gut-retching decision a no-brainer. Zach was going to call the marriage quits. His marriage had been dead for a long time anyway; the only thing left was the paperwork and the lawyer fees. Zach's wife had become immersed in a socialite's lifestyle, free of responsibility and free of children. Zach had tried to see it her way, tried to appreciate what she labeled as the finer things in life, jet-setting with the elite. But he had found the lifestyle not only selfish but boorish as well. Zach longed for a family with children. He wanted to teach his son how to fish or his daughter how to dance, and his wife refused him.

Zach's wife would pout at his announcement, maybe even throw a temper tantrum. But he also knew she would get over it. The minute she stepped on a plane to be whisked away to Paris, or Italy, or wherever the elite go to be elite, she would have the sympathy of many a man. Yes, he had no doubts that she would get over him quickly. While the process would not be easy, the end result would be worth it. Zach would tell Kristin when he got back. He could wait.

Kristin was finishing up her makeup when she realized she had been daydreaming. "Crap," she said out loud to herself in the mirror, "I'm gonna be late. Damn Zach Newton. Damn that stupid surgery."

She was supposed to meet Judy for dinner at a new restaurant that just opened up downtown. They (whoever "they" were), were trying to revitalize the downtown area, and there was always a new restaurant trying to make its way. She grabbed her purse and keys and ran out the door.

"Judy, I'm sorry I'm late."

Judy was at the entrance of Barney's, waiting patiently.

"I was in a surgery that seemed to last forever."

"No problem, Kris. It's great to see you." Judy motioned to the hostess that they were ready to be seated.

After the hostess seated them, Kristin continued. "Actually, it was a harvesting—a botched harvesting, I might add. What a mess." Kristin reached for the drink menu.

"A harvesting? Really? Man, you've come a long way since your old psych days. What do you mean by botched? Do I want to hear this?"

"Let me look at the beer list first. I need a drink. Have you tried any of these? I haven't been here before." Kristin silently looked over her choices.

Judy also looked over the list. "I've tried the German blonde ale, which is pretty good. I'm not much of a beer connoisseur, though.

"Kill-A-Man Irish Red!" Kristin pointed to the name of a beer. "That's me, that's gotta be me."

"What?"

"Let's order our food first. If I start talking now, we'll never get to the menu."

Kristin handed Judy one of the menus that the hostess had left on the table.

"Judy, you don't know how glad I am to see you. How broad are your shoulders?"

"As broad as you need, you know that."

Kristin and Judy were the best of friends. Even when their lives seemed to take different paths, the time apart did not weaken their bond. Judy was a few years older than Kristin, and more than once Kristin had tapped into Judy's tower of strength for support.

"Are you ladies ready to order?"

"I am. What about you, Judy?"

"You go first; I'll have it figured out by the time you finish."

Kristin read from the menu. "I'll have the thick-cut rib-eye, medium rare. For my side, I'll have whatever the vegetable of the day is. And I would love a Kill-A-Man Irish Red, please. Oh, and Caesar dressing on my salad."

"Got it. And for you?" The waitress turned to Judy.

"I think I'll have the blackened salmon. I believe yours is the best I've found lately."

"Why, thank you. It's one of my favorites, too. What would you like for your side and salad dressing?"

Judy pondered the lists of sides. "The red-skinned mashed potatoes for my side, and balsamic vinaigrette on my salad. And I think I'll try a Kill-A-Man Beer myself. Sounds too tempting to pass up. As a matter of fact, it just might become my new favorite drink."

Judy, Kristin, and the waitress all snickered.

"You don't know how many times I've heard that. I'll get your drinks out to you right away."

"Great. Thanks," Judy replied.

With the waitress gone, Judy nudged Kristin to open up. "So, what's going on? You okay? Is it Eric?"

"No. Eric is okay, as good as can be, considering everything." Kristin shrugged her shoulders. "Just today, just work. We're in a boatload of trouble over that harvesting today."

"Yeah? I've never seen one, but I've heard a lot about them. You know, there's an idea out there that harvestings happen to people who are very much alive. I don't know if it's true or not, but the way things are going in medicine I wouldn't be the least surprised."

Kristin took a deep breath. "Judy, I swear I saw the patient grimace. Almost like he was in pain while they were working on him, cutting into him, suctioning the blood out of his body. So creepy." Kristin had to literally shake herself, feeling a chill go up her back. "And then, after the heart was on its way to be implanted into someone we realized there was another person's paperwork in this guy's chart! It's just a mess!"

Judy shook her head. "Shit, Kristin. Not good. What's going to happen?"

"Not sure. But that's not everything. The paperwork that was wrong was the paperwork from a recent harvesting."

"Here you go ladies, Kill-A-Man Irish Red. Here's to killin' a man. Hope you enjoy." The waitress placed the drinks on the table with a big grin. She always took pleasure in serving that particular beer to women. It was like an inside joke for females only.

Kristin rolled her eyes at the waitress' statement. "Thanks." She took a drink, a gulping big drink. "This is pretty good. I might have to have another."

Judy tried hers. "I agree. I think it's better than the German blonde."

Kristin took another swallow before she continued. "I didn't see everything in his chart. If I remember correctly, he was found passed out. Couldn't find any drugs in his system, but he wouldn't wake up or breathe on his own. Or at least that's what the tests said. And the tests also said he had a good liver, but when he was opened up and the surgeons saw it, they knew something was very wrong. I looked over the paperwork again. I found a report that had one patient's name on one side, but a different patient's name on the other." Kristin shook her head, sighed, and took another drink of her beer. "You know, there was also something vaguely familiar about him."

"Like what?"

"Not sure. Sometimes I'll get a patient for surgery whom I actually knew when I worked on psych. Maybe he was one of those guys."

"What was his name?"

"You promise not to tell?"

Judy and Kristin had worked on the psych unit for so long they could recite confidentiality laws in their sleep. But they were the best of friends and could trust each other with any secret.

"It was like two last names. Melvin Michaels, but that's not right. What was his name?" Kristin leaned forward, trying to whisper to Judy. "David Michaels? That doesn't sound right, but it was something like that. Melvin Davis?"

Judy tried to yell in a whisper, *"Davis Melvin? Do you mean Davis Melvin?"*

Startled by Judy's sudden action, Kristin jumped in her seat. She looked at Judy with wide eyes. "You know him?"

"Yes, and so do you. He's been admitted to the psych unit so many times, we used to say we were going to give him a key and make him a staff member. You don't remember him? He's a—was a—drunk. And a child molester. Never could figure out why he didn't rot in hell. We just discharged him a couple of days ago. His drug screen was negative? I could've told you his liver would be shot."

"That's how we figured out the paperwork was screwed up. His liver was a mess and the harvesting surgeons wanted to know what his liver panel said." Kristin was trying to recall Davis from the psych unit, but she couldn't pull him up from her memory. "Maybe I can't remember him because of tubes sticking out from everywhere."

"People have a way of looking different when they're half dead." Judy and Kristin both took big swallows of their Kill-A-Man.

"You got that right."

The server came out with their meals. "Would you like another?"

"Yes, I would love another beer. You know we're gonna have to walk around a little before I drive home. I'm such a lightweight. Two's usually my limit."

"No problem. I'll have another myself." Judy finished her beer and handed the empty glass to the waitress.

***

Benny was at home talking into the phone. "Where are you, Maggie? I have something very important to share with you. This is the *tenth* time I've called. I'm telling you, you want to hear this."

Maggie stared at the phone wondering if she should pick it up. He wouldn't leave her alone. She knew that if she answered it, he would take it to mean that maybe the relationship had a chance. She couldn't give him that idea. Not anymore. She turned off the ringer on the main phone and unplugged the phone in her bedroom. She made a cup of hot tea, found the book she was reading, and went to bed.

Maggie's phone continued to ring in Benny's ear off and on late into the night, with him leaving message after message after message.

***

Chapter 5
Monday

There is no disguise that can for long
conceal love where it exists
or simulate it where it does not.

Francois de La Rochefoucauld

Zach looked out the window of his plane, replaying the events that had unfolded over the weekend. He was anxious to get back home, and back to Kristin.

"You want a what?" Zach looked at his wife in ironic disbelief. Zach and Alex had spent their weekend days either scuba diving, sunning, or at the spa. Their evenings included the warm breeze of the ocean, sparkling wine, and romantic music. It was a weekend for lovers and Zach could think of no one but Kristin. Alex seemed to be in her own world, too, Zach thought, when she was not finding fault with him. The nights had been cold; each of them retreating to their own side of the bed, to their separate fantasies. Zach knew his fantasy well; he longed for the warmth of Kristin. It mattered little to him that he had no desire for Alex.

Zach felt the engines of the plane start to roar as it wheeled to the tarmac. Zach looked at his watch. It had been just a few hours ago that Alex had made her announcement, after another cold and sleepless night.

"I said I want a divorce."

Zach had just come out of the shower, towel wrapped around his waist and rubbing his head with a smaller towel drying his hair. Alex stood at the balcony door with an empty champagne glass in her hand. Zach didn't know what to say.

"Look, Zach." Alex walked to the wet bar and mixed herself a mimosa. "This isn't working for me anymore." She eyed Zach in his towel. "Damn it. Why did you decide to come out in a towel?"

Zach had to chuckle. For a second she reminded him of earlier times when they couldn't get their fill of each other. "Alex, I'm sure it's just the champagne."

"Ya think?" Alex took a sip of her drink. Making it obvious she had been thinking the same thing she added, "It's not what it used to be."

"Ya think?" Zach couldn't help but mock her; he had become tired of placating her.

"Asshole. I'm trying to be nice here. But you're making it a little difficult." Alex added more champagne to her drink.

Zach sat on the bed with a sigh. "Look, I'm sorry. I agree with you, it's not what it used to be. And more important, I think we want to go in different directions."

Alex tried to lighten up, grinning at Zach. "Well, at least that's something we can agree on. You're not putting up much of a fight, though."

"Would you feel better if I did?"

Alex didn't respond.

Zach continued, "The truth is you're not happy with me and want to be somewhere else. I can't give you what you want. And you don't want to give me what I want."

Alex stirred her drink with her finger, not sure why she felt sad.

"We've talked, we've fought, we've yelled, but my desire to have a family and kids and maybe a dog and a big back yard will never change."

Alex felt a tear run down her face. "I can't give you what you want, Zach. You know that sounds like prison to me."

"And to me it sounds like heaven." Zach stood and moved toward Alex to hug her. "Look, I'm tired of fighting, and tired of you feeling like I'm your prison guard. I'll get dressed, pack my bags, and get a flight out of here today. You stay a couple more days. When I get back to the States, I'll go see a lawyer, try to make it easy on both of us."

"I thought I would be happy once we talked about it, but now I'm just sad that our good days are gone." Tears were trickling down Alex's face. Zach hadn't seen Alex this vulnerable in a long time. Zach reached for a tissue and helped wipe her tears.

"Me, too, Alex. Me, too."

"Sir, would you like a drink?" The airline stewardess's voice startled Zach. He hadn't even realized the plane had left the ground.

"Yes, thanks. Maybe just some water." Zach put the tray down in front of him.

"I hope you enjoyed your stay at Saint Croix."

"I did, thank you. But I'm definitely ready to get back to the real world." Zach took a sip of his water. "Sometimes I think the real world is where the fantasies begin."

The stewardess laughed, rolling her cart to the next row of people. "It's definitely where you pay for them."

Zach nodded at her and laughed, too. His mind was already in the real world, impatient to see Kristin.

***

Bear was up early on Memorial Day. On every United States holiday that honored the country's servicemen and women, he always made it a point to pay tribute to them by raising the American flag first thing in the morning, and not taking it down until sunset. Ever since they were young corporals in the army, Bear had spent every Memorial Day with Bull. The first one was the most memorable. It was the end of the Vietnam War and they were young military policemen. They got the lucky job of patrolling the bars near their camp when the soldiers went for a little rest and relaxation. It was Memorial Day weekend and the war was as good as over. Everybody was antsy to get out of Vietnam. The drinking was heavy and the bars were hopping. At every bar entrance was a young, barely dressed Vietnamese girl calling out,

"GI, Come here GI, Good beer, sexy girls. Come in, all you GI Joes."

Bear and Bull would have preferred watching the entertainment themselves, but it was their job to make sure no one got out of hand. They had to be content with walking up and down their designated beat, trying to look all business. All of a sudden one of the girls from a club ran out screaming for help. A soldier and an airman were fistfighting, breaking the tables and bar stools, glass shattering on the floor. Instead of stopping the fight, the bystanders were cheering it on. Bear and Bull ran in, attempting to separate the two. Not wanting to arrest anyone, they took great pains to figure out the problem. The owner was livid, cursing at the men in broken English, wanting to know who was going to pay for all of the damages.

Bull and Bear found that the fight was over which service was the best to join. Not believing such a lame reason could be the cause of so much destruction, they talked the two men who were fighting into letting Bull and Bear referee their fight with their buddies placing bets. Half the money would go to the club owner for damages and the other half would go to the winner. What a great night it turned out to be—organized violence at its finest. People came in all night long, volunteering to fight, placing bets. The club's owner got enough money to remodel the whole bar and nobody got arrested. The good old days, Bear chuckled to himself, knowing all too well that during those Vietnam days there weren't very many. Bear planned on grilling Bull his favorite, Beer-can Chicken, or as Bull liked to called it, Beer-in-the-butt Chicken. He sure did miss his days of running with Bull. Their last day together as partners was the day Bull saved his life. Bear was thinking about that day as he was getting dressed, struggling to button his shirt. If it wasn't for Bull and his quick thinking, Bear would have lost more than his arm. He would have lost his life.

***

Fred and Tom were not happy. This was Memorial Day and instead of enjoying the day off they had been on the street since Saturday morning wondering how a person could just disappear in thin air. They thought they had found their informant on Sunday, in a dumpster behind Fantasy Fever.

But once they got a good look at the dead man, they realized it wasn't their man after all. And here they were on Monday, wading through the scum, talking to the whores and pimps to find out just what could have happened to Davis Melvin.

***

Benny woke up on his couch. He felt as if an ax had cracked his skull wide open. He had drunk so much the night before he passed out with the phone in his hand. It took him a minute to remember that he never did reach Maggie. He immediately called her; there was no answer. He got off the couch, turned on the Beatles, and took a shower. While the warm water fell on his body he decided he could be nice no more, he would have to make Maggie see things his way. No more phone calls. He would make a plan, think it through, and visit her tomorrow.

Chapter 6
Tuesday

If we are to judge of love
by its consequences,
It more nearly resembles
hatred than friendship.

Francois de La Rochefoucauld

Andrew decided to go out for lunch before paying Maggie a visit at her outpatient clinic. He could barely tolerate the hospital cafeteria. It was always loud, the food greasy, the people unsophisticated. He appreciated a finer dining experience, with a wait staff who valued his business. While Andrew enjoyed his entrée of curried lamb, he mulled over the events of the morning. At first he couldn't believe his ears when Judy told him about Davis. Andrew didn't particularly like Judy. Andrew thought she was always so smug, like most nurses. But he also knew that Judy was a great resource when it came to the truth about the latest gossip. He had just talked to Davis on Friday. Davis had said he wanted to get clean and sober, that he was tired of the way he was living. Sure, most bad boys came up with this "novel idea" when they were looking to get out of the hospital, but Andrew just knew that Davis meant it this time. Davis had had enough. Andrew thought that retching a bucket of blood had finally turned Davis around. He had seen a few who survived esophageal hemorrhaging and lived to tell about it. There weren't many, though. Maybe Davis started bleeding over the weekend again and it was too late. Andrew wanted to talk to Maggie about it. She had not been at treatment planning that morning. He decided he would stop by her office on the way back from lunch, maybe even let her know that she should have listened to him. That she was wrong about discharging Davis, and he had been spot on.

"Can I get you anything else, sir? Sir?" The waitress was standing in front of Andrew with the check.

Andrew looked up at the waitress. "Oh. No, thanks. I'll take the bill." Andrew pulled his credit card out of his wallet and handed it to the waitress. Once Andrew got his credit card back he slipped it into his wallet with the receipt. Andrew always saved his lunch receipts for tax purposes. He tried to not think about work while he ate, but some days he couldn't help it. And when he thought about work while he ate, he saw it as a business lunch, justifying the tax write-off. As he drove away from the restaurant he put his wallet in the glove box. He pulled his hospital badge out, and laid it on the passenger seat. He was always forgetting to put it back on after lunch. Driving through the hospital parking lot he glanced around for an empty space. He was hoping there would be a few open spots because of lunch. Slowly he wove his Mercedes between the rows of parked cars hoping for a plum location. Not seeing anything, he glanced at the doctors' parking lot. He knew there would be some extra ones. Always were. But was he allowed to park there? Hell no. Andrew despised the fact that he had to park with the rest of the hospital staff. He felt it was beneath him. *The hospital's suits are idiots. After all, the therapists are just as important as the doctors. Why didn't they see that? The therapists do all of the psychiatrists' work, anyway.*

Andrew hated the doctors, and the nurses, too, for that matter. Psychiatric hospitals should not have nurses in charge; they have too many stupid rules for everything. Having to find a parking place in the back forty and thinking about nurses reminded him of Judy's comments from the morning, and what she knew of Davis's untimely demise.

"One less piece of scum wasting taxpayer money, I say."

Judy was expressing her opinion to a couple of the case managers before the treatment team meeting started.

"Judy, that's a terrible thing to say. He should have had a chance to get right with the Lord, before he died. God rest his soul."

"Michelle, the way I see it, now he can do it face-to-face. Better there than here! Before he abuses another child, ruins another life."

Andrew shuddered at Judy's hard-core, non-caring attitude. "So what exactly happened anyway?"

"I always thought this hospital was a death trap, now I believe it. Shit's going to hit the fan on this one. Medicaid, Medicare, Joint Commission, we got a big problem here. It seems Davis ended up in the main hospital Saturday, some medical problem. Somehow his records got switched up, or a doctor said he was brain-dead or something like that, and by Sunday morning a group of organ harvesters were on him like a pack of vultures. Just wait until the paper gets a hold of this; they already have it in for this hospital. This will screw us for sure. It's all the damn vultures that hover around: managed-care companies, lawyers, harvesting teams. That's who's killing people, but it's the hospital staff that'll take the fall. Pretty slick setup, if you ask me. The only people who really care will be the ones to get their butts chewed. You can't keep a patient long enough anymore to really help them, but if something goes wrong, look out."

Andrew was in shock. "He looked good to me when I saw him on Friday. I wanted him to stay for the weekend, which I noticed he didn't." Andrew was holding up a list of patients who needed treatment planning for the day.

"So what do you know?"

"All I know is they found him unresponsive in some back alley. Heart still beating but faint. That was pretty much confirmed through the ED report. But he had to be intubated. Ended up on ICU. Next thing I hear, he's an organ donor. The only reason I know about the organ donation thing is because a friend of mine works in the OR. She was on the case. She said she thought she saw him grimace. The whole thing sounds pretty creepy. You hear stories about how they take your organs before you're really dead, now it's happened here. *Sixty Minutes,* here we come!"

"Maybe he was brain-dead. God rest his soul." Michelle tried to offer Judy some reassurance.

Andrew was only partially listening. Judy could go on and on, given half the chance. He was too busy going over his last session with Davis. He'd just known that Davis was going to stay sober, he could feel it. It had been such a good session. Andrew remembered feeling especially impressed with himself on the way home Friday afternoon. But something was tugging at his brain about that drive; Andrew tried to remember those thoughts, but he couldn't pull anything up into his consciousness.

Andrew did remember that when Maggie had come back for rounds on Thursday, she was feeling better and Andrew was able to talk her into letting Davis stay over the weekend. That would give Davis a few extra days to stay in a supportive environment and get through a Friday and a Saturday night without using. Maggie had been more concerned about the people he could hurt if he was out. Maggie had called the sheriff's department hoping they were looking for him; she would have been more than happy if he could go directly to jail. No jail, no outstanding warrants. Maggie knew Medicaid probably wouldn't pay; he was a frequent flyer, but she didn't care. She had learned long ago that managed-care companies' ideas of managing care was more about managing money. Andrew wondered what had changed her mind.

Andrew finally found a parking place, about a hundred frigging miles from everything. He got out of his car, made sure it was locked, but forgot his hospital name badge on the passenger side. As he trudged to Maggie's office, Andrew couldn't believe how muggy and dense the air felt already. It wasn't even June yet. He looked up in the sky for clouds. He had lived in this area for so long, he knew the air could only take so much humidity and heat before exploding into thunderstorm. Hopefully he would get back to his office before that happened. Andrew walked into Maggie's office building, and not seeing a receptionist, walked down the hall. As he knocked on Maggie's door, he could hear what sounded like arguing. The voices stopped immediately. Andrew knocked again, harder. After a few seconds Maggie cracked the door open. From the look on Maggie's face, Andrew could tell she was distressed. Andrew looked past her and saw the back of a person, a man.

"Maggie, uh, Dr. Taylor, what's up?"

"Andrew, what are you doing here?" Maggie tried to motion with her hands that things were okay, but her eyes betrayed her.

"I want to talk to you about one of our patients…" Andrew's eyes motioned to the man in the office. "Are you okay?"

"I'm good, fine. But I'm busy right now. Maybe we can talk later. I'll be free soon. Half an hour or so."

Andrew looked back at Maggie, trying to read her concern.

Maggie said again, "Really, things are okay."

"Okay. I guess I can come back. I'll be around. Maybe you could call me when you're done here."

"I'll be on the unit soon. Why don't I just meet you there?" She closed the door, almost in Andrew's face.

Maggie turned toward the man in her office.

"Benny, look, I'm tired. I need time to think. I need time alone. If you love me, as you say, you would give me that time."

Benny didn't respond. As a matter of fact, he became incredibly quiet. *Who is this Andrew fellow at Maggie's door? She has his phone number? What does he want? Is Maggie dumping me for this guy? Why is she playing all these games?*

"Okay, Maggie, my love. I understand. I'll give you time. You'll see that my love for you is actually timeless. Once you see that, once you understand, you will want to go to any length to prove your love to me, as I have done for you." Benny walked toward Maggie as he spoke, backing her up into a corner. He was so close to her, she could feel his breath on her lips as he spoke. He reach for the buttons on her blouse, at first toying with them; then slowly unfastened the top one, then the next. At first Maggie attempted to break away, but Benny pinned her to the wall. Coddling her breasts, he exposed her nipples. His grasp became firmer, as he licked each one, nipping at them, sucking on them. And then he stopped. She didn't fight, or run. Her eyes were wide, but she didn't move. He had never pushed himself on her before; this was not the Benny she knew. Maggie looked into his eyes. They were on fire. His eyes pierced her soul.

"You will want me and you will love me." At that moment he turned from her, leaving her office. He would have more time for her, later.

As he walked down the hall he felt his whole body to be an inferno, a rage from within. The power he felt when he thought of taking Maggie was overwhelming. He had never attempted to force himself on her, and the urge to dominate her was fierce. He could feel he was becoming the man he needed to be to have Maggie. And she needed to be broken. No more demands from her, no more tests. He had passed with flying colors. Now it was her turn for tests, her turn to prove her love to him.

Andrew was down the hall taking a sip of water from the water fountain. He wasn't sure if he should leave Maggie alone or hang out in case she needed something. He wasn't even sure what he would do. He just knew things weren't right and he didn't feel too good about any of it. As he was bending down for another sip, he heard the door slam. He turned to see who had been arguing with Maggie. A flash of Davis getting in that car on Friday afternoon came into Andrew's mind. It's the guy who had been with Davis on the

street corner. Benny walked past Andrew, barely acknowl-
edging him.

Instinctively, Andrew followed Benny out the door.
Andrew was curious about him. What was this guy doing
with Davis on Friday and Maggie today?

It was getting dark out. Andrew looked up at the sky
to see big black clouds. Lightning cracked in the distance,
but a storm was rolling in fast. The air was thick and the
humidity stifling. He looked in Benny's direction and followed him into the hospital, going through a back door by
the loading docks. Andrew rarely went to the main hospital
unless he had to attend a meeting, and he never went in
by the way of the loading docks. He caught up with Benny
enough to see him go through a door down a hallway that
wasn't familiar to him. Andrew stopped himself from going
into the room; he had no clue what was on the other side.
He wasn't even sure what he would say to this guy if he
found himself eye to eye with him. Andrew didn't like not
having the upper hand when dealing with people. Being a
therapist made it easy to have the upper hand. People would
talk, pouring their hearts out to him, putting themselves in
a vulnerable position, waiting for his response. He didn't see
this guy doing that. As a matter of fact, Andrew was the one
feeling vulnerable, very vulnerable. Out of his comfort zone,
for sure. He started to walk away. He decided he could save
this for another day. He was going to leave the way he came
but the rain poured down, lightning and thunder exploding
in the sky.

"Shit, I need to get out of here."

"Just where do you need to go?" Benny had come out
of the door and was looking over Andrew's shoulder at the

electrical sky show. He wondered why this guy had followed him from Maggie's.

Andrew jumped at Benny's voice. "Man, you scared me. I need to get back to my office. I came over to get a cup of coffee. I thought I was taking a shortcut. I think I'm just lost now."

"Come with me. I'll show you a good shortcut. I could use a cup of coffee myself." Benny led Andrew through some double doors.

"It's okay to go this way? Looks like a bunch of medical supplies."

"Yeah, they let us cut through here all the time. It's where they clean instruments. Sterilize stuff. Here, I'll show you."

Benny escorted Andrew through the maze of bloody drills, retractors, and forceps. Andrew's stomach started to turn. Another reason he was a therapist. No blood.

"So. What do you want with me?" Benny turned to look at Andrew.

Andrew jumped again, this time because of a sudden boom of thunder. "You? No, I came for coffee, really. I just got lost. Why would I follow you?"

"You were at Maggie's office." Benny started to move toward Andrew. "You know Maggie. She wants to break up with me. It's you. I thought it was that creep that was causing her grief, making her want to leave me. No matter, he was scum anyway. The world is better without him."

Andrew backed up as Benny moved closer. Benny's voice was low and he appeared to be talking to himself while he inspected his hands and fingernails.

Andrew tried to put on his best therapist face, his stomach feeling queasy about the whole situation. "Yeah, I know Maggie. Look, why don't we talk over a cup of coffee? Which way did you say was the cafeteria?" Andrew attempted to walk past Benny.

Benny stared at Andrew, stepping in his way. *He's admitting it! This is Maggie's new boyfriend. And he wants to have a cup of coffee to discuss it?* "You think I'm going to discuss Maggie with you over a cup of coffee? Is that why you were lurking around her office?" Benny's fury escalated.

Andrew could feel Benny's wrath penetrate into his bones. His adrenalin soared, heart pounding in his chest, forcing blood through every cell in his body. He had to get out of there. His eyes darted past Benny, looking around for exit signs. Sinks, hoses, drains, trays of surgical instruments all lined up, row after row was all he saw. *Where's the damn exit?* Andrew's brow beaded up with sweat; his fine hair lay limp and flat against his head. Benny had maneuvered Andrew into a corner in the decontamination department. He had made a fatal mistake as a therapist. He forgot to have a way out when dealing with a mentally deranged person. Benny walked toward Andrew, causing Andrew to back away. Andrew was seeing the wrath of evil before him and was frozen by his fear. As Andrew moved backwards he unconsciously hunched his body over attempting to dwarf himself, trying to curl into himself to hide. All of a sudden Benny stopped.

Andrew was hunched over, unable to stand straight. *What in the hell am I in? Metal walls; like a cave, a very small cave.*

Andrew looked up at Benny.

"Hey, man. What is this? Look. I don't want Maggie. I just work with her. Really. We can discuss this man-to-man. C'mon." Andrew tried to get a handle on what was happening, realizing he was in a very small space with no way out except through Benny.

A sudden stillness overcame Benny. He was standing in the doorway of a walk-in instrument sterilizer.

Andrew was trapped, like a fox in a snare.

Benny slammed the metal door shut, ignoring Andrew's pleas. Benny punched at the control panels, "Twenty minutes, unwrapped, 270 degrees Celsius," and walked away.

*** ·

Benny left the decontamination department as three of the people who worked there were coming back from their break. He nodded his head toward them, hoping they didn't see him come out of their department. He slowed his pace wanting to hear what they were saying.

"This hospital would save a lot of money if they'd let us smoke inside."

"You got that right. We got drenched in that rain storm. Good thing about working in this department. If we mess up our clothes all we gotta do is get fresh scrubs."

"Yeah, lucky for us. But now we gotta hurry and get those OR instruments cleaned and sterilized. They'll be coming down, yelling at us that we don't have their stuff ready, and we don't need that crap."

The three employees disappeared into their department.

***

"I'm sure glad you decided to come home. We're hurtin' for another detective. We've been short and bustin' our butts. Overtime only goes so far and it sure as hell don't get me laid."

Eric couldn't help but smile at Bull. He had met Bull at the police department for his interview, but his stepfather's old partner, Brian "The Bull," decided he was starving and proclaimed that the interview could take place just as easily over lunch as in a stuffy office. Bull had taken him to the department's favorite hangout.

Bull looked just like his nickname, but his looks didn't give him his name. No one ever pronounced his name, Bulle, correctly. Instead of "Beauly," people would say "Bully," and soon everyone was calling Brian Bull. He was a massive man at six five, with a broad chest and shoulders and a deep, heavy voice to match. He liked his nickname and his looks, becoming a power-lifter just to make sure his nickname stuck. But he was actually one of the most humble and noble men on the force. He just enjoyed using his larger-than-life qualities to intimidate the hoodlums he had to deal with on a daily basis.

"I sure do miss havin' your old man on the force. We could tell you young'uns some real stories." Bull took a bite of his sandwich, fondly named "The Bull's Revenge." Orange, spicy barbecue sauce trickled down Bull's chin. He was ready with a napkin. "Yep, all them bad-asses crawled under their mamma's skirts when the Bull and the Bear were on the prowl." Bull took a big swig of his water while eying Eric. "How's that sandwich, son?"

"To tell you the truth, I think it's one of the best roast beef sandwiches I've ever eaten." Eric was surprised a corner bar could come up with something so tasty.

"This joint takes really good care of us. I like how they named some of the sandwiches after us lifers. You got the Beast of Bear, right? Yep, that's a good one. I like mine because the sauce tastes just like the sauce on Hooters' wings, and I can't ever get enough of those Hooter wings."

"Are you telling me it's the wings you go to Hooters for? Personally, I always liked the view."

"Nothin' wrong with being honest, boy. A gorgeous woman's body is somethin' to behold. Definitely got me there the first time. But I go back for the wings. Hell, these days you can see a little T and A just about everywhere you go, whether you want to or not. Nothin's left to the imagination. And some of it ain't too kind on the eye. Hell, nothin's as good as it used to be." Bull finished up his water and motioned the bartender for more. "Except maybe these sandwiches. Yep. Jake asked us personally what we wanted our namesake sandwiches to taste like. It tastes better with a cold beer, of course. We'll have to come back when we're not on the clock. Bring Bear with us."

Bull took another bite of his sandwich, ready to catch the sauce on his chin. "Yep, when me and Bear were running the roads, it didn't get much better. In those days you could tell the good guys from the crooks; the lines were clearer. Those were the days, that's for sure. But hey, I'm glad you're here. We need some young blood, and can't get no better than a young Bear cub. Now that Bear has retired, my favorite fishing pole is calling my name louder and louder. I just might teach you a thing or two and call it a day. It will work out good for both of us." Bull took a drink of the water that had been brought to him.

Eric was busy enjoying his meal and letting someone else talk.

Bull loved to talk. "You noticed how much downtown has changed?"

Eric nodded, his mouth full of chips.

"Yep. This downtown area looks like a different city. They've really done a lot to improve things. If my memory serves me correctly, if we were sitting in this same place fifteen years ago we could be getting a lap dance right about now."

Bull held his arms out in front of him pretending a woman was standing over him dancing. Eric couldn't help but laugh. *Here's a man who used to give me piggy back rides and now he's pretending he's getting a lap dance.*

Bull laughed at himself. "Yeah, the town's really done a good job cleaning up around here, except all of the red light district regulars just moved down the road about ten miles. It's going to take more than the city's hot shots to clean it up completely. Hell, you and I both know it's a lot of those city hot shots who keep that crap alive. They don't call it the oldest profession for nothin."

"I guess at best I'm conflicted. If all the crime went away, we'd be out of a job." Eric tried to be analytical.

"You got a point there, little Bear, here's to the hookers and their johns." Bull tipped his glass of water toward Eric. Bull saw Eric's empty plate. "You need anything else before we get outta here?" Bull was reaching into his front pocket for tip money.

"It's quiet right now; we could probably call it a day. Hell, I'm thinking we could even have a beer to celebrate your new job and start fresh tomorrow."

Before Eric could respond, Bull called out to Jake.

"Hey, Jake. Jake. Two Sam Adams." Just as he got the barkeep's attention, Bull's phone rang. He flipped it open and put it to his ear.

"Whatcha got?" Bull listened intently. "You gotta be kiddin' me..."

He waved at the barkeep. "Forget the beer."

Into the phone he replied, "Be right there."

Bull was standing before his phone was back on his belt. "We gotta go. They found a friggin' cooked body at the hospital."

Eric looked at Bull, not quite catching what was said.

"In some kind of contraption that sterilizes instruments. Come on, Dorsey, you got your first case."

Eric and Bull jumped into Bull's car.

"Hell, I've been to this damn hospital so many times I could probably drive it blindfolded." He looked over at Eric and winked. "But I won't. It's against the law, ya' know." Bull laughed at his own humor. "Hell, sure wish we coulda had that Sam Adams. I got a great stogie I was ready to burn. From your old man, actually. He sure can pick out cigars."

"Yeah, Bear does a lot of things pretty good." Eric was looking out the side window, wondering how gruesome a scene they were going to find.

"Bear ever tell you about the time we were staking out a big drug bust, and we had to go in a couple of nights early? The main supplier showed up unexpected. We had to go in or we'd lose him. You know me and your old man. We had worked too hard on that stakeout to let that asshole get away. We called for whatever back up we could get. As soon as we busted down the door, some drug-crazed maniac jumped down from the stairs and landed on top of me. Son of a bitch had a knife and stabbed me right in my neck. Bear picked up that scrawny pecker by his neck and slammed him against the wall. Told the back-up cops to clean up the mess. Then he picked me up and threw me in the back seat of this car here and drove like a bat outta hell to the emergency room. Your old man saved my life that night."

Eric had heard the story before, but he never objected to hearing it again. When they arrived at the hospital, Bull and Eric went through the main lobby. A uniformed police-woman and two other men were waiting for them.

"Whatcha got?" Bull directed his question to the petite policewoman as they started down the hall.

"Pretty gruesome, sir."

"Who are you?" Bull asked the two men who walked with them. He hated beating around the bush.

The tall, younger man put his hand out to shake Bull's. "Ellis King, CEO of the hospital, and this is Palmer Jones, hospital security."

Palmer nodded to Bull and Eric.

"Call me Bull. This here is Dorsey," pointing to Eric.

Bull turned to the policewoman. "So talk to me, whatcha got?"

Before the policewoman could talk, Ellis interrupted. "Look, Bull. You need to talk to your people here. By the time I got down here to see what had happened, the police had already roped off the area. They would not let me in until a detective got here. You need to let them know who I am."

Bull looked square into Ellis' eyes. "They did right." Bull was rarely impressed with titles.

Ellis was taken aback by Bull's response and reacted by self-consciously adjusting the cufflinks on his shirt. "Well, I'd like this incident taken care of as soon as possible. The decontamination department is the nuts and bolts of this operation." Ellis paused, expecting an immediate agreement to do his bidding. No one spoke. Ellis continued, "The longer you take to rectify this problem, the more money is lost throughout the hospital. It could cost me thousands of dollars. Because of this mess, my hospital's business has already come to a grinding halt."

Bull looked at Ellis, giving him a once-over. He knew the type. Hair combed perfectly and sprayed down; probably shaved the hair from his chest—a metro man. College boy for sure, probably on his daddy's dime and name, four hundred-dollar suits, two hundred-dollar cufflinks, and soft, smooth, manicured hands; not only to feel up the politicians for a little shakedown but to seduce his wife's friends for a blow job at the club.

Bull ignored him. He turned to the policewoman. "Whatcha got?"

Everybody looked at Ellis. His face turned beet red at the rebuff. He was not used to being disregarded so blatantly. Ellis made a mental note of Bull's abrasive behavior with a plan to call the city manager.

"C'mon, let's hear it," Bull said, not aware of the mental commotion he had caused in Ellis's head. Flipping open her notepad, the policewoman referred to her notes while they walked toward the decontamination department.

"Call came into 911 at 1337 hours from Linda, secretary of Ellis King, CEO of hospital. She stated that employees working in decontamination department opened a walk-in instrument sterilizer and found what appeared to be a person, on the floor and not breathing." The policewoman paused, looked up at Bull, and grimaced. "I believe the word she used to describe the body was 'cooked'."

Bull and Eric looked at each other. "Dorsey, looks like you got yourself a humdinger."

"Great, can't wait." Sometimes Eric hated his work. He had already decided this was going to be one of those times.

The group of five had stopped at the swinging doors of the decontamination department. The hall was full of hospital employees, some gossiping in circles, some standing in a line waiting to give their names to the policeman at the door. The policeman had a surgical mask on but Bull could see that his face was pale and his eyes watery. Eric had noted the same thing and knew this wasn't going to be pleasant. From the double doors came a sweet aroma akin to half-cooked meat.

Bull said to the young officer, "You got some back-up coming? You don't look so good."

"I'm hangin' in. It's not gonna be any easier on them." The policeman got out his notebook to document the group's arrival.

"Central supply gave us these masks; you may want to use one. It helps a little." Earlier he had tucked some extra masks in his waist belt. He pulled them out and handed them to the four men.

To Bull and Eric, Ellis said, "This is the man that would not let me in."

To the young policeman, he said, "You know who I am? Ellis King, CEO of this hospital."

The young policeman looked at Bull, wondering exactly what that meant. Bull just rolled his eyes, letting the policeman know it was not worthy of comment or worry and took two masks from him, handing one to Eric.

The policeman looked back at Ellis. "Yes, sir," and handed Ellis and Palmer each a face mask before writing everyone's name down in his notepad.

As the four men finished tying the masks, they passed through the yellow tape and double doors. In front of the open sterilizer, they stood speechless. The image of Andrew lying in a crumpled heap challenged their senses as well as their view of humanity. Wet clothing encased a smoldering corpse. Andrew's face and arms told the four men of his horrific suffering. His arms were a patchwork of oozing red, angry blisters, melted skin, and half-cooked muscle. The hair on Andrew's head was plastered to erupted bubbles of skin and open, weepy sores. A crater of waxy cartilage and bone was where his nose should have been; his ears were spongy blobs. Yet it was his eyes that hit the four men the hardest. Eric thought they looked haunted. The steam had vaporized away any color in his eyes, leaving them blank; meaningless. They reminded Eric of hardboiled eggs. Palmer was the first to react. He tried to keep the vomit from leaving his mouth. "Excuse me," was his muffled attempt to speak as, cupping his hand over the mask, he ran out the door.

Ellis King was too irritated to react to the hell in front of him. "This is great," he mumbled to himself, walking out into the hallway.

He saw the head of the decontamination department talking with the policewoman. "How the hell did that jackass end up in my brand-new, state-of-the-art, walk-in steam sterilizer?"

The policewoman and the department head looked at Ellis, not hearing what he had said. "Sir, if you could wait a minute. I'm in the process of getting statements. I'll get to you in a minute."

Ellis was not in the mood to wait for answers. This needed to be taken care of immediately. He already had one catastrophe that was going to put his raise at risk. He had been trying to get a handle on the surgical services' harvesting screw-up from the weekend when he got the call about this. He had spent major dollars on this walk-in sterilizer. It was designed to save the hospital millions of dollars. Turnover times in the OR would improve, procedures could be done quicker, fewer staff would be needed, and the overall overhead would come down. Now, because of this fiasco, the budget could easily be screwed. He had no time for this crap. His yearly evaluation was coming up soon and if his budget numbers didn't crunch to his advantage, not only would he not get a raise, he would not get the bonus promised him. His money was dependent on the timeliness of every admission and discharge this hospital had. If the hospital was put in limbo and all operations halted for even twenty-four hours he could possibly never recover. No, this would not do. He was getting nowhere fast. He would go back in and talk to the detectives. Ellis saw the medical examiner go through the double doors after giving his name to the officer guarding the door.

"Paul, hey, Paul!" Ellis attempted to follow the hospital's medical examiner through the doors.

"Sir, you need to wait out here." The policeman blocked Ellis's entrance.

"Excuse me? I was just in there."

"Yes. But now they're collecting evidence. They're not gonna want any extra people around till they're done."

"I am not extra people, I am the CEO, damn it. This is my hospital and I'll go where I want."

Ellis barged through the doors before the policeman could stop him. Eric was taking pictures of the scene. Bull was donning gloves, preparing to collect specimens from Andrew's body. Paul was helping Bull. Everybody looked up as Ellis barged in. He walked toward Eric, wanting to avoid Bull.

"Look, this is bad, bad for the hospital. What can you do? I have sick people to take care of. How fast can you get this body out of here? I can't have this department closed down indefinitely.

Eric looked at Ellis, almost dumbstruck. Then he saw the policeman behind Ellis.

"You tell him he couldn't come back in?"

"Yes, sir."

Eric nodded to the police officer. "I'll take care of it."

Eric said to Ellis, "Look, we'll be done as soon as possible. You coming back in here asking us questions just hinders the process." Eric tried to be diplomatic. "I appreciate that you have a lot on your shoulders, that you are the CEO of the hospital, but encouraging us to hurry doesn't really help much. We just lose our focus."

Ellis attempted to emphasis his point. "You don't seem to understand…"

"Look, King, Mr. CEO, I believe it is you who doesn't seem to understand." Bull stopped what he was doing and stood up. "Dorsey, here, is giving you a break, trying to be politically correct and all that. I, however, don't give a rat's ass." Bull walked toward Ellis. "I don't care if you are the CEO, the FBI, or the CIA. You're obstructing my work and I'll arrest your ass if you don't get outta my way."

No one had ever spoken to Ellis King the way Bull was talking to him at this moment. Ellis felt his face turn beet red again. "Get your work done and get the hell out of my hospital. I've got phone calls to make." Ellis turned and stormed out of the room.

Paul started laughing. "Bull, your boss is going to kick your ass, you pissing off the CEO, the FBI, and the CIA, all in one day."

"Shit, it won't be the first time." Bull looked at Eric. "Dorsey, you're way too nice. Is that how they do it in the mountains?"

Eric was smiling. "Naah, I figured we could just play a little good cop, bad cop. Next time I'll let you be the good cop."

Bull broke out in a broad smile.

"Dorsey, I think I'm gonna like having you in the department. You can think on your feet and you like to have fun at the same time."

Bull got back to his work. "All right, let's get this over with. The stink ain't gonna get any better. Dorsey, after you get all the pictures, go out and get any witness names and statements you can. Me and Paul here will get done what we can till you get back."

"Sounds like a plan to me." Eric finished taking the pictures while Bull and Paul continued to collect the needed evidence.

"Okay, I think I got all the pictures we need." Eric put the camera away. "I'll be outside, see who knows what."

Bull nodded but stayed focused on his work with Paul. "Paul, grab a test tube. Gotta hair, here, doesn't look like it was in the sterilizer. Wonder whose it is."

Bull picked up the hair with tweezers and dropped it in the test tube. Paul placed a cap on the tube. Bull grabbed a label, jotted down the date, time and location of the hair, and placed the label on the tube before packing it away with the other specimens.

Outside people continued to mill around. Some were just curious and couldn't believe what they had heard. Most were there so they could be the first to nourish the hospital's pervasive rumor mill. These people were always hungry for the latest gossip; it fed their egos as well as their boring existence. It was their duty to be the experts of scandal and pass it on to the hospital's underbelly where the lies became truths.

"Sergeant, any chance you've been collecting any names I need to talk to?"

"As a matter of fact, yeah. It seems everybody wants a piece of the action. Wish we had this kind of public response when somebody dies from a gang killing." The sergeant handed Eric a list.

"I tried to weed out the looky-loos from the folks that might know something."

"Great. Thanks." Eric took the list, which included staff positions and phone numbers. He counted over ten names that had been collected. He shook his head; this was going to take him a while. He started with the folks who actually worked in the department.

"Sara Conway, Ali McKinley, Kyle McGee."

Three of the people who were standing in the crowd poked their heads up when they heard their names called. Eric waved them over.

"Hi. Name's Detective Dorsey. You three work in this department, the decontamination department?" Eric was reading the signage on the door. All three nodded.

"I'd like to talk to you one at a time. I'll start with Kyle McGee. That you?" Eric pointed to the only man in the group. "But if you ladies won't go too far, I'll get to you next."

Sara shook her head. "If I can go next that would be great. I clock out at five and my kid's at day care. I get charged sixty dollars for every five minutes I'm late, and this joint don't pay enough for sixty dollars every five minutes."

Eric looked to Kyle for his approval but was speaking to the woman. "I suppose I can talk to you first. Don't want to make you late for the day care."

Kyle shrugged his shoulders. "No matter to me."

"Well, as long as you keep me till time to go home. If you're done with me early, the bastards will probably make me clock out. You know these are some cheap-ass bastards we work for." Sara looked to Ali for support. Not getting any, she continued, "They hired me to work eight hours a day, but lately if there's no work they've been making me go home early. How am I supposed to pay my bills when they do that?"

Sara stood right in front of Eric, shaking her professionally polished finger at him as if he should have an answer for her.

Eric did his best to maintain a sense of authority. It was going to be a long night. He wished he never opened his mouth.

"I'll do my best. How much time before you clock out?"

"Exactly twenty-eight minutes," Sara said, looking at her watch. "And I gotta change clothes, too."

"I can do short and sweet; then if I need to ask you more questions, I'll call you later."

"Sounds good to me. Tomorrow, my husband will be home and can get the kid. So if you need to talk to me again, come here tomorrow, same time, and then I'll stay on the clock. Get some overtime. I'll get those sorry bastards to pay me extra. I deserve it."

Eric wanted this over. "Tell me what you know."

"It was a little slow. So, me and Ali and Kyle decided to get a smoke before we started cleaning the next load. And you know we have to go off the hospital grounds to smoke, right? Which is pretty stupid if you ask me. But anyway, while we were outside, it started raining. We got drenched, so we had to change our scrubs before we started back to work. When we got back, we found what we found. You know, if they didn't make us leave the area to smoke we would have seen what happened."

Eric listened to Sara hoping to hear something worth writing down. Maggie walked into the hallway. She stopped a few feet away from the commotion not knowing what to do next.

The gossip chain had been swift. Somebody was found dead in the hospital. Some of the rumors said murder, others said suicide. She came to help counsel anybody if they needed her, or maybe, and God forbid, identify a prior patient. Maggie needed to get her mind off her afternoon with Benny. He had scared her—so much so that it was like a shock of reality through her system. The police would tell her to get a restraining order, but she could count on two hands the number of her patients killed by their spouses or lovers after restraining orders had been signed. Commitment papers to a psych hospital? Only if she could prove he was a danger to himself or someone else. She needed another head to help her think this through. After she had finished seeing her patients for the day she gave Liz a call, but her machine picked up.

"Crap." Maggie talked into the phone. "Liz, Maggie here. I really, really need to talk to you this afternoon. Give me a call with a good time I can..."

"Maggie. Hey. Sorry, just finishing up with a patient."

"Oh. Hi, Liz. That's okay. You have some time this afternoon or this evening? I really need to talk with you about Benny."

"You know it. This is my busy afternoon, but I can see you this evening."

"Sounds great. My eyes were opened today, Liz. I think he's going over the edge. Whatever hold he had on me is gone. But he's not well. I need your brain power to help me figure out what to do."

"Sure. Okay. Is seven good? If I need to, I can cancel a couple of appointments."

"Seven is okay. Your patients come first. I'm just an idiot who should have known better." Maggie did want to see Liz earlier, but there was no way she would let Liz cancel a patient.

"What's going on out there?" Zach walked through the door, immediately forgetting he had been gone for five days.

"Well, hello to you, too, happy wanderer. I thought you weren't due back for a few more days. What do you mean, 'what's going on out there?'" Maggie closed her phone. She was more than happy to have Zach around.

"There's tons of people milling around the hospital. Police, fire truck, and I think even a TV station or two."

Maggie and Zach went outside.

Judy was in the parking lot. When she saw Maggie and Zach, she walked toward them.

"Hi, Dr. Taylor. Welcome back, Dr. Newton. Did you guys hear?" Judy didn't wait for an answer. "They found some man dead in the hospital. Not just dead, like a sick patient dead. But like a murder or a suicide dead."

"You serious?" Maggie asked in disbelief. After her encounter with Benny she wondered if something was in the water.

"As a heart attack." Judy tried to catch her bad joke. "Sorry. I heard the guy was cooked in a sterilizer. Some contraption that sterilizes instruments. A real crispy critter."

Judy put her hand to her mouth as if it could stop her words. Judy's wit was often faster than her ability to control herself.

Zach and Maggie just shook their heads. Because of Judy's insightful expertise on the job, they often overlooked her unusually blunt verbiage.

Judy made a feeble attempt to overcompensate. "I didn't know autoclaves were so big."

"Maybe one of us should go over there." Maggie said to Zach. "It sounds pretty traumatic."

Maggie and Zach were both on the mass-casualty response team in the event that the hospital needed expert debriefers.

"I'll let you go check it out, Maggie. I want to get settled in first. I feel as if I've been gone forever. Have you made rounds yet today?"

"No, and I missed treatment planning this morning."

"I'll tell you what. You go check out the 'crispy critter' situation," he paused, with a wry grin to Judy, "and I'll go make rounds."

"And something else, too, I wanted to tell you guys. I almost forgot," Judy said, making a face back at Zach. "Dr. Taylor, you remember that patient, Davis Melvin? We just discharged him last week."

Maggie nodded, "What about him?"

"It sounds like he gave his organs up for a good cause over the weekend."

"What?"

"Remember I told you I was going to see Kristin this weekend?"

The mentioning of Kristin's name caught Zach's attention. "You saw Kris this weekend?"

"Yes, I did. As a matter of fact we had dinner together." Judy knew full well the sparks that flew between Zach and Kris. Even though Kristin had confided in her, she'd sensed it from the beginning. "Anyway, she worked this weekend and was involved in a harvesting. And the patient was Davis Melvin. I didn't think he would have any decent organs to harvest."

"Oh my God." Maggie was beside herself. What had happened to him over the weekend? Maggie tried to clear her head. Nothing seemed to make sense. Benny's behavior, the dead man in the sterilizer, and now Davis Melvin.

Judy went on. "Kris said the hospital could be in a mess. Somehow Davis Melvin's chart got paperwork that wasn't his and the worst of it is it's the paperwork that's needed to progress to a harvesting. They are still looking for the correct paperwork with his name on it. Probably will be an investigation, at least by Medicare and Joint Commission. I just wanted to give you a heads up since he had just been here."

"Thanks, Judy. I think. We certainly don't need that sneaking up on us." Zach rubbed his forehead with his left hand. "Wow. Maybe I should have stayed away."

"Oh, no, you don't. Thank goodness you decided to come home early." Maggie noticed a white line where Zach's wedding ring should be. "Zach, where's your wedding ring?"

Zach couldn't help but grin. "Down the drain, with the marriage. I'm glad you reminded me. Judy, give me a minute or two to make a phone call. Then I'll meet you on the unit for rounds."

Judy couldn't believe her ears. Kristin must not know that Dr. Newton and his wife were splitting up. Surely she would have said something over the weekend. She couldn't help but smile. "Sounds like a plan to me. See you in a few." Judy said to Maggie, "See you later, Dr. Taylor. And don't forget to bring back all the juicy dirt."

"You're a mess, Nurse Judy."

"And Zach, now that you're on the loose again, please try to stay out of trouble." Maggie left Zach to make his phone call and walked to the main hospital.

The decontamination department was on the far side of the hospital, right below the operating room where Benny worked. People were everywhere, in the hallway, in the lobby. Maggie scanned the groups of people, with her eyes coming to rest on Eric, who was talking an employee. He looked like someone in charge, so she decided to wait until she could talk to him. While she waited she instinctively sized him up. Tall and clean-shaven, Eric looked at ease in a coat and tie. Maggie was thinking he could easily look just as comfortable in a flannel shirt and a pair of jeans. Maggie was so busy taking Eric in, she didn't notice that he was watching her study him.

Eric waved at her. "Can I help you?"

"Oh. I'm sorry. I wasn't staring. Uhm, daydreaming. Well, not daydreaming, really."

Maggie needed to regroup. She put her hand out to shake Eric's.

"I'm Maggie Taylor. A psychiatrist for the hospital. The gossip is somebody found a dead person on the premises. I'm here to help, if anyone needs to talk. Or maybe identify a body, just in case it's a psych patient, heaven forbid."

"Nice to meet you, Dr. Taylor. Eric Dorsey. Looks like I'm one of the lucky detectives on this case."

Maggie looked at him with uncertainty.

"Please, call me Maggie. Lucky?"

"Sorry. First day on the job. You familiar with the cliché, trial by fire? Well, no pun intended." Eric could see Maggie was still not getting it.

"You don't know, do you?"

"Know what?"

"How this guy died."

"I heard rumors, but I don't know anything for sure. I learned a long time ago to not believe everything I hear."

"Very wise. So, what did you hear?" Eric wasn't sure what Maggie Taylor was about, but it might be worth pursuing.

"Look, I'm here to help, not to discuss gossip."

"Maybe gossip. Maybe a lead."

Maggie was frustrated. "All I want to do is help. But you're not letting me. I guess this was a bad idea." Maggie turned to walk away.

Eric sighed. "Wait. I've got a bunch of folks I still need to talk to. You heard something, maybe gossip maybe not."

Maggie turned backed to look at Eric. He went on. "I know one thing; you probably don't want to identify this guy, pretty gruesome. If you can stay, great. If not, let me get your number, I'll give you a call."

"You can call me at the hospital. That number is in the phone book." Maggie wasn't in the mood for a cat-and-mouse game.

"Here, take my card. You may decide you need to call me." Eric handed a card to Maggie.

Maggie looked at the card. "This says Asheville. You said your last name is Dorsey?" Maggie remembered a conversation with Judy from a few days ago. She looked back at Eric.

"Oh, yeah. I still have my old cards. Haven't even had time to get my new cards yet."

Maggie grinned at Eric. "You are having a rough day. You just moved here from Asheville? I bet you have a sister named Kristin, too."

Eric's whole demeanor changed. "You know Kris?"

"Actually I do. But I know her friend, Judy, better. Judy keeps trying to get your sister to come back to work with us. She's a great nurse."

"Yeah, she's a great sister, too. Look. I really need to get these people questioned. And as much as it might help to counsel them, I need to get to them first, before their memories are tainted. No disrespect meant. And I really want to hear what you heard. So call me, or I'll call you. What do you say?"

Maggie looked at Eric. He was kind of cute and down-to-earth. Maggie liked that. A real person. No pretense. "No hard feelings. I guess I wasn't thinking. You're right, of course."

Maggie started to walk away again, pausing for a second to look back at Eric. "Sure, you can call me. I'll tell you what I heard, but I'm sure it's just gossip."

"Maybe, but maybe not, Maggie Taylor." Eric noticed a sparkle in Maggie's eyes he hadn't noticed earlier. He couldn't help but smile back at her. He also noticed she had soft dark eyes and full pouty lips. For the first time in a long time, Eric thought he felt a twinge of magic. Waving to her, he wondered if maybe that gaping hole in his heart could possibly one day close.

"Look, I need to get outta here. Are you gonna question me or what?" Eric was jarred by the voice of Sara, the woman he had begun to question before Maggie had caught his eye.

"Oh, yes, ma'am. I'm sorry. Let me get your name and number so you can leave. I'll call you if I need to speak with you again."

"Remember what I said. Tomorrow, same time, then I'll get me some overtime. And I'll listen out, too; call you if I hear anything. My name is Sara Conway. That policeman over there has my number, but you can reach me here, too. Got that?"

She read over what Eric had written and, seemingly satisfied, walked away. Over her shoulder, she yelled out, "Remember, tomorrow, same time."

Maggie watched Eric as he turned his attention back to the woman he had been questioning. Something drew Maggie to Eric but she was having trouble naming it. Trying to ignore her own curiosity, she sighed and shook herself. She had enough problems, she decided, no reason to add more.

Benny had been hovering around, wondering if anyone had connected him to the dead man in the sterilizer. Killing that idiot was not part of his plan, and now he wanted to make sure no one had seen him. He did not expect to see Maggie in the mix. Her interactions with Eric captivated him. He was studying all of the people standing around the sterile processing entrance when he saw Maggie talking with

Eric. He watched them smiling at each other. Benny's mind had taken notes. *Maggie's flirting with that guy. She didn't answer her phone all weekend. She said it was because she was ill, but she didn't look all that sick. She looks fine, a picture of health, really.* Benny shook his head. *After everything I've done for her. Maybe Maggie isn't the person she claims she is. Maybe Maggie's teasing me, so she can laugh with her lovers about me, after they make love; after they fuck. Maybe Mother was right all along. Women are whores. Maggie seems to have men everywhere. My Maggie May, a whore!* Benny watched Eric and Maggie without blinking. *I'll forgive you, Maggie May, because I love you. You know you're my air, my oxygen. You need a hard cock to suck? I'll give you mine. I'm becoming the man you want me to be. I've killed your pain. I sucked the life out of that scumbag patient of yours just to prove my love to you; just like you wanted. I'll make to love to you the way you want. I'll make love to you and you will be mine. You are my destiny, and I am yours. So, it's okay, my Maggie May. I will forgive you, but soon it will be your turn to prove your love to me.*

Benny stepped out of the shadows, stopping Maggie cold.

"Oh. Benny. Hi. You startled me."

"Well, hello, my Maggie May. Yes, I see you've been quite busy."

Benny's expression was cold, nodding his head toward Eric.

Maggie looked at the commotion behind her. "Can you believe what's happened?"

Benny didn't answer, staring at Eric.

"Oh, him? He's one of the detectives. New in town. He's also related to one of the nurses you work with, Kristin Dorsey. Small world, huh?"

"Did you get his phone number, too, Maggie May?"

"What? You're not jealous, are you? Benny, there's no reason to be jealous. Look, what's between you and me has nothing to do with anybody else."

Benny didn't respond.

"Walk me to my office, Benny. We can talk on the way." Maggie thought that with Zach there, Benny wouldn't stay too long. It would also buy her some time until she could meet with Liz later that night.

"Is he the reason you want to break up with me?" Benny continued to eye Eric.

"What? No, Benny. I just met him today."

"I saw you talking to him. Flirting with him."

"Don't be silly. I'm just trying to help. Someone's been killed, didn't you hear?"

"Yeah, I heard. I doubt it's murder, though. Lover boy over there will probably find out the klutz tripped and fell, hit his head or something." Benny looked at Maggie. "Look, Maggie, we need to talk. I see you flirting with other guys. But I'm the only one who will love you the way you want to be loved. I've proved my love to you. I know you love me back. Our souls belong together. I know you know it. You have to give me more time, you'll see."

As Benny talked she realized he had slowly backed her up against a wall. Thoughts of the afternoon came rushing back. She felt a chill run through to her spine. She looked into his eyes and tried to appeal to him.

"You're scaring me, Benny. Please, don't scare me. Let's go back to my office and talk. Where we can have some privacy." Maggie needed to buy some time. She didn't want to be alone with him, but now that Zach was back she wouldn't have to be.

"That's more like it, my Maggie May." Benny grabbed onto Maggie's arm, and holding it firmly led her away from the crowd. Once outside, he walked in the direction of his car, holding Maggie tightly by her arm.

"Wait, my office is this way," she pointed in the opposite direction.

Benny tightened his grip. "Look, whore. We're not going to your office. We're going to my place, where we can get some real privacy. Snoopy people, boyfriends, might be hanging out at your office, like that maggot in the steamer." He looked at Maggie with disgust.

What he had said didn't register with her. "Benny, wait. My arm, you're hurting my arm." She tried to stop and pull away, but his grip was too strong. "You're hurting me, Benny, let go."

Benny slapped Maggie across the face. The blow was stunning; emotionally, as well as physically. Fear crept into her eyes.

Benny grabbed both of Maggie's arms and made her look into his face.

"I tried to do it your way, you whore bitch, but you wouldn't listen. Now we're going to do it my way. I showed you how much I loved you. I gave you that scumbag patient of yours on a silver platter, and all I've seen you do is shove your cunt up in men's faces."

She looked at him in disbelief. With a firm grip under her arm, he guided her to his car. "But you're lucky, my Maggie May. Because I've decided to forgive you. I'm going to let you show me how much you love me. Very, very soon.

I saw you look at that detective. You wanted his dick in your mouth, didn't you?"

Benny looked at Maggie for a response. When she didn't answer, he squeezed her arm. "Didn't you?" Benny was getting louder. "And what about the loser that was hanging out at your office earlier? What did he want to talk to you for? You were probably sucking his cock over the weekend while I was bending over fucking backwards showing you how much I love you, you fucking bitch."

They had reached Benny's car.

"Now, my sweet Maggie May, you have to show my mother that she was wrong. We have to show her that she is the crazy, demented one; that it's not me, and not you. So it's time for us to kiss and make up."

Benny turned sideways without releasing his grip on her arm. "Reach into my right pocket and get my keys, sweet Maggie May. It's time for you to start showing me just how much you care."

His rant exposed the full extent of his madness to Maggie. Her mind needed to be clear to help herself, and to help Benny, too. "Okay, Benny, okay. Maybe you're right. But you're hurting me. I'll get your keys."

As much as he scared her, Maggie still saw a little boy in pain. She knew his past. The doctor in her wanted to help. Maybe she should go along with him; maybe she could help him. After all, at this point who else would he trust?

"That's more like it, my Maggie May. You treat me right, and it will make it easier on both of us."

Maggie reached into Benny's pocket for his keys. She could feel the bulge coming from his crotch. She looked at Benny who was smiling at her.

"I told you I've become the man you want. No more will you have to go looking for your desire. I'll be your desire, now and forever."

Maggie handed him the keys and he triggered the keyless entry.

"Get in, my Maggie May, it's time to love me."

She didn't put up a struggle and sat in the passenger's seat. He immediately activated the child safety locks, then manually unlocked his car door and got in. Maggie's thoughts were racing. Once he turned the engine over, the Police boomed through the speakers.

"Every breath you take, every step you take, I'll be watching you..."

"This is one of my favorite songs, Maggie May. But don't worry." Benny maneuvered his car out of the parking lot while he talked. "I don't want to hurt you. I've been telling you we belong together. I just need a chance to show you. Earlier today, when I came by your office, you acted as if you weren't going to give me a chance. I'm glad you're changing your mind. And now that you're with me, you won't have a chance to whore around. You know, Mother didn't want me to be like them. She said all men were bastards. She wanted to me to be different, better. But you like a hard cock, don't you, Maggie May?" Benny looked at Maggie. "How many men have you been sucking, anyway? I'll forgive you, of course. But it will be better for both of us if you come clean."

"What? I haven't been with anybody."

Benny backhanded her. "Don't lie to me. I told you I would forgive you. Don't act as if I don't know. That maggot who was at your office earlier, the one they found in the steamer. I could tell you were fucking him. Why else would he want to see you? And why would he want to follow me unless it was about you? He got what he deserved. You won't be sucking his dick anymore. So that's one."

Maggie thought she was going to throw up. "That was Andrew in the sterilizer? You did that because you thought we were having sex?" Her eyes watered. Her mouth stung from the slap, and she could taste fresh blood from a cut on her lip. She wondered if getting in the car with Benny had been such a good idea after all.

"Don't play innocent with me. I saw you in action with that detective guy. You were eyeing him, I could see that. Probably couldn't wait to have your cunt in his face. I'll take care of him, too."

"No, Benny, you have it wrong, all wrong."

"Then why do you want to break up with me? Who ever heard of somebody breaking off a relationship for nobody? I never have. There's always someone else waiting in the wings. That I do know. And I bet it's that detective. You just got them lined up, don't you, Maggie May? But no matter, you're with me now. And we will have to let your detective fella know that, one way or the other."

Benny pulled into his driveway. He turned to Maggie. "We can do this the easy way, or we can do this the hard way, but in the end it will be my way. Up to you, my sweet Maggie May."

As much as Maggie wanted to run, she could tell this was not the time. He might be expecting it; and he would be ready to stop her. She wanted to clear her head so she could grasp what was happening to her; what was happening to him. Then she could plan a way out, and maybe she could save Benny from himself as well.

"Benny, I'm all for the easy way. I guess you're right, I haven't really been fair. I know you love me..."

"And..." Benny coaxed her to finish the statement they used to say together at the end of every date.

"And...I love you." Maggie had to force the words out of her mouth.

"That's more like it, my Maggie May. How about a glass of carmenere to toast our new beginning?"

Benny helped Maggie out of the car, directing her into his apartment. Maggie stood next to Benny as he got a bottle of wine and two wineglasses. Under the kitchen light Benny saw blood on Maggie's lips.

Spitting on his finger, he gingerly wiped the blood off her bottom lip.

"We'll get some ice to that cut, don't want it to swell and bruise."

Once the blood was gone he continued to rub his fingers on her bottom lip, pushing down on her bottom lip, making her mouth open wide. "Is this how you looked for those other men, mouth wide open, ready to suck them? I understand now. It was all just a cute trick to show your boyfriends. I killed that patient for you, to show you how much I loved you. But I see now that was nothing more than a game to you. You thought I was your puppet. You and your boyfriends laughed at me, because I couldn't make love to you."

Benny's finger continued to circle the inside of Maggie's lips, forcing his finger high into where her gums met the inside of her mouth. Maggie backed into the counter, eyes wide with fear. He poured each of them a glass of wine, handing one to Maggie.

"Have a sip, my Maggie May. It will relax you."

As Maggie took a sip from her glass, Benny used his finger that had been in her mouth and drew an imaginary line from her lip down her throat to one of her breasts. He took a sip of wine himself as he started to gently pinch at her breast watching for the nipple to react. He smiled, taking another drink as he saw the small nub protrude from her blouse.

"Ahh, yes." Benny looked into Maggie's face. "But that's all changed now. See, Maggie May? When we met, I thought you were different from all of the rest; someone who didn't need nastiness in your bed. I thought that my mother would have been quite proud that I picked someone like you. How I wished she could have met you. But not now, now that I've found you're the kind of woman who needs to spread her legs and hump like a dog. How could I have been so wrong? I'll get hard for you, Maggie May, but it comes at a price. But just for you, so you won't have to go to other men humping and licking their cocks; we'll pay that price, me and you together. I'll make you the type of woman my mother would like. And you'll be paying me back, showing your ultimate love for me."

Benny finished off his wine and poured himself another glass. Maggie tried to settle her mind so she could grasp everything he was saying, drinking very little. He began pacing in the living room, appearing preoccupied and seemed to be forgetting that Maggie was even there. Maggie started inching for the door. Benny was lost in own world, talking to himself.

"I've thought long and hard about how to make these things happen in unison. How can you prove your love to me and make you the woman my mother would be proud to have for a daughter?" Benny turned toward Maggie just as she reached for the door knob.

"Circumcision will be the easiest way, don't you think?"

He asked her the question as if he were asking which wine would be better served with dinner. He walked to the door and nonchalantly escorted her back to the living room, as if he were redirecting a child.

"Benny, what on heaven's earth are you talking about?"

Benny handed Maggie her glass of wine, sitting her down on the couch. "Maggie May, what's wrong? You're not drinking your wine. This isn't like you. Drink up, drink up."

Benny grabbed onto Maggie's hand holding the glass. Forcing the glass toward her mouth, he pressed it between her lips. Trying not to drink much, Maggie let the wine dribble down her chin and onto her blouse. Benny seemed to be oblivious to Maggie's refusal. He got up and retrieved the open bottle of wine from the kitchen.

"Here, I know you want another glass." Benny poured Maggie another glass of wine and continued with his idea. "It's the only way, Maggie May. You'll see. And it's the perfect plan."

"Wait, Benny. What are you talking about? I thought you said the word 'circumcision.' I'm sure that's not what I heard. I want to help you. Please, let me. I can help you find a good therapist."

"No!" The back of his hand popped her across the face. Her wineglass sailed across the room, wine splashing the furniture, glass shattering against the bookcase. Startled, Maggie backed up into the couch as far as she could go, coiling herself up into a fetal position.

She felt her old demons returning, a flashback flooding her mind. She tried to fend off the instinct of retreating into her childhood days, when she didn't fight back. She began to cry.

Benny reacted to Maggie's tears. "Look, baby, my Maggie May. Don't cry. I don't want to hurt you, I don't. I'll give you some medicine so you won't feel anything. Don't you see, if I cut your clitoris off, you won't be able to enjoy sex anymore; you won't want it. It's the only way." He stood up, getting her another glass of wine. This time he took the vial out of his pocket and emptied the contents into the glass of wine. "Here, Maggie May, my baby, you need to have a drink. You'll feel better if you finish your drink, I know you will."

Benny bent over, moving Maggie's hair away from her face. He nudged her to turn toward him. She slowly faced him, her face red and tear soaked. She almost looked infantile. Benny handed her the wine laced with GHB.

"Have a drink, Maggie May, you will feel so much better, I promise."

Maggie obediently took the glass and drank.

"Once it's all over, we will truly be happy together, and our souls will finally be fused together as one." Benny poured himself another glass of wine and took a drink. "I can't believe it took me this long to figure it out. I knew something wasn't right between us. It hit me while I watched you with that detective. I could sense your desire. It's your desire, your lust, that's keeping us apart; and I can see now that it would keep us apart forever."

Benny looked at Maggie, trying to explain his madness as perfect sanity. "And you owe me, Maggie May. You asked me to kill a man to prove my love for you. And I did, because our love is everything to me, but now it's your turn. Cutting off your clit will be the ultimate sign of your love for me. And that is the sign I deserve."

Maggie closed her eyes, tears rolling down her cheeks. Benny took a tissue out of his pocket and dabbed at her tears before encouraging her to take another drink from her glass. "It will be okay, really it will. It will sting—just a little though, just like a mother's love." Benny looked away from Maggie for a moment, reflecting on what he had just said. "My mother use to say that to me when I was little. You know, Maggie May, I never really comprehended what she meant until this moment. Soon it will be just you and me forever. I'll take good care of you. You'll have to quit your job, of course. Maybe not go out for a while, until you're all better. But it shouldn't take too long."

Benny was stroking Maggie's hair. "I'll learn to cut your hair how you like it, buy your clothes for you. I'll treat you like a queen, Maggie May. You'll never want to leave me again. You'll see."

Maggie was getting drowsy and losing her concentration. She was also losing her sense of fear. Benny's words were getting blurry. She vaguely remembered being afraid and wanting to leave, but now she was feeling dreamy. Maybe he would let her take a nap before he took her home. She tried to keep her eyes open and focus on what he was saying. Benny saw that she was reacting to the GHB that was in her wine.

"It's time for you to rest, my Maggie May." Benny stood up. He picked Maggie's legs up, placing them on the couch. As her torso slumped to the side, Benny grabbed one of the couch pillows and positioned it to catch her head.

"You have a peaceful sleep, my Maggie May."

She was grateful to lie down; she couldn't believe how sleepy she had become. Her eyelids fluttered. She tried to talk, but the words wouldn't come.

"Soon, my Maggie, soon."

Benny walked to his sound system putting on his favorite CD mix. He looked at himself in the large mirror that also reflected a sleeping Maggie. He had been feeling his pants tighten across his crotch and wanted to look at it. A smirk engulfed his face as he massaged his growing bulge. It was time for the homage to begin. Rod Stewart was singing in the background, remembering the sweetness of Maggie May in the tender years of his youth. Benny started to sing with Rod. Benny was ever so grateful for their friendship. It was because of Rod that Benny knew Maggie was meant to be his.

He pulled out another bottle of wine, popped the cork, poured a glass, and made a toast.

"To you, Rod. To you, to me, and to Maggie."

Benny sang with the music as he strutted to his bedroom.

"Wake up, Maggie, I think I got something to say to you..."

He wished she had passed out in his bedroom instead of on the couch in the living room. He was going to have to drag her to his bed. He folded the sheets back and attempted to crease them evenly; making a place to lay Maggie for the procedure. Benny contemplated preforming the procedure while she lay on the couch just so he wouldn't have to move her. But he knew it had to be the bed. The symbolism is part of the homage. Anything less could cause bad luck, failure.

Singing out loud with the music, Benny crooned,

"You made a first class fool outta me, I'm as blind as a fool can be, you stole my heart, but I love you anyway."

He turned around when he thought he heard a noise. Cocking his head to listen, he finally responded. "Is that you? I knew you were getting my messages and would come if you could."

He had to refold the sheets multiple times after eyeing them from different angles. They had to be perfect. When he was finally happy with his work he pulled his box of drugs from beneath the bed. He retrieved candles and incense from his nightstand. He placed a candle on each side of the bed. The incense and box of drugs were placed on his dresser.

"Oh, can't you see, you belong to me; how my poor heart aches with every breath you take...."

Benny picked up the remote and turned the music up looking toward Maggie. From across the room he couldn't tell if she was breathing or not. He walked over to her while he continued to sing with the Police. Bending over her, he made sure he could detect breath sounds. When he was satisfied with his assessment he decided he might as well move her to the bed. He was going to have to do it sooner or later. He was also going to have to make a run to the hospital and pick up some sterile equipment; might as well get that done, too. She had enough GHB in her for about four hours. He would have to dose her up again at least once more. Let her wake up, get some fluids in her, then dose her up again. Homage needed to be paid to all of the Great Ones; sharing with them what Maggie was willing to sacrifice for him. The men who wrote and sang their music just for Benny; giving him direction in his life: Rod, Sting, John. Of all of them, Benny owed the most to John; for it was John who took a bullet for him, as only a father would, saving his life for just this moment. And now Yoko was here. Too bad his mother was not here to attend. The selflessness of Benny's caretakers would be reciprocated by this celebration of Benny and Maggie's new relationship.

Benny anchored his arms under Maggie's armpits, flexing at his elbows to pull Maggie off the couch. He had to pause a few times to adjust his grasp while dragging Maggie's limp body across the rug toward the bedroom. As Benny tried to get a better grip, John Lennon came on with his love song to Yoko.

"I want you...I want you so bad. I want you, I want you so bad. It's driving me mad, it's driving me mad...She's so heavy."

When Benny heard the song he seemed to find new strength. He was able to get a better grip on Maggie and pulled her into the bedroom. He flopped her on the bed face down. After pulling her torso toward the headboard, he rolled her over, picked her legs up and maneuvered her whole body lengthwise in the bed. The sheets that he had refolded almost to the point of exhaustion were a mess. Benny needed to catch his breath.

Seeing the disarray that was caused to the neatly folded sheets by moving Maggie infuriated him.

"What a fucking mess."

He talked to Maggie as if expecting her to answer. "Look at this shit. I spent a lot of time trying to make it perfect for you. You'll just have to lie in it the way it is. I'll fix it later."

Benny left Maggie in the bedroom to get a drink. He needed a quick break before he went to the hospital. He looked at his watch. Eight thirty. The OR was probably starting to slow down; it would be easy for him to slip into the sterile core to get the necessary instruments. He shouldn't need much. A knife handle, a couple of sterile blades, a couple of packs of sutures. He already had a suture removal kit, plenty of gauze, and some Bacitracin. Working in a hospital made it easy to have those things as household items.

Benny thought he heard more noises. Cocking his head, he strained to hear. "Maxwell's Silver Hammer" was playing. He walked over and turned the sound system down. After a few minutes, Benny nodded his head with reassurance.

"Yes, Yoko. I hear what you're saying. Of course Mother will be honored. After all, it was Mother who made me the man I am today. I wish she could be here to take part in the bonding of Maggie to me forever. I think she would like it. Don't you?"

Benny was silent waiting for an answer.

"You don't think "Maxwell's Silver Hammer" should be Mother's song? But it's so fitting. After all, it was a hammer that freed her from her miserable life. I think I did her a favor. And you gotta admit, the song is downright funny."

Benny went to his bedroom to look at Maggie. Satisfied that she would be okay, he dug his car keys out of his pocket, turned off the music, but continued to sing the chorus.

"Bang, bang, Maxwell's silver hammer came down upon her head. Bang, bang, Maxwell's silver hammer made sure that she was dead."

As he sung, he motioned swinging a hammer and started laughing. Benny continued to talk as he left his apartment, pausing to make sure the door was locked behind him. "Look, Yoko, I want to honor you, too. I know it's been hard on you without John. You've been selfless in all of this, and you deserve my devotion."

He paused before opening and entering his car. "Well, don't answer me, but think of a song. I know you're listening." Benny then jumped into his car and sped toward the hospital.

***

It was eight in the evening and Liz sat in her office wondering what had happened to Maggie, hoping everything was okay. She called Maggie's cell phone as well as her home phone but got no answer. One more phone call to Maggie's office. If she wasn't there she would try again tomorrow.

Zach was walking out the door when he heard the phone ring. He looked back and scowled at the office phone. He had a lot of business he needed to take care of; clearing his things out from his home, getting a new apartment, making things right with Kristin. Even a phone call could get in the way. It couldn't be for him, he reasoned, hardly anyone knew he was back. He doubted it was for Maggie at this late hour, but if it was they could call her cell phone.

Closing the office door, he decided to let the answering service triage the call.

Liz let it ring until she heard the answering service. "Cape Fear Psychiatry. Can I help you?"

"Has Dr. Taylor checked in lately?"

"No, she hasn't. If you'll leave your name and number and the reason for the call, we'll contact her for you."

"No, no message. Thank you."

Hanging up the phone, Liz decided not to worry, except the feeling of uneasiness sat heavy in her head and wouldn't let go. Not wanting to overreact, she made a deal with herself. If she didn't hear from Maggie by noon tomorrow, she would call the authorities.

Chapter 7

Wednesday

Love can no more continue without
a constant motion than fire can;
and when once you take hope and fear
away, you take from it its very life and being.

Francois de La Rochefoucauld

Kristin tossed and turned in her bed. She peeked over at the clock that read one fifteen. The more she tried to relax her mind so she could sleep, the more she obsessed over the conversation she had had with Zach just a few hours earlier. She needed a good night sleep and didn't want to wake up exhausted. She felt as if every synapse in her brain was firing at breakneck speed. Her mind was bent on playing the phone call over and over again in her head.

She had just finished a four-mile run and was walking around the block to cool down.

"Hello?" The brightness of the sun obstructed the number on the phone's screen.

"Kristin. It's me, Zach."

Kristin pulled the phone away from her ear and tried to read the number on the screen. "Zach who?"

"Zach Newton, Kris. How many Zach's do you know?" He was laughing at her.

"Why are you calling me, Zach Newton?" Kristin was irritated. Irritated because he was laughing at her; irritated because she loved him. "And I know more than one Zach, thank you very much."

"I'm sorry, Kristin. I don't mean to laugh. I didn't call you to make you mad at me."

"So, what did you call for?" Kristin wanted to be off phone as soon as possible.

"We need to talk. I just got back from my trip..."

Kristin cut him off. It was more than she could bear. "Look, Zach. I'm in the middle of my run. I can't think of one thing that you need to tell me."

Zach saw that he was going to have to jump in with both feet. "Kristin, my wife and I are splitting up."

"What did you say?" She wasn't sure she heard Zach correctly.

"Look. I want to see you to tell you everything, tonight if possible. But the bottom line is that Alex and I are divorcing. To be honest with you, I was going to bring it up to her, but she beat me to it. I want to see you tonight."

Kristin tried to take everything in, her mind reeling. "You and your wife are breaking up? And you want to see me? There's gotta be something wrong with that, Zach. Don't you need some room to breathe? I know I would want some."

"Kristin, I don't want to play games. I'm no good at it. I stayed away from you while I was married. You stayed away from me. You left your job because of me. We need to talk. Please don't say no."

Kristin couldn't refuse. She wanted to, but the last wall was coming down.

"Oh, Zach. Okay. But not tonight, tomorrow."

Kristin needed to think this out before she saw him, maybe even call Judy to talk it through.

"Okay, great. Seven okay?"

"What about lunchtime?" Kristin wasn't sure she wanted to see Zach in a moonlit night full of stars.

"I'll take what I can get. Is a late lunch okay? Say about two?"

"Two's good. Where do you want me to meet you?"

"Meet you?" Zach wanted a date and not in the afternoon. He didn't like the way this was going. "Kristin, I'd like to come pick you up if I could."

"What about picking me up at my mom's? Tomorrow is my day off and I told her I'd come over in the morning." She had not planned on going to her mother's but she didn't know if she wanted to be alone with Zach quite yet. She was afraid she would do something stupid, such as kiss him.

"Okay. That sounds good. I'll see you then." He paused for a second. "Kristin?"

"Yeah?"

"I really can't wait to see you."

"Me, too. Okay, Zach. Bye." Kris closed her phone and put it back in her pocket. She couldn't believe what had just happened. She finished her walk around the block recalling different memories of Zach Newton. When she got back to her apartment, she stripped off her sweaty clothes and took a hot shower. While she cleansed herself of the day, her mind drifted back to an earlier time of knowing him, when life was still fresh and their futures distant. They had been the best of friends during their freshman year of high school, meeting in French I. Their friendship was spontaneous and easy, spending time with each other, studying, being each other's confidante. Only once did their lips ever touch. Kris had walked over to Zach's to catch up on some French homework she had missed, only now it was French IV and they were seniors. Zach and Kris were sitting on the living room floor, TV going, French books open.

"Almost done on your research paper?" Kristin asked Zach.

"Just got it done. And boy, was it a pain in my ass."

"Really? I didn't think it wasn't too bad. I kind of enjoyed it, actually. I had Monet, who did you have?"

Zach pulled out a manila folder from under his stack of books. "You got Monet? You lucky dog. I always thought Madame Collier liked you better than me. This clinches it." Zach looked at the name written on the front of his folder. "I got some lame writer named Francois de la Roachclip…or something or like that."

When he saw Kristin trying to suppress a giggle, he couldn't help but smile back, and continued his rant.

"I can't even pronounce his name. And I'm still not sure just what he did exactly, except come up with a couple of goofy quotes. I had to work extra hard at not plagiarizing."

Kristin tried to sympathize with her best buddy. "Does sound kind of boring. You need someone to proof it for you?"

"You willing?"

"Aren't I always, *monsieur*?"

"*Oui, mademoiselle.* Huh, how you say…" Zach flipped the pages in his French book.

"*J'ai su que nous étions des amis pour une raison.*"

"What? You knew we were friends for a reason? We better be friends for more than just proofing your boring paper, Zach Newton! Here, let me help you some more with your French, monsieur." She held up the couch pillow she had been leaning on.

"*L'oreiller dans votre visage*, Monsieur Zach Newton, is... 'the pillow in your face.' Ha!" At that Kris let the pillow fly straight toward Zach.

He caught it before it hit him in the face. "Oh, yeah, Mademoiselle Dorsey? 'L'oreiller dans votre visage' back at ya! Double ha!"

Playfully, he threw the pillow back at her, making contact with the top of her head. Without thinking, she lunged at him. Before they knew it, they were rolling around on the floor, tickling each other and laughing at themselves. Kristin was on top, straddling Zach, leaning toward him with her hands propping her up.

"I'm gonna knock the snot outta you, Zach Newton!"

"Yeah? You and whose army?" Zach grabbed her arms out from under her and she fell forward, her lips inches from his.

They felt the sexual tension immediately. They just stared at each other for a second, feeling each other's hearts throb through their shirts. Zach put his arms around Kristin and brought her close. And he kissed her. A long, soulful kiss.

"Zach? You and Kristin want a snack?" Zach's mother, hearing the sudden quietness, decided she needed to give fair warning. Hearing Zach's mother, they immediately broke their embrace, sitting up and flipping pages in their French books.

"No, Ma, we're not hungry."

Kristin tried to suppress a giggle by covering her mouth.

"Are you sure? Kristin, do you want something to eat?" Zach's mom walked into the room.

"I'm fine, Mrs. Newton. Thanks, though." Kristin felt her face flush. "As a matter of fact, it's about time for me to go. It's getting dark out. Mom's going to want me home soon." Kristin looked out the window. Neither Zach nor Kristin had noticed it had started to snow.

"The weather's getting bad; you can't walk home in this. Zach, go ahead and take Kristin home, but be careful. You shouldn't be out in this, either."

Zach helped Kristin gather her books, putting his book report on top. "Think I can get this back by Tuesday?"

Kris put her coat on, only half listening. "I guess so. Sure."

They were both abnormally quiet on the way home. Kristin couldn't help but think of how her heart raced and how his lips had felt on hers. When they got to her home, she turned to face him. She was expecting something but not really sure what.

Zach looked back at her. "Okay, girl, here you go. Be careful."

As she started to get out of his truck, he called her name. "Kristin?"

Kristin's heart skipped a beat. "Yes, Zach?"

"My paper? Tuesday?"

"Oh. Yeah, okay." Kristin turned from Zach's truck, walking through the falling snow to her front porch. As she walked she could feel her face grow warm as tears blurred her vision, spilling onto her cheeks. She looked down, watching her tears and the snowflakes mix together on the brown manila envelope that held Zach's French report. Through her tears she blinked her eyes a couple of times, trying to focus on the title. *True Love Is Like Ghosts, Which Everyone Talks About and Few Have Seen and Other Quotable Quotes by Francois de La Rochefoucauld.* Her emotions went into immediate overload. That kiss, that glorious, wonderful, spectacular kiss had just ruined the best friendship of her life. And it was also at that moment that she knew she had fallen in love with Zach Newton.

The next time she saw Zach, she could tell things were different between them. He thanked her for proofreading his paper, but instead of them becoming closer, he seemed to drift away, spending more time with his girlfriend and his studies, putting distance and time between them.

After high school Zach went to pre-med, then medical school. Kristin was aimless, not really knowing what direction to take. Eventually, she settled into nursing school. She had volunteered at the local hospital as a teen and thought she could enjoy helping people who needed her. Through the years she buried Zach Newton deep inside her memory. She rarely allowed herself to think about those days, that kiss. During her psychiatric rotation in nursing school she had come to the conclusion that forward motion without looking back was best for good mental health. Kristin did her best to live that creed.

It was also during her psychiatric rotation that she and Judy became such good friends. Judy was a no-nonsense practical woman back then, too, strong in her convictions and didn't mind verbalizing them. They both loved psychiatric nursing. They appreciated the level of insight it gave them into their own psyches as well as into the behavior of others. They made a pact to practice psychiatric nursing together. After graduation and passing their boards they were hired at the local psychiatric hospital and quickly became experts in the field. It was there that the memory of Zach became flesh for Kristin. She would never forget that day either. Kristin and Judy had had a miserable, butt-kicking day. Their shift was over, but they sat among stacks of patient records, still needing to complete their notes for their workday.

"There you guys are. I've been showing the new psychiatrist around and wanted to introduce him to you." Maggie walked into the room where Judy and Kristin were busy writing and entering patient data.

"Dr. Newton, this is Judy and Kristin, two of the best psych nurses money can buy. Ladies, this is Dr. Zach Newton, my new partner."

Kristin looked up. "Oh, my God."

"Kris. What a surprise! I didn't know you worked here. This is great. Maggie, do you know who this is? She was one of my best buddies in high school. Wow! Let me give you a hug!"

Without thinking twice, he walked up to Kristin, wrapping his arms around her. She tried to hug him back but was in shock at seeing the love of her life standing before her.

"So, this is the great Zach Newton. As I live and breathe."

Judy walked up to Zach to shake his hand. Kristin tried to kick her, wanting her to shush. Through the years of their friendship Kris had shared with Judy her feelings for Zach. Little did she know Judy would come face-to-face with him.

"You guys know each other? How cool," Maggie continued. "I'm taking Zach and his wife out for dinner tonight. Why don't you guys join us? You can catch up on old times."

Kristin's heart sank. His wife. She could feel sadness seep into her bones. "Thanks, Dr. Taylor. But I promised my mom I'd come over."

"How is your mom, Kris? And Bear?"

"Good, Zach. I mean, Dr. Newton."

"Kris, call me Zach. You sure you can't come to dinner with us? I'd love for you to meet Alex."

Kristin wouldn't have been able to eat even if she wanted to. "I'd love to, really. But I promised my mom. I'll have to take a rain check."

"Judy, I think I'm finished with the charts. I need to go. I'll call you later, okay?"

Judy looked at Kristin. She saw an obvious change in Kristin's demeanor from just a few minutes ago. "Sure, Kris. You go on. I'll make sure everything's done."

"I'm going to take you up on that rain check, Kristin. It'll be great to talk about the good old days."

"Yeah, great. Good seeing you, Zach. Really. See you tomorrow, Dr. Taylor, Judy." Kristin needed to get out of the room. She felt as if she was suffocating.

***

After her shower, Kristin rummaged through her dresser finding a T-shirt and a pair of pajama bottoms. With her head full of Zach, she mindlessly walked into the kitchen. She opened the refrigerator, moved things around, found nothing of interest. Her pantry proved the same. She knew she should eat but wasn't one bit hungry. She decided she needed to talk and picked up her phone.

"Hey, Jude, you busy?"

"Kris, hey. Just watching TV. What's up?"

"Zach called me today. He told me he left his wife. He wants to see me."

"Hey that's great!"

"It is?"

"I wondered if that was the phone call he needed to make today before rounding."

"You saw him today?"

"Yeah. He got back from his trip early. Didn't go into much detail, but I noticed his wedding band was missing. He made rounds with me in the afternoon so Dr. Taylor could go check out that gruesome murder in sterile processing. Did you hear about that?"

"Yeah, I did. Eric and Bull got the case. They came up to the OR to talk to some of us. It made our day come to a screeching halt, as a matter of fact. This has been a hell of a day all the way around."

"The earth definitely must be off its axis. Is it a full moon tonight or what? If it isn't, it sure is missing a good chance."

"You got that right. Judy, he wants to meet me tomorrow to talk."

"I hope you said yes."

"I did, but I'm nervous as can be. My appetite has vanished. I hate this crappy love-sick feeling."

"It'll be okay."

"Ya think?"

"Kris, you've been trying to ignore your feelings about Zach Newton for so long now that they're all tumbling out at one time. But if tomorrow is too soon to see him, tell him so. You gotta take care of yourself first, you know."

"I know. But my problem is that I do want to see him. I just don't want to be a blubbering idiot. I want to be able to hold my own, whatever happens."

"Wish I could be there for moral support. But I know you don't want or need me there. And I'll share this with you, too. He was in a pretty good mood when I saw him. Almost giddy. I haven't seen him this happy in a long time."

"Really?"

"It wasn't very pretty, Kristin. There's something not quite right about a giddy man."

"Oh, Judy. In your eyes, all you gotta do is be a man to have something not quite right with you."

Judy laughed at Kristin's statement knowing it was all too true. "Well, I can't argue that point. But I do know that you love Zach and have loved him for a long time. You're going to have to deal with this eventually. If it's not going to work then you have got to get him out of your brain. It's not good to let it haunt you, dictating your life as it has. You're going have to meet it square on."

"I know. Crap."

"Sorry. You want to come over and eat some ice cream? I'm more than happy to do some sympathy eating with you."

"Naah, I'm already in my PJs. Thanks, though. I'll be all right." Kristin knew Judy was right. She was going to have to deal with this head on.

"Thanks for your ear, Judy. I'll probably call you after I see him. I imagine I'll either be laughing or crying. Maybe tomorrow night you'll go with me to that restaurant we went to on Sunday and have a beer, or six. What was the name of that beer?"

"Kill-A-Man! I love that beer, for the name alone. Sounds like a plan to me!"

Kristin chuckled at Judy's enthusiasm over the name of Kill-A-Man beer. "Okay, then, I'll give you a buzz. He's picking me up from Mom's at two. I'll call you after. You'll be the driver in case I need to cry in my beer?"

"No problem."

"Thanks. Night, Judy."

"Night, Kris, try to get some sleep."

But Kristin couldn't sleep. She tossed and turned most of the night. It wasn't until two thirty in the morning that she was able to finally quiet her brain enough to drift off into a restless slumber.

***

Andrew's wife was frantic at two thirty in the morning. It wasn't like her husband to be out like this. She called the hospital's emergency room but got no results. She finally called 911.

"My husband didn't come home from work today. I'm really worried about him. What should I do?"

The dispatcher tried to be sympathetic, but he had had this phone call more than once. Usually the guy was out doing his girlfriend. But he'd learned that no wife, ever, ever wanted to hear that. "Well ma'am. Did you call the emergency room at the hospital?"

"Yes, I did. His name is Andrew Hardin. Do you know anything about him?"

"Sorry, ma'am, but I don't."

He didn't even try to reason with these women anymore. "Let me patch you in to the night watch commander, see if he knows anything."

"Okay. Thank you very much. I'm very worried about him. This is just not like him. Not one bit."

It never is, the dispatcher thought to himself as he forwarded the phone.

After the night watch commander got all of the specifics from Andrew's wife he put her on hold. Ten years ago, he would have listened patiently, soothed the fretful wife, and been done with it. But not anymore. Violent crimes were the norm, and if there was a delay in service resulting in something bad, guaranteed he would be in the middle of a nasty lawsuit against the department. He had to at least check the previous shift report. Didn't want some lawyer saying something stupid like he was negligent. He was too old for that. He planned on retiring in a couple of years. He wanted to be able to keep all his money and not have to give it to some yahoo because he was out screwing his girlfriend and got run over on the way home. As he was reading the report, he got back on the phone.

"Where did you say he worked? At the hospital?"

"Yes. He's a therapist there."

The night watch commander saw there was a dead man found at the hospital earlier in the day, but no ID as of yet. "Well, ma'am, I don't see his name here. If he doesn't show up in twenty-four hours, give us a call back and we'll file a missing persons report."

"Can't you do that now? My Andrew would not be this late."

"Ahhh, he'll probably walk in any second, and instead of being worried you'll want to hit him over the head with a frying pan."

"God, I hope so. This is just not like him. I'm telling you. I know my husband. You people just don't care." Andrew's wife slammed the phone down in frustration.

The night watch commander made a mental note to pass this call on to the day folks in the event she called back. He also wondered why the dead guy at the hospital was nameless.

***

Eric was slam tired. It was two in the morning and he was just getting home. Walking into the den, he saw Bear still up and reading.

"Rough first day?"

"You got that right, Bear. What're you doing up? Not worried about me, I hope."

"I don't sleep as good as I used to. I just try and go with it. Sleep when I'm tired; get up when I'm not. Guess it's from my crazy days as a detective."

"Great, can't wait." Eric flopped himself down in a chair.

"Somebody steamed someone in a sterilizer, a sterilizer that sterilizes instruments, for God's sake. Can you believe that?"

"Son, I can believe just about anything. As nice as some people can be, there are just as many rotten souls stinkin' up the earth." Bear got up and walked to the kitchen. "Let me get you and me both a beer."

He came back holding two beers with one hand. He walked over to Eric holding out the beers so he could take one of them. Eric rarely saw Bear without his prosthetic arm. It took him by surprise.

"I could have gotten it, Bear." Eric looked into Bear's face. "Thanks."

Bear ignored the sympathy and sat down, taking a drink. "Got any good leads yet?"

"Not really. We'll probably have to wait for someone to file a missing persons report to figure out who it is. No ID. No wallet. He's so gruesome we'd rather not march half the hospital through the morgue to find out his identity. As far as who did it or why, who the hell knows? It doesn't go with a run-of-the-mill robbery, that's for sure. It took us all evening and half the night to talk to people, gather the evidence, et cetera, et cetera. I'm sure you know the drill. What a first day at work." Eric took a drink from his beer, then another. "This sure does hit the spot. One good thing about the day was that I got to see Kris. We had to go to the OR and talk with some of the folks there. Off the record, of course, she told me she was very happy she was getting the rest of the day off." Eric laughed at his sister. "Is she a mess or what?"

"She's a mess, all right." Bear chuckled with Eric.

"Looks like you're gonna have your hands full for a day or two. How's old Bull? Hanging in there?"

"He's doing great. Still has a lot of punch in him. Hope I'm doing as good as he is when I'm his age."

"Yep. There's nobody quite like old Bull. I'm just glad you're there to take care of him for me. He's not as young and spry as he used to be, not that he'd admit to it."

"Are you kidding? He is as sharp as he ever was. Kind of fun to watch. He's one of a kind, that's for sure. I know I'll learn a lot from him."

"No doubt about that, son." Bear finished off his beer and stood up, stretching. Eric noted that even without his arm, Bear was still a massive man. "It's time for me to hit the sack. Get some sleep yourself, son. You're gonna have some busy days ahead of ya."

***

Benny was back from his hospital run. The first thing he did was to check on Maggie. Her breathing had become stronger. He would let her wake up a little before giving her another dose. While he waited for her to wake up, he went to the kitchen and made himself a sandwich. He was too excited to be hungry but knew he should eat. He could already tell he was going to like having her here, waiting for him when he came home from work. The minute he walked into his apartment he could feel the difference. He sensed a completeness, a fullness, like after a satisfying meal. *Yes, I'm going to like this arrangement just fine.*

He opened another bottle of wine and poured himself a glass. He opened up his bag of stolen equipment and placed the items on the kitchen counter. He was surprised how easy it had been to obtain the items he needed. He had been so focused on Maggie that he didn't appreciate the ramifications of a closed sterile-processing department. The surgery department had had to shut down, with only one team on duty for the emergencies that couldn't be transferred to another hospital. And they had all crashed in the doctor's lounge. *I did myself a favor and didn't even know it, steam cleaning Maggie's boyfriend.* When he saw that the surgical team paid him no attention, he walked straight into the sterile core where the supplies were kept. He found the blades, sutures, and Betadine easy enough. The knife handles he had to hunt for. Once he found them he saw a bin marked "forceps" and grabbed a couple pair of those as well. Probably would help to make a cleaner cut. *Wouldn't want her twat all jagged, even though she probably deserves it.* The last thing he grabbed was the necessary equipment to start and maintain an IV in Maggie's arm. He wouldn't be able to intubate her; he would be too busy with the ceremony. He would have to rely on his drugs to keep her sedated.

He added gauze, Bacitracin, and his beloved GHB to his collection. He attempted to line up all of the paraphernalia he had accumulated for the ceremony in a symmetrical fashion. First he lined them up in the order he would need them. The vial of GHB, alcohol, IV needles and tubing, two bags of Lactated Ringers, Betadine, knife blades, knife handles, forceps, sutures, Bacitracin, gauze. He then switched the forceps with the knife handles. Then he switched the blades with the forceps so they would be next to the knife handles. The lines he saw frustrated him. He rearranged them, smallest to largest. Still not pleased with the lines, he tried largest to smallest.

"Fuck! This is crap. Get it right!" Benny's arm swung out in full force knocking everything off of the counter. He drank what was left in his wine glass and poured himself another. Sweat beaded up on his forehead. He went to the thermostat cranking up the air-conditioner. *Damn, it was hot for the beginning of summer.*

He picked up everything he had knocked to the floor and retrieved a ruler from a kitchen drawer. After carefully taking measurements of the items as well as between the items he was able to complete the task. He decided on smallest to largest. As long as the distance between each item was the same and he kept everything smallest to largest during the procedure Benny decided it would be okay. He would keep the ruler close by for guidance if he needed it. Too bad the ruler was plastic. He wouldn't be able to sterilize it very well without it melting. Benny decided that the lines being right were more important than the sterility. If the lines weren't right, nothing would be right and everything had to be perfect. If it wasn't perfect the circumcision of Maggie's clitoris could not be completed. *If her clit gets infected because of the ruler I'll just have to deal with that.*

He went to the bathroom for some rubbing alcohol. At least he could clean it up some. As he went to the bathroom, he saw that Maggie had moved. *Good, she's waking up. I need to get some water in her, don't want her dehydrated.* He looked at his watch. It was two thirty in the morning. *Perfect, twelve hours from now, the ceremony will all be over.*

He went back into the kitchen, getting a glass of water to give to her. She was coming around but still pretty groggy. Her face was bruised where he had backhanded her. "Here Maggie May, have a sip of water."

He helped her sit up in the bed. She felt like she had the hangover from hell. Reaching out for the glass of water, she put her hand over Benny's to help direct the water to her lips. Her face hurt and she couldn't remember why. She wondered if her stepfather had come back for her. She looked to Benny.

"Help me, Benny, I think he's after me again."

"Who, my dear Maggie May? Nobody's after you."

"Yes, I think he is. My stepfather, he's come for me. He's going to hurt me again." Maggie had regressed to a little girl, scared, wanting to hide. She curled up into a ball on the bed.

"My Maggie May. I won't let anybody hurt you, not anymore. Not your stepfather, not those men you fucked, no one. I'll keep you safe with me. Do you trust me, my Maggie May?"

Maggie looked up into Benny's eyes, searching for comfort. Her mind was blurry. He looked like Benny, but he felt like her stepfather. She didn't want to trust him; the feelings were the bad feelings. "You're Benny?"

"Promise. And I'll keep your stepdad away from you." Benny petted Maggie's hair and brought the glass of water to her lips, encouraging her to drink. "But you're going to have to trust me."

Maggie's mouth was very dry. She sat up to get more water. Any energy she exerted seemed to be too much and she lay back down after sipping the water.

Benny stood up. "I'm going to get you something to eat. I don't think it's a good idea for you to eat much, though. Maybe some soup. Would you like some soup, Maggie May?" Without waiting for an answer he walked out of the bedroom.

She was so worn; she could only think her answer. *Soup is a good idea, warm chicken noodle soup. That's what I need.*

It will make me feel better. Maggie had trouble fighting the sleepiness that egged her to lie down. Ignoring her gut feelings she closed her eyes.

While Benny heated up the bowl of chicken noodle soup he got out a bottle of Valium. He needed to save the GHB for his ceremony and Valium would keep her sedated just as well. She would just have to swallow the pills. He was tired and wanted to take a nap, she would have to take a nap, too. While the soup heated, he pulled out a box of saltines and took out four crackers to go with the chicken noodle soup. As he stirred the soup, he ate a few of the crackers himself, careful to eat them over the sink. He didn't want the crumbs to fall to the counter or on the floor. He found his ruler and after measuring distances, he arranged the crackers, bowl of soup, napkin, and spoon in a systematic fashion on a serving try. Satisfied with the appearance of Maggie's meal and with the valium in his pocket, he went back into the bedroom where she had fallen asleep. He sat the tray down on the bedside table and nudged her gently.

"Come on, Maggie May. Wake up. We need to get this soup in you. You'll sleep soon enough."

She stirred and tried to wake herself up. He placed a pillow against the headboard for her to lean against. Once she was up, he placed the serving tray on her lap and spooned the soup into her mouth. Once she got a taste of the soup, her hunger intensified. She took the spoon from Benny to feed herself.

"There you go, Maggie May. Have some crackers, too."

Benny picked up a cracker and put it in her other hand. She ate it immediately. She wasn't sure if her stepfather was somewhere in the shadows, waiting. If he was, he might take her food away, as he used to. Benny handed her another cracker. "Try not to get the crumbs on the bed. We need to keep it clean for later."

Benny brushed the crumbs that had fallen on the bed in the palm of his hand. Maggie quickly finished off the soup and crackers without talking. She picked up the glass of water.

Benny fished the Valium out of his pocket. "Here, wait. Take these first."

"What are they?" Maggie looked at the little blue pills in Benny's hand, thinking she should know what they were.

"Medicine. You'll feel better."

Maggie's head told her no. "I think I'm starting to feel better, actually. That soup and crackers helped a lot." Maggie tried to shake her feelings of fear and doom, not remembering enough to understand where they had come from.

"Maggie May, I told you I would protect you. But it's important that you do what I say." Benny's voice was firm.

She didn't want the pills. She looked at Benny and tried to remember how she got here, in this bed. Maybe she should get up, try to leave. She tried to swing her legs over to the side of the bed. "I think I want to stand up. I'm feeling better now."

"No!" Benny blocked her legs from hitting the floor. "I told you that you must do what I say. I'm running the show here."

She looked at him and subconsciously rubbed her jaw where he had hit her earlier.

"I'll get your stepfather."

"My what?" Maggie's mind was muddled between her past and her present. "My stepfather?"

Benny had not expected Maggie to become so lucid. He grabbed one of her wrists. "I told you. You do what I say. It's time to take your pills."

He held out his hand with the pills in front of her. She knocked the pills out of his hand and tried to twist away. He jumped on her and straddled her, banging her head on the wall behind the bed. He grabbed the hair on the top of her head.

Benny held her head up by her hair making her look into his eyes. "Now that wasn't very smart. We are now going to have to go back into the kitchen, get more pills, and you're going to have to go with me."

He pulled at her hair, jerking her head up, hyper-extending her neck. Maggie's eyes were wide, her body tense. Benny's face softened as he started to stroke her neck with his free hand. Slowly his hand moved toward her chest. His eyes followed his hand as he fondled each breast through her blouse, caressing them. Benny looked at her face.

"You like that, my Maggie May?" He pulled her hair taut.

Maggie didn't answer. Her hell had come back.

"Did you like it when your boyfriends did it, too? We're going to make it right. You will see." Benny continued to hold on to Maggie by her hair, and attempted to loosen his belt with his free hand. Unable to unbuckle his belt with one hand he leaned toward the bedside table and pulled out two wrist restraints, another benefit of working in a hospital. "This is so you don't do anything stupid." Benny tied Maggie's wrists to the posts of the headboard.

"Please Benny, no. I'll be good, I promise."

"We'll see if your behavior improves."

After Benny was sure Maggie was securely tied to the bed, he stood up facing the mirror. He could see Maggie behind him, tied to the bed, watching him in the mirror. The image excited Benny. He took his belt off. As he unzipped his pants he watched himself. He talked in a detached manner while he began to stroke himself.

"You know, Maggie, in the beginning I didn't think you cared about a hard cock. Cocks are nasty when they're fat and full. I thought you were a better woman than that. You acted like you were better than that. And then you gave me a test to prove my love for you. You're just like my mother in that way."

Benny continued to stroke himself as he became harder, looking at Maggie in the mirror. "I sucked the life out of that scum just like you wanted. It was great, Maggie May. I wish you could have been there. I was making love to you while they were sucking the blood literally right out of him. I was making love to you and my dick was hard and I wanted to come in you." Benny masturbated openly while he talked.

Maggie stared at Benny in disbelief. Benny caught Maggie's eyes in the mirror.

"You want some, Maggie May? The whore in you can't help it, I know." Benny turned and faced her, continuing to stroke himself. "My mother was right, you know. She tried to teach me when I was young. Now I finally understand. I can help you, just like my mother helped me."

Benny straddled Maggie again. He unbuttoned her blouse, rubbing himself between her breasts. Maggie turned her head away. Benny grabbed her jaw, turning her face back toward him, making her watch.

"You have to understand, Maggie. The purification must begin."

She watched in horror as Benny continued to masturbate. His moaning intensified as he feverishly worked himself into a frenzy. Benny let out a moan as he climaxed, semen spewing onto Maggie's breasts and dripping from his hands. Benny closed his eyes for a few seconds, savoring his orgasm.

"I proved my love for you, my Maggie May, and now it's time for you to prove your love to me. We must continue the purification process. It's the only way." Benny got off Maggie and continued to talk. "We both need our sleep, Maggie, for tomorrow is a big day. John, Rod, and Sting are all going to be here. And we have to be ready. I wanted to save my cum for you tomorrow, but watching you watch me, knowing you wanted me, seeing the whore you are, was too much. You're just a whore, Maggie May, just like all women, just as my mother said. You don't have to take the pills if you don't want." Benny reached into his dresser again and retrieved more restraints. "You wanna be wide awake, Maggie May? That's okay, too."

Maggie didn't respond. She knew whatever she said wouldn't matter. When she was watching Benny in the mirror she remembered what had caused her fear. She felt her sanity slipping again. Her stepfather had come back.

***

It was seven in the morning. The night watch commander was reporting to his daytime replacement.

"All in all it was a pretty quiet night. We did get one phone call that might be a missing person's report. Probably nothin'. Only reason I'm mentioning it is because the guy works at the hospital. I guess they're still workin' to ID that guy they found there yesterday. I heard we're supposed to have our ear out for that kind of info." The night watch commander handed Pete a piece of paper with the information about the missing person phone call.

"I'll make sure it gets passed on." Pete took the piece of paper and folded it before putting it in a breast pocket. I'm going in to meet with the captain in just a minute. But I got to get a cup of mornin' Joe first."

The night watch commander yawned. "Time for me to go home. See you tomorrow. What did they used to say on *Hill Street Blues*? Get them before they get you. Somethin' like that."

"Yeah, somethin' like that. See ya tomorrow."

As the night watch commander walked out the door, Pete picked up his coffee mug and headed out the door behind him. On his way to the coffee pot he heard a woman almost panic-stricken. He walked toward the high-pitched chattering sounds. A harried-looking, overweight woman sat at the desk of a policewoman.

"You don't understand. This is not like my husband. He would never, ever stay out all night. He is a good husband, he loves his family. I don't want to wait twenty-four hours. I want to file a missing report now, damn it. Something is very, very wrong."

Pete walked up behind Andrew Hardin's wife and caught the eye of the policewoman. "I tried to tell her, sir, that she could come back in about twelve hours. Maybe we'd hear something, or maybe her husband would be home by then."

"I don't want to wait twelve hours. I want you to look for him now." Isadora looked around the room at all of the policemen shuffling paper, pretending to ignore her. She stood up, flailing her arms at them. "Look at all of you, standing around with your important papers. You could be out looking for my dear Andy. Instead all you do is shuffle papers and drink coffee. He could be hurt somewhere, dying even. But all you do is stand here. I'll get a lawyer, I will. It's my right as an American citizen. I'll sue you if my Andy is hurt. It will be your fault." Isadora Hardin's heavy breasts heaved as tears streaked down her face. She held herself as she silently wept. Her nose started to run. Isadora tried to stop the flow of mucus, sniffing deeply, rubbing her arm across her face. Heaving, she slumped back down into her chair.

Everybody in the room watched her, dumbfounded. Pete moved in quickly. He hated to react to anyone threatening a lawsuit, yet he knew he had to do what he could to make sure that didn't happen. He grabbed some tissue off of the policewoman's desk, handing it to Isadora.

"Ma'am, here. Come with me to my office. Let's see if we can figure this out together."

Isadora looked up at Pete, grateful to have someone's ear. "Oh, thank you, thank you."

She looked up at the ceiling and crossed herself.

"Thank you, Lord Jesus. You sent someone to help me find my dear Andy."

As Isadora got up, Pete looked at the policewoman. "I'll take it from here."

"Yes, sir." As they walked to Pete's office the policewoman rolled her eyes. Lawyers were ruining law enforcement.

***

Kristin woke up startled. She looked at her alarm. *Almost nine o'clock! Crap!* She jumped out of bed, grabbing the clock. She couldn't remember if she had forgotten to set the alarm or not. She hated getting up late and especially today when she was supposed to meet Zach. She needed to be on her game today. She wanted to get some exercise in, run some errands, and have plenty of time to visit and relax with her mom and Bear before she met with Zach. She looked at the clock again and wondered if she needed a new one. She took the clock with her into the kitchen and after putting a pot of coffee on, reset the clock to see if it would go off. She called her mom to tell her she would be over shortly. She stopped short of telling her about the lunch date. She made a cup of coffee and when the alarm clock went off in the middle of her conversation she jumped, already having too much on her mind to remember resetting the clock.

"Damn alarm clock." Kristin said out loud to her mother.

"What's wrong with your alarm clock?"

"Oh, nothing, probably. It didn't go off this morning. I probably forgot to set it. So you think Eric will be home for lunch?"

"I doubt that. He's got his hands full with that murder at the hospital."

"Oh yeah, how could I forget that? What a way to start a job. Does he even know who it is yet?"

"I don't think so. He was gone this morning before I got up. Bear said he didn't get in until late. I'm afraid we might see him less now than we did when he was in Asheville."

"You might be right, Mom. But I hope you're not. I'll try to be over around noon. I want to get a run in before I come over. Do you need me to pick up anything on the way?"

"I think we're good. I already did some extra grocery shopping over the weekend since Eric was coming home. Still have plenty of everything."

"Okay. If you change your mind and I'm not here, leave it on my voice mail. I'll pick it up on my way over."

"All righty. I'll see you in a bit."

"Okay, Mom. Bye."

Kristin closed her phone, grabbed her coffee, and headed to her bathroom to find the running clothes she wore yesterday. Aside from her panties and socks, Kristin always wore her running clothes two or three times before she washed them. They were going to be sweaty in a matter of minutes and she didn't see the need to wash them every time. She took them off the bathroom door hook and quickly changed. After she put her hair in a ponytail she rummaged through her drawer looking for a fresh pair of socks and a bandanna to use as a sweatband for her head. She grabbed her shoes, a bottle of water, and her cup of coffee and headed outside to the front porch. She sipped her coffee while she put on her socks and shoes. She twisted her bandanna into a rope and tied it around her head. She stood up, and still sipping at her coffee, started to stretch the muscles in her legs. She held her stretch until she could feel the burn in each muscle. This was going to be a great run; she could feel it in her bones. Her mind was high on Zach, her adrenalin flowing. And though she rarely allowed it, today she let her mind venture far into her fantasies of loving Zach.

As she runs, she relives that kiss from so long ago on that snowy day. So many times her mind had played that scene over and over until she could take it no more. But today not only does she permit it, she yearns for it and wants more. Kristin's desire for Zach's touch finally overpowers her deepest thoughts.

She feels Zach's mouth on hers as he holds her in his arms. He kisses her neck, her shoulders, and slowly moves toward her chest. He unbuttons the first button on Kris' blouse, then the next. In her mind she allows him to continue, thirsting for his touch, hungry for his love.

He looks at her, searching her eyes. "I've always loved you, Kristin. Always. I want to make love to you."

Kristin can't answer. She kisses his lips. As she runs she sees them lie on her bed. He continues to unbutton her blouse, helping her to take it off. He slides her bra straps off her shoulders, kissing her breasts as he continues to undress her. She watches him as he takes off his shirt; her mouth begins to water as her desire for him grows.

Kristin looked around her.

"Oh my God."

She had already run five miles. She was sweating, her legs fluid, but there was no pain; she felt as if she was gliding. A runner's high—the ultimate running experience. A runner's high and she was making love to Zach Newton. It about took her breath away. She was afraid she had imagined too much. Maybe it would bring bad luck to the afternoon.

"Please, God, no. Please be on my side."

Against her desires, she brought herself back into the real world. She knew it was the only one that counted. It was important for Kristin to keep her expectations low. It was the only way. Kristin finished another mile, and attempted to think with her head, trying to hide the dreams of her heart. By the time she finished her cool-down, Kristin was more wistful about her meeting with Zach. She had denied her feelings for such a long time that she was almost afraid of them, afraid that if she allowed them to exist they would somehow betray her. She couldn't handle her own feelings turning on her; it was easier for her if she refused them life. Kristin got back to her apartment, made a fresh pot of coffee, took a hot shower, and readied herself for her meeting with Zach.

***

Zach bounded out of bed. This was going to be the best day of his life. He had to get to work, see his patients, then go over to Kristin's parents' house. It would be great to see them again. He had only seen them once since he got back into town and when Kristin found out about it, she let him know she did not like it. While Zach got ready for work he reminisced about his high school years. He and Kristin had been great friends—the best, really. He thought about that kiss in his living room their senior year, that kiss that changed everything. He hadn't seen it coming, wanting to kiss her as he did. It had scared him. He wanted to keep their relationship a friendship. He saw how relationships worked in high school. They loved you, and then they hated you. He didn't want Kristin to hate him, ever. He loved her. So they had to stay friends. And then he saw her again, when he came back as Maggie's partner. The minute he saw Kristin he realized how much he missed her in his life. He tried to rekindle the friendship with her, but she made it very clear to him that she was not interested. When he found out she was leaving the psychiatric unit for the operating room, he tried to talk with her about it. It seemed they were never alone at work. He had wondered if she was avoiding him intentionally. It wasn't until her last day on the psychiatric unit that he'd caught up with her in the parking lot, leaving for the last time.

"You're going to the OR?" Zach asked Kristin point-blank.

Kristin was very matter-of-fact. "The hospital has an opening in their operating room school. I think it's a great opportunity to learn something new in nursing."

Kristin always tried to maintain a professional demeanor with Zach. She couldn't let her guard down.

"But you love psych nursing."

"So, I'll learn to love OR nursing. What's it to you anyway, Dr. Newton?"

"Kris, what is it? We used to be best friends, we confided in each other about everything. I really miss that. I miss you."

Kristin felt her emotions intensify. She didn't expect him to talk so openly. Tears welled up in her eyes. She tried to show her anger instead of her pain. "Zach Newton, what do you know about missing me? You kissed me that one time and I practically never saw you again. I lost my best friend over one stupid kiss. And then you left me, and you got married. And I hated you. And I loved you." Kristin gasped, putting her hand to her mouth, trying to stop the words from leaving her brain.

All at once he understood. The whole time he was busy taking care of his feelings he never once thought of Kristin's. He looked at Kristin. She was trying so hard not to cry. He wanted to hold her but was afraid she would back away if he tried.

"I need to go, Zach. Please, let me go." Kristin was really asking Zach to leave her soul; she just didn't know how to release him from her being.

"Sure, Kris. Look, I'm sorry. I think I did this all wrong. Maybe one day we can talk about it."

"Yeah, okay, maybe." She needed to get away. Her guard had been dismantled, and she didn't want Zach to see her pain. She was still a few yards from her car. "See ya." Kris turned around and walked away.

"Yeah, See ya, Kris," Zach yelled out to her. And then she was gone. And he found he missed her madly.

But this was the day, Zach Newton declared as he drove himself to work, that he would take Kris in his arms and kiss her, and love her; and he was so happy that he thought he was going to burst.

***

"Yeah, Bull. Pete here. Look. We got a Mrs. Isadora Hardin here. Says her husband, Andrew Hardin, never made it home last night. He's a therapist at the hospital. After hearing what she's got to say, thought I'd give you a call. You might be interested." Pete was on the phone while Isadora waited in his office. After getting a general description of her husband and knowing the basic description of the man found in the sterilizer, Pete thought it was worth a phone call.

"We'll be waiting." Pete put the phone down.

"Mrs. Hardin, I gotta couple of detectives who are on their way here to talk to you."

Isadora nodded. "Thank you so much for listening to me." Isadora blessed herself and looked up to the sky. "Thank you, Lord Jesus."

"Would you like a cup of coffee while you're waiting?" Pete got up to fix himself the cup of coffee he had started to get before meeting Isadora Hardin.

Before Isadora could answer, Eric and Bull knocked on Pete's door as they walked in.

"Hey, fellas." Pete was stirring the Sweet'N Low in his coffee. "This is Isadora Hardin. Her husband never made it home last night. Here's his stats."

Pete picked up a piece of paper from this desk and handed it to Bull. One thing Bull had learned over the years was that when Pete had a hunch it was usually a damn good one. Pete's stats matched the victim's.

"Mrs. Hardin, does your husband carry a wallet, wear any jewelry? Wedding ring, necklace?" Eric thought it peculiar that the man found in the sterilizer had no identification on him, nor did he have a hospital badge. The only thing they had to go on was a wedding ring that had a bunch of letters inscribed on the inside. BBNTB. Letters that had no rhyme or reason to Eric or Bull, but they meant something to someone.

"My Andy quit carrying his wallet with him. His patients were always asking him for money. In the beginning he didn't mind giving out a dollar here, a dollar there. But after a while he said it was all the time, and it was getting to be too much. So since he was their therapist and he didn't want to lie to them he just started leaving his wallet in the car so he wouldn't have any money with him, except maybe some change in his pocket. So I guess that's not good now, if he has no ID on him." Isadora shook her head, arms crossed over her big bosom, hugging herself.

"What about jewelry?" Bull wondered how much more besides height and weight and no ID would Isadora's husband and the steamed man have in common.

"A wedding ring, of course. He's a good man. Not like some of those men that don't wear wedding rings, so they can go and fool around."

Isadora looked at her own wedding band before looking at the ring fingers of Pete, Bull, and Eric. Seeing no ring on Bull's or Eric's left hands she looked at them with raised eyebrows. Bull rolled his eyes, but Eric was quick to respond.

"Mrs. Hardin, neither of us are married."

"Of course you're not. I didn't say anything. And if you're not, you should be. Marriage is good for a man." Isadora winked at Eric.

Bull was getting impatient. "The ring, Mrs. Hardin. He wore a wedding ring? Anything peculiar about it, different?"

Isadora was enjoying the conversation she was having. Sometimes a little bit of flirting went a long way. She did not like Bull interrupting. She looked at him, wrinkled up her nose and frowning. "No, sir. I don't think his ring is peculiar at all. I think it's a very nice wedding ring. I picked it out myself." Isadora looked at her own rings again, twisting them on her finger. She sighed loudly, her huge breasts heaving, becoming one with her chubby abdomen.

Bull shook his head and rolled his eyes before turning away from her to fix himself a cup of coffee. He had little tolerance for the drama, and he was frustrated with himself for provoking the situation. Pete and Eric's eyes met for a minute, Pete trying to suppress a wry grin. Bull always had a way with women. Eric scratched his head, wondering what to do next.

Before the three men could decide what to say next Isadora calmed herself and started talking. "My Andy, he has such a way about him. The day he gave me my ring, he was so nervous. I'll never forget it. I was outside working in the yard, and he drove up in the driveway. He jumps out of his car holding up a little plastic bag." Isadora began rock herself back and forth.

"He held up the bag, and yelled out, 'I got 'em.' 'You got what?' I said. 'The rings, I got our wedding rings!' I had to laugh. I said, 'That's not very romantic, Andrew Hardin.' He came up to me, both of us hot and sweaty from the summer heat, and he opened the package. He opened up my ring and said, 'Black, black, no take back.'" Isadora's nose was running, as tears flowed down her plump cheeks.

Bull had kept his back to Isadora while she talked, not turning to face her until now.

"Black, black, no take back?"

Eric's mind clicked off what was engraved on the dead man's ring. BBNTB. Black, black, no take back.

Eric bent down on his knees in front of Isadora. This was going to be bad. "Mrs. Hardin, was there anything engraved on your husband's wedding ring?"

Isadora looked up into Eric's eyes. "I thought it would be a funny joke to put that on his ring. The whole saying didn't fit so I just did the first letters of each word. Andrew thought I was very clever." Isadora smiled widely through her tears.

Bull interrupted. "And the letters were, Mrs. Hardin?"

"What do you think, Mr. Bull?" Isadora was indignant. "BBNTB, of course."

***

The visit to the morgue with Isadora Hardin was one of the worst things Eric could have imagined. Bull thought it was a scene from a bad movie. They both agreed that the smartest thing they did was have a policewoman drive Mrs. Hardin to the morgue so they wouldn't have to deal with her after she saw her cold, steamed, and very dead Andy in a body bag.

Once Isadora told Eric and Bull about the engraving on the wedding ring, they were positive they had an ID for their steamed and sterilized man. And as much as they didn't want to do it, they knew they needed Isadora to identify her husband. With a policewoman in attendance, Eric and Bull gave Isadora a rundown of the person they found in the sterilizer, along with a description of the wedding ring, and lack of ID. While she listened, she sobbed and held herself. It was when they got to the morgue that Isadora Hardin lost it. Eric thought they had prepared her well for what she would see, but that was obviously not the case. The minute the morgue refrigerator opened, Isadora's sobs turned to howling, her massive breasts bouncing up and down on her protruding belly. By the time the body bag was unzipped and exposed Isadora's cold, steamed, and very dead Andy, Isadora was past hysterical.

The morgue refrigerator had an electrical design that allowed the hospital to lay the deceased horizontally four bodies deep. The morgue employee pushed button number three. The pulleys began to creak and squeal as they were called into action. Bull and Eric's eyes met, both wondering when they would hear lightning and thunder just to add to the moment. After the rack marked 'Andrew Hardin' lurched to a stop, Bull unzipped the body bag. Isadora knew immediately it was her beloved husband.

"Oh, my God. My God. My dear sweet Andy! My Andy. Oh, Lord Jesus." Isadora started to hyperventilate. She bent down to touch her husband. "Let me see your eyes, your beautiful blue eyes. Open your eyes, Andy, and wake up. Andy!"

Before anyone could stop her, Isadora lifted her husband's eyelids. Staring back at her was nothing more than dull yellowed eyeballs, devoid of all color. Isadora jumped at the sight, screaming out in a mix of pain and horror. Her arms flailed up toward the ceiling as she cried out. "Jesus, Mary, Mother of God, my Andy, my Andy!"

Isadora collapsed. As her heavy body lurched toward her dead husband, her arm closer to the morgue refrigerator collided with the panel that activated the electrical projections. Out came Andrew's bottom bunk mate. The massive weight of Isadora and her husband combined was too much for the old rickety electrical frame. The hefty load caused the rack to snap. Both Isadora and Andrew tumbled to the floor, flopping on top of the corpse under them. There in a very big pile lay two very dead cold bodies and Isadora Hardin.

The morgue employee yelled out, "Holy shit," and picked up the phone to call for help. Not knowing for sure whom to call, he called into the overhead system.

"Code Blue, the morgue. Code Blue, the morgue. And maintenance, too. Uh, stat."

The policewoman, Bull and Eric kneeled beside Isadora to make sure she still had a pulse and was breathing.

A team of nurses slammed open the door of the morgue with a crash cart. It took a second to register the three bodies on the floor. "What the hell?"

The morgue employee tried to explain. "It's that one", pointing to Isadora. "I didn't know who to call. The others are already dead."

" 'That one'" is very much alive. She just passed out, it appears." The policewoman got off her knees after checking on Isadora.

The leader of the code team looked at the morgue employee with distain. "You're wasting our time, boy." She went over to check Isadora's pulse. "She's got a great pulse. And you got a mess on your hands. See ya."

"Wait. Can't you help me wake her up? Or do something?"

The team leader looked at the morgue employee as if he had three heads. "Are you high? I'm not going to open this crash cart for a live person. Don't you have an ammonia ampule?"

The policewoman spoke up. "Here, I have one." She pulled one out of her breast pocket. She broke it and put in under Isadora's nose. Immediately Isadora started to snort and cough. The policewoman looked at the nurse. "Can I get a wheelchair and some help picking her up?"

The team leader looked at one of the other nurses standing next to her. "Go get a wheelchair from the ED and swing by the chaplain's office to get someone in here. What a mess."

The team leader looked to the morgue employee, an obviously young and inexperienced person. "What's your name?"

"Forest."

"Forest, where's your boss?"

"At lunch. He said it shouldn't be a problem since there were three law enforcement people here with her."

The team leader shook her head, talking to Eric, Bull, and the policewoman.

"That's what's wrong with this hospital. Management is so damn busy around here passing the buck nothing ever improves. No accountability in this joint, if you ask me. I'll go find his boss."

Bull was ready to get going. "Well, Dorsey. Looks like it's time for us to get the hell outta Dodge. What do ya say?"

Eric turned to the policewoman. "I know you're going to think this is a silly question, but will you need us? We got a lot of road to cover before we sleep tonight."

"Not only do I think that's a silly question, I think that's a stupid question. However, I won't hold it against you. I'll take care of things from here. I'll make sure Mrs. Hardin gets back home with some relatives."

"Great. Let's get out of here, Dorsey." Bull and Eric walked out the door as the nurse from the code team was returning with a wheelchair, a chaplain, and a maintenance worker. Everyone was so busy with their tasks at hand no one thought to wonder about the body that lay crushed under Andrew and Isadora Hardin. It was a shell of a man who never knew love or caring, a man whose innocence died so early in his childhood that he never had a fighting chance. It seemed to be Davis Melvin's lot in life as well as in death; he was always in the wrong place at the wrong time.

***

"I say we go to the back of the hospital and find out some more about this therapist. What the hell was he doing way over here in sterile processing? That doesn't make sense."

"We might as well walk. Kristin still has a couple of friends on the psych unit."

Eric and Bull walked around to the back of the campus of the hospital. They could have easily driven. Over the years, the hospital grew bigger and bigger, adding services and technology, buying up land, expanding offices just to meet the demands of managed care companies, tightening its budgets and constantly looking for ways to improve the bottom line.

"Now that I think about it, yesterday, when we were first called to the scene, I met one of the psychiatrists who work here. Any reason for her to be way over there? That makes it just too easy. But they say sometimes the culprit hangs out at the scene of the crime to watch." Eric shook his head. "Bull, that would just be wrong. Pretty woman. Surely nobody that saintly-looking could be evil."

"I've seen plenty of saintly-lookin' evil women in my day. Don't let her hook you yet. We'll check her out, that's for sure."

Standing at the door of the psychiatric unit, Bull pushed the doorbell.

"Yes, may I help you?" came through the speaker.

"Yeah. Detectives Bulle and Dorsey here. We need to talk to someone in charge."

"Okay. I'll be right there. Detective Dorsey? Eric, is that you? Judy here."

"Hey, Jude. Yeah, it's me, Eric."

"Well, hey, little bro, I'll be right out."

Bull looked at Eric. "Well, la-de-da. You got connections."

Eric kidded Bull back. "That's right, I'm little bro, and don't you forget it. You probably know Judy. She's one of Kristin's closest friends. But you better watch out, she can take you on and maybe take you out."

Bull just laughed. "Yeah, right."

Judy was at the door in a matter of minutes. She unlocked the door and gave Eric a big hug. "Man, is it good to see you. You look great!"

"Thanks, Jude. You look pretty good yourself." Eric returned her hug before turning to Bull. "You know Bull, here? I'm sure you've met at least once over the years. He's Bear's old partner, mine now."

Judy held out her hand to shake Bull's. "Yeah, we probably have met a time or two."

Judy had actually remembered him from Eric's wife's funeral, but she didn't want to say. Definitely a man's man, she couldn't help but think when she saw how he interacted with Kris and Eric's family at the funeral. Strong and rugged, but gentle; a dying breed, for sure. Bull shook Judy's hand.

"Yeah," Bull agreed. "I think I've seen this pretty face a time or two."

"All right. Now, you can cut the crap." Judy laughed at Bull and shook her head. "You don't even know if you have to butter me up yet."

"What? Can't I pay a pretty lady a compliment? This is not buttering up." Bull acted as innocent as possible.

Judy just rolled her eyes. "So what brings you guys here? I'm a busy woman."

"We want to start with whoever is in charge of this place." Bull eyed Judy, getting serious. He noted Judy had a little sass in her. He liked that in a woman, someone who could give it back.

Judy eyed Bull right back. "Well, right now, that would be me. All of the managers are over at the main hospital in a meeting. What can I help you with? One of our patients have an outstanding warrant or something?"

Eric jumped in the conversation. "Not hardly. We need to talk about Andrew Hardin."

"What about him? He surely wouldn't do anything wrong. He's one of our therapists."

Eric continued. "You're going to find out soon enough, I guess. He's the guy we found in the sterilizer yesterday."

"No way! Oh, my God! Maybe you guys should come in. Let me call a few people. Does his wife know?"

Eric nodded. "That's how we confirmed it. Earlier to-day."

Bull chuckled, thinking of the morning. "Yeah, that was fun."

Judy looked at Bull quizzically.

Eric said to Judy, "Don't ask. You don't want to know."

Judy just shook her head. She knew she would hear the story eventually from Kristin and showed Eric and Bull into a small office next to the nurses' station.

"Let me make a phone call." Judy got on the phone and left a message on someone's voice mail.

"I called the patient-care manager and left a message for her. You guys can go through her about anyone you need to talk to."

Eric thought about Maggie Taylor. "What about Dr. Taylor? Is she around? I'd really like to talk to her."

"I can see if she's in her office." Judy called the number.

"Hey, Dr. Newton, is Dr. Taylor available?" Judy listened to his reply. "Well, when she gets in will you have her call me? It's kind of important. No, nothing you can do, but thanks. That was her partner, Dr. Newton. He said that she was already a few minutes late for her first appointment but that he would leave her a message to call here ASAP. Eric, you remember Zach Newton, Kristin's best buddy from high school?"

"Oh yeah, I remember a thing or two about him. I know he broke Kristin's heart."

"I didn't think anybody knew."

"Well, I had to live with her. Bull, maybe Zach can talk to us. Maybe he knows something."

Bull cocked his head to the side, stuck his bottom lip out, and shrugged his shoulders. "Maybe."

Eric asked Judy, "Where's his office? Is it in walking distance?"

"Not a bad walk. I can probably point to it outside. What about when my manager calls back?"

Bull pulled his calling card out and handed it to Judy. "Have 'em give me a call. Do us a favor and keep all of this under your hat until we talk to a few people. When you see it in the paper, that's when you can say something. Deal?"

"Deal."

Judy knew how to keep a secret. Her job often depended on it. Judy walked Bull and Eric back to the front door. After unlocking it to let them out, she pointed in the direction of Maggie and Zach's office. "It was good to see you, Eric, but we need to get together when good things happen, not just bad." Judy gave Eric a hug.

"I agree with you on that. We'll probably come back to talk to you, but I know where you live." Eric returned Judy's hug with a smile.

Judy turned toward Bull, always showing her manners. "It was nice to see you again, Bull, and likewise, maybe next time it will be under better circumstances."

Bull attempted his charm again. "Miss Judy, the pleasure was all mine. And I agree, the next time it should be with a beer in our hands and a breeze at our backs."

Judy couldn't help but smile; maybe male chivalry was not all bad. She waved them off before locking herself back up on the psychiatric ward.

It was getting close to noon; Zach still needed to make rounds at the hospital before he met with Kristin. Maggie had patients in the office, but she had yet to show up. Zach called her house phone and then her cell phone. He didn't want to worry, but he couldn't figure out why she was late. As he was sitting at the empty receptionist desk with two of Maggie's patients waiting for her, Eric and Bull walked in. Eric recognized Zach immediately, a little older but definitely Zach Newton. Eric held out his hand.

"Zach, it's been a while." Zach stood up to shake Eric's hand.

"Well, hey, Eric, yes it has. How you been, buddy?" Zach had heard about Eric's wife through the grapevine, but never got a chance to talk to Kris about it.

"Hanging in there. This is Bull, my partner."

Bull and Eric pulled out their badges.

"We need to ask you some questions about your partner, Maggie Taylor, and a guy named Andrew Hardin."

The two patients in the waiting area both leaned forward to hear what was being said. Zach noticed their attempts to eavesdrop.

"I hope nothing's wrong. I've been trying to get up with Maggie all morning."

He peered over to the waiting patients. "Maybe we should go back into my office."

Once they were behind closed doors, Bull spoke first. "This is the deal. The guy in the sterilizer was a therapist here named Andrew Hardin."

Bull paused to see what kind of effect that information had on Zach.

"You've got to be kidding." Zach's face read shock and disbelief, nothing more.

"You think Maggie has something to do with that?"

"Well, Zach, she was there yesterday, when we first showed up."

"She was there as part of the trauma team, a debriefer, if you will."

Eric continued. "Do you know why Andrew Hardin would be over there, in the sterile-processing department?"

"Not a clue."

It was Bull's turn. "When was the last time you saw Andrew, or Maggie, for that matter?"

Zach was getting frustrated. His good feelings were going down the tubes fast. He let out a big sigh. "Let me think. I just got back into town yesterday and I made rounds late afternoon. I distinctly remember seeing Maggie, because we discussed who would go over to the hospital to see if they needed a trauma counselor. She's not your man, Eric."

Bull asked, "You got a time for that?"

Zach sighed again. "Maybe four. Let me think about that, though. When I made rounds, Andrew was not around. I hadn't seen him since before I left for my trip."

Eric was taking notes on what Zach was telling them. Just then the phone rang.

Zach picked up the phone. "It might be Maggie."

"Hello? Oh, hi, Liz. No, we're actually looking for her, too."

Zach was quiet while Liz told him about Maggie missing her appointment the night before. She also broke a big therapist rule. She told Zach that Maggie had become afraid of Benny and that she was trying to break off the relationship.

"Liz, I wouldn't worry right now about confidentiality. I'm just worried about her, even more now that I've talked to you." Zach looked at Eric, shaking his head. "No, I'm glad you called. I'm going to talk to someone right now. Don't you worry. I'm sure she's okay." Zach put down the phone. "This doesn't sound good." Zach said it to himself more than anyone.

Eric asked first. "What is it?"

"Maggie's got this boyfriend, Benny Cole. Personally I think he's a little creepy. But they seem to hit it off, so to each his own, you know?"

"Liz said that Maggie told her Benny was becoming more and more controlling. He wanted to know her every move, didn't want her going to therapy anymore...Maggie even got a weird feeling that he wanted to kill someone for her, a child molester, Liz says. Anyway, Maggie called Liz yesterday, and she was supposed to meet Liz at her office at seven last night but never showed up. Liz said she waited until now because, well, because she didn't want to overreact." Zach got up and started to pace. "But this isn't like Maggie. Not at all. And that Benny Cole. He's a strange one. Maggie told me he was a victim of child abuse. She is, too. I think that's what brought them together to begin with."

"Who's this Benny Cole fella? Where does he work?" Bull didn't like how this was sounding. A dead therapist. A missing psychiatrist. A fruitcake. Not good.

Zach's color drained from his face. "Benny works here, in the operating room. Right above the sterile processing department."

"Son of a bitch. We need to find that fella, now."

Bull, Eric, and Zach all walked to the front receptionist office. Zach had forgotten that two of Maggie's patients were still there and now another had joined them. Zach turned to them.

"Maggie—Dr. Taylor—is home sick. She just called. Please call back to reschedule. I'm sorry."

They all wanted to ask Zach questions.

"She's just sick. With the flu. She'll be better in a few days. If you need prescriptions, if you would be so kind as to call and put them on the answering machine, later on today. I'll listen to them and call them in for you so you don't have to come back. Just leave the name of the pharmacy, too." Zach talked as he ushered them out the door.

Eric asked Zach, "You know where this guy lives?"

"I can show you." *Crap*, Zach thought, *I'm going to miss my date with Kristin. She'll never talk to me again.*

"Good enough, let's go. Where the hell's our car?" Bull looked around, forgetting they had parked on the other side of the hospital near the morgue.

Eric grimaced, "I think we walked here from the morgue."

"Jesus Pete. Let's get the lead out."

Bull, Eric, and Zach practically ran across the campus of the hospital, knowing full well that time could be working against them.

Judy just happened to be looking out the window when she saw the three men sprinting by the unit. She couldn't help but think that something must be very, very wrong.

***

"I want you...I want you...I want you so bad
it's driving me mad, it's driving me mad...
I want you..."

The time had come. Once Benny used the extra restraints to tie Maggie to the bed she seemed resigned and settled into a restless sleep. Only then was he able to nap off and on himself. But now it was daylight. The sun streaming into the window energized him. He was trying to maintain himself until later in the day but he was so excited about the events and the upcoming ceremony he could feel his pants tighten across his crotch. He took a quick shower, masturbating to relieve himself. He dressed in the bedroom, watching Maggie sleep. Once he grabbed a cup of coffee, he gathered his supplies to start an IV in Maggie's arm. As he held her arm taut to look for a vein, she woke up. At first she struggled, forgetting she was tied to the bed.

"Maggie May. Hold still now. I need to start an IV." Maggie looked to Benny then looked away. She allowed herself to lie limp. She didn't care anymore. Feeling she had relaxed some, Benny tried to soothe her. "That's much better; you'll see, my Maggie May."

He took a tourniquet and applied it to her upper arm. He already had a bag of fluid and tubing primed and ready to be connected. Once he saw a vein protrude through her skin he inserted an IV needle, poking around until he saw blood return. Maggie tried to lie as still as possible, ignoring the pain of him searching for the vein with the needle under her skin. He quickly taped the needle in place and started a slow IV drip.

Maggie raised her head. "Benny, can I have something to drink? I'm very thirsty."

"I'm afraid not, Maggie. The ceremony will begin soon. I don't think you should have anything on your stomach. I'll be giving you some medicine though, soon. You'll forget you're thirsty. I don't want to hurt you Maggie May. You must believe me; this is for you, for us."

Benny walked away.

Maggie could hear music in the background.

"Wake up, Maggie, I think I got something to say to you...It's late September and I really should be back at school..."

Rod Stewart, one of her favorites. Benny had told her that he and Rod were good friends, the best. *One day we'll go visit him, as soon as he finishes his tour, didn't Benny tell me that? Or was I dreaming? Maybe Rod's coming today, isn't that what Benny had said?* Maggie was feeling drowsy, dreamy even.

Benny walked into the room with all of his medical supplies. He could tell by looking at Maggie the drugs that he had put in her IV were starting to take effect. He went back into the living room and turned up the music.

"Can't you see, you belong to me, my poor heart aches, every breath you take..."

He knew John, Sting, Rod, and hopefully Yoko, and his mother would be arriving shortly. He needed to get the place in order. He closed the blinds and curtains. He took his ruler out of his pocket and measured the distance of the candles he had placed the night before. Once he was satisfied with their placing, they were lit, one on each side of the bed, four on the dresser. That was probably why the night went so badly. He had brought the candles into the room but did not measure them for accuracy. That alone should be a reminder of how important even the little things are, he told himself. He then turned his attention to his medical supplies. The tray had everything on it he should need: forceps, knife blades, knife handle, a suture, bandage, bacitracin, gauze. He took the ruler out of his pocket and added it the paraphernalia on the tray. He looked at Maggie on the bed. She appeared to be sleeping peacefully. "Oh, my beautiful Maggie May, what other words can I say?"

Benny walks over to her, sitting down on the bed beside her. After unzipping her pants, he pulls them below her thighs. Seeing a few tufts of pubic hair peeking from under her panties excites him. He feels the crotch of his pants start to pull, getting tight. He looks up at her face, her arms restrained to the bed. He continues to take her pants off, then her panties. He straddles her sitting on her belly facing her legs, the mirror in front of him. He rubs his hand in her crotch, fingering her clitoris, making her wet. He unzips his pants, and strokes himself, watching himself getting harder, bigger. He moans aloud as he massages himself faster. He hears footsteps running into the bedroom as he jerks at himself, knowing he's about to climax. As he ejaculates all over himself and Maggie, he beams at the three men as they enter into his bedroom.

"John, Rod, Sting. I'm so glad you made it. See what I have for you?" Bennie smiles at them, rocking back and forth over Maggie.

***

Kristin was sitting on the back patio at her mother's. It was well past two. She tried hard not to cry.

What is it, God? What did I do to deserve this? What sin did I commit that I'm being punished for?

Kristin was beside herself. The tears rolled down her cheeks. She tried to make sense of the situation, replaying in her head the conversation she had with Zach. *He called me, damn it. I didn't call him. He called me and wanted to see me. I'm such a fool.*

"Are you okay, Kris?"

Kris looked up at Bear with her tear-streaked face. She opened her mouth to talk, but all she could do was stutter. "Bear, it hu-hu-hurts so ba-ba-ba-bad." The tears were unstoppable, her sobbing uncontrollable.

"Hey, hey. What is it?" Bear sat down beside Kris, rubbing her back.

Kris hated it when she was so out of control. Doing her best to stop her tears, she wiped her eyes with her arms and tried to sniff in the mucus before it dripped out of her nose.

"Bear, I just love him so much, and it hurts so bad. 'Cause I can't have him."

"Who, Kristin?"

Kristin looked up at Bear. Didn't he know? Mom knew, Eric knew.

"Zach, Bear. Zach Newton. He was supposed to meet me here today. Take me to lunch. But he didn't. I got stood up." Kristin was getting mad again. "He's a stinking, no-good jerk. I'll never let him do that to me again. Damn it."

Bear sat back, rubbing his chin. "Well, I got a message for you from the stinking, no-good jerk. But if you don't want it…" Bear stood up to go.

"Wait. What did you say?" She grabbed at Bear's prosthetic arm to stop him from leaving. Nobody thought about Bear's arm anymore.

"Are you sure you want a message from a stinking, no-good jerk?" Bear rubbed his bald head, teasing her.

She let out a big sigh. "Yes, Bear. I want the message from the stinking, no-good jerk. What did he say?"

"Well, if you're sure. He said that he's very sorry he's running late. But he has your brother for an alibi. And he will explain it all later."

"Is that it? When later? Did he say when later?"

"Yes, he did, as a matter of fact. He said don't leave your mom's. He's coming here for dinner with your brother, so if you get mad, Eric will take the punch for him."

Kristin growled at Bear. But she was growling with a smile.

"You got a beer, Bear? I need a beer."

"Well, yes, I do, young lady. Yes, I do. I'll even have one with you."

***

Epilogue

Hope is the last thing that dies in man;
and though it be exceedingly deceitful,
yet it is of this good use to us,
that while we are traveling through life
it conducts us in an easier and more pleasant
way to our journey's end.

Francois de La Rochefoucauld

"Kris, I think that's your phone. Want me to get it?" The ringing stirred Zach from his peaceful nap.

"Huh? Oh, yeah, please. It might be Eric."

As Zach reached for the phone on the table beside them, Kristin stretched her arms high above her head. It was late afternoon, and the sun was beginning to set. A few hours earlier they had checked into their hotel at the beach, looking forward to their next few days together. Their plan was to take a walk in the waves as soon as they got there, but a playful kiss led to a passionate touch, and they spent the afternoon making love. After they were full of each other and could rest without wanting more, the breeze coming from the open balcony door beckoned them to the recliners outside. She grabbed a pair of shorts and a T-shirt, putting them on in the semi-darkness of the room. They both laughed when they saw that she had put on Zach's boxers and T-shirt.

They were big and baggie, but he liked them on her so much he talked her into keeping them on. They had fallen asleep in the recliner, her head resting on his broad chest. As she reached high above her head to stretch, he could see the full curve of her breast through the sleeve of his T-shirt.

"Hello, Kristin's whipping boy. How may I help you?" Zach answered her phone, rubbing the nape of her neck with his free hand. "Nope. Come on up. We're in 405." Zach's hand moved slowly down Kristin's back, around to her tummy, and under the T-shirt. "You want to talk to Kris? She's right here."

Kristin leaned back on Zach, taking pleasure in Zach's caress.

"Okay. I'll tell her. See you in a few." Zach put the phone down. He leaned into Kristin and kissed her neck. "We gotta get some clothes on. Your brother is going to be up here in a few minutes."

"Crap. I guess we can come up for air and food for a couple of hours." She turned toward Zach, finding his mouth with hers and kissed him before standing up. "It's so nice out here, maybe we could sleep on the recliner tonight."

"Now, that's not a bad idea."

They went inside the hotel room. Kris found her shorts, T-shirt, bra, and panties. She slipped off Zach's boxers and T-shirt and slipped on her own clothes. She then went into the bathroom to freshen her makeup. Zach put on his shorts and shirt, and got a beer out of the refrigerator. He went back out to the balcony to relish the view, the weather, his contentment.

As Kristin came out of the bathroom, there was a knock on the door. Zach heard the knock from the balcony and walked into the room. Kristin opened the door.

Eric and Maggie walked in.

Kristin was taken by surprise that Maggie was with Eric but tried to hide it.

"Hey, little bro. Glad you made it down." Kristin gave Eric a hug. "Dr. Taylor. Good to see you. How've you been?"

Zach tipped his beer in the direction of Eric and Maggie, amused to see Maggie with Kristin's younger brother. "Can I get you guys something to drink?"

Maggie knew her presence might catch them unawares. "A glass of water would be good, thanks. How's it going? Zach, Kristin."

"I'll take what you're drinking if you got another." Eric pointed to the beer in Zach's hand.

"Pick your poisons." Zach walked to the refrigerator and opened the door. Eric took out a bottle of water for Maggie and a St. Pauli's for himself.

Kristin walked to Eric taking the bottle of water. "Let me put it in a glass for you, Dr. Taylor. I've got some sliced lemon, too, if you want."

"Please, Kristin, call me Maggie. And I would like a slice of lemon, actually. Thanks."

Maggie and Kristin went into the kitchen to fix Maggie's water.

Zach leaned toward Eric as the women walked out of hearing distance. "I'm glad you brought Maggie down. She could use a little relief."

Eric smiled at Zach as he took a drink of his beer. "Maggie's good company. And we both needed some time away. The craziness of the case and all."

"Well, you guys did a good job putting him away. I know it was hard on her." Zach motioned to Eric to continue the conversation on the balcony.

Once outside both men leaned on the rail, looking out at the waterway spilling into the Atlantic Ocean. The sky was so clear they could see for miles. The beauty and serenity of the beach was such a contradiction of the real world, Eric thought, as he took another drink. He shook his head.

"Not good enough, the way I see it. As far as I'm concerned, not guilty by reason of insanity is just as bad as not guilty."

"Well, the important thing is that he's locked up. It doesn't matter if it's prison or a forensics unit. I doubt Benny Cole will ever see the light of day. By the way, the paper said Benny had some crazy delusions about knowing Rod Stewart, Sting and John Lennon. He actually thought we were them, didn't he? When we stormed in there and got Maggie?"

Eric nodded, "Yep, crazy as a loon. Unfortunately— the way I see it anyway—it's what helped seal the insanity defense." Eric shrugged his shoulders, took another drink from the beer he was holding and turned his attention to watch a sailboat out on the water.

"Is this an all-male party? Or can the girls join in, too?" Kristin poked her head out the balcony door.

"Shoot, the party doesn't start until the girls show up." Zach motioned Kristin and Maggie onto the balcony. "I think this is the best room in the whole place."

Just at that moment a slight breeze of warm salty air came from the ocean waves. It seemed to give all four of them a sense of tranquility. They all sighed at one time. And then they laughed at themselves as well as at one another.

Maggie spoke first. "Do we have to go back? It's so peaceful here." She leaned on the balcony rail taking in the view.

Kristin sighed again. "It is wonderful, isn't it?" She sat down on the recliner where she and Zach had fallen asleep earlier.

Zach looked at Eric. "We could stay here, but we have no food. I suppose we could live off of the fruit we have but then we wouldn't be able to make sangria. I say let's go the grocery store, pick up four big fat steaks, salad, and more beer. Then I'll be ready to stay forever."

Eric agreed with Zach. "That sounds like a plan to me."

Eric turned to Maggie, gently rubbing her back. "Why don't you and Kris stay here? You guys can enjoy the peacefulness, Zach and I will get the groceries."

Maggie nodded her head, and Kristin agreed. "While you guys are gone we'll get started on the sangria."

"Good deal, then we'll really get this party started." Zach bent down to kiss Kristin's mouth. "We'll be back in a few, save some sangria for us."

"You got it." Kristin kissed Zach back, already hungry for his touch again. Magic, she thought, just like her mom and Bear, and she could feel it to her core.

Eric turned to Maggie and gave her a quick kiss on her lips. "We won't be gone long."

Eric and Zach were out the door.

Kristin gave her brother a funny look as he walked out and then looked back at Maggie.

"I hope you're okay with this." Maggie was almost apologetic to Kristin.

"Are you kidding?" Kristin stood up with a big smile on her face.

"I think it's wonderful. I hope it feels like...magic, for you and for Eric. You both deserve it. Come on, let's make some sangria!"

Maggie followed Kristin into the kitchen, wondering how Kristin could know that magical was exactly the word she had been thinking.

***

"I'm wasting my time in here." Benny was sitting in his therapist's office, staring out the window.

"What makes you say that?"

The therapist's office lights were low; a haze of smoke from a lit cigarette in the ashtray hung in the air . Benny had been on the forensic unit for a month, and the therapist had not yet been able to get into Benny's brain. Three times a week Benny was escorted by armed guards to George's office and three times a week Benny would sit in the dark and smoky office, staring out the window without speaking. At the end of the hour the guards who had been waiting outside the closed office door would come in and escort Benny away. George didn't like having the guards at the door. He felt that having them so close hindered the building of a therapeutic relationship, even if the door was closed. George knew it was a moot point to argue since it was protocol for this unit.

Eventually everyone started talking; the forensics unit was a lonely existence at best.

George took a drag off of his cigarette as he studied his patient in the shadows. He had been intrigued with Benny's case the minute he learned about it on the news. He had followed the trial from the beginning, wondering what made this monster's brain tick. He had followed many a madman's story. Jeffrey Dahmer, Ted Bundy, Charles Manson. He was dying to get inside Benny's brain, maybe even write a book. This could be his lucky break, but he needed to get into Benny's reality, and Benny wasn't budging.

Benny thought George was an idiot. He continued to stare outside. He didn't belong in this place. He didn't need or want therapy. Nobody visited him. Not Yoko, not Rod, Sting, nor John. Not even Maggie May. Benny cocked his head. Someone was talking to him.

At first George thought Benny was talking to him, finally opening up.

"What? I didn't get that."

George leaned forward, putting his cigarette out in the ashtray. But George soon realized Benny wasn't talking to him at all.

Benny was seeing someone George did not see. "Look, I know you're right. I tried to show you, but I failed. Yes! I said 'failed,' damn it. Why do you have to rub it in?"

Finally, George thought, he was getting somewhere. "Benny. Benny. Who do you see? Who are you talking to?"

Benny didn't hear the therapist; he was too busy listening to the voice.

"Why are you here to harass me? If you loved me you'd help me. I tried to prove you were right. Help me now, so I can get it right. So I can show you I'm a man."

Benny stood up, his face contorted. "Please, Mother, don't yell at me. Yes, you can help me be a man. The way you used to do."

George tried to intervene. "Benny, it's your mother? What does she want, Benny? What is it?"

Benny's tears turned to anger. "Mother, help me, damn it. Do I have to beg? Is that what you want? Me on my knees? You want me to cut my dick off for you, Mother? I'm not your little boy anymore! I am a grown man! Don't tell me I'm a failure anymore!"

Benny raised his arms toward the sky furiously shaking his hands. His whole body seemed to expand. Benny was so loud the guards opened the door and stepped in.

George turned toward them and motioned to them to be still. For a few seconds nobody moved.

George was perplexed. Benny's hallucinations had taken him so far away from George's office that he wondered if Benny could ever come back. He wasn't sure if he should let Benny work through this hallucination by himself or if he should try to bring Benny out of it. He definitely didn't want the guards involved. George reasoned it would enhance the therapy session if he could involve himself in the experience. It was a decision he would never get to regret. He took another drag of his cigarette before he placed it in the ashtray. He motioned to the guards to back up into the hallway, away from the door.

"Benny. Here. Look at me." George walked over to Benny. "Tell me what's happening. What do you see?"

Benny looked at George. The last thing George saw was the rage in Benny's eyes. Benny grabbed him by his head, snapping his neck.

The guards rushed Benny, placing him in a two-man hold. When they'd placed Benny in shackles, the guard closer to the phone called for backup as well as medical attention for George. In no time the office was full of hospital personnel. One group attended to George's lifeless body; the other group circled around Benny. Benny curiously looked at the chaos around him as they led him out of George's office.

***

Benny sat on his bed, head cocked and listening. The shackles were off of his feet and wrists. He was alone, secluded. He didn't seem to mind, he was too busy listening.

"I can still make you proud, Mother. Maggie May and I belong together, no matter what they say. Once the homage is complete she'll be worthy of your love." Benny eyed a spider hanging from a corner in the room. He was fascinated by her delicate spinning, creating a web that would soon trap her prey.

"Of course, I'll have a plan. And I won't rest until I have Maggie May as my own. She didn't look at me once during the court case. But I think I know why. The whore in her wants out, wants to run free. She needs me to tame her, Mother, the way you tamed me. I know it will please you to see I can be a man to her, humble her."

"Dinner. Go to the far side of the room, Cole."

Benny obliged the guard while his dinner tray passed through the slit in the door. He had no plans to leave, at least not yet. His plan to catch Maggie had to be like the spider web; delicate, powerful, and flawless...

ABOUT THE
AUTHOR

This is K. A. Stevens's first medical thriller. Most of her knowledge about psychiatry and the surgical services come first hand, as she has practiced as a registered nurse in both areas for thirty years.